BLOOD AND BETRAYAL
A DARK FANTASY ANTHOLOGY

S. K. SAYARI   A. M. DILSAVER   R. L. DAVENNOR
CHRISTIANA MATTHEWS   JAY ROSE
AISLING WILDER   INE GAUSEL

Edited by
EMMA O'CONNELL • S. K. SAYARI
Illustrated by
FICTIVE DESIGNS

ZASRA
PRESS

Copyright © 2020

Paperback edition ISBN: 978-1-7777139-0-4

Electronic Edition ISBN: 978-1-7777139-1-1

Published by Zasra Press, a registered trademark of Ardent Dawn Publishing Ltd.

First Edition: June 2021

This is a work of fiction. Names, places, and incidents are products of the author's imagination or used fictitiously, and are not to be construed as real. Any resemblance to actual events, places, or persons, whether living or dead, is entirely coincidental.

Cover Art by Maria Spada Design https://www.mariaspada.com/

Illustrated by Fictive Designs https://www.fictive-designs.com/

Compiled and edited by S. K. Sayari, edited by Emma O'Connell. Proofread by Caitlin Wade.

All rights reserved.

No part of this book may be reproduced in any form or by any electronic or mechanical means, including information storage and retrieval systems, without written permission from the authors, except for the use of brief quotations in a book review.

Introduction © S. K. SAYARI 2021
THE PATH OF DARKNESS © A. M. DILSAVER 2021
BEAUTY'S CURSE © A. M. DILSAVER 2020
BLOOD OF THE STARS © S. K. SAYARI 2020
CURSED IN BLOOD © JAY ROSE 2020
DEATH'S REQUIEM © INE GAUSEL 2020
FEED THE SEA © AISLING WILDER 2020
HARVEST © CHRISTIANA MATTHEWS 2020
HEART OF SHADOWS © A. M. DILSAVER 2020
NEVERENDING SUMMER © INE GAUSEL 2020
PAVANE FOR A PRINCE © CHRISTIANA MATTHEWS 2020
SEAWHISPERS © R. L. DAVENNOR 2020
THE BLEEDER'S WIFE © AISLING WILDER 2020
THE DOE PRIESTESS © S. K. SAYARI 2020
THE LAST SINGER © AISLING WILDER 2020

THE PRICE OF PROPHECY © INE GAUSEL 2020
WITCH-DRAGON © S. K. SAYARI 2020
WYRMS OF AVASAL © S. K. SAYARI 2020

CONTENTS

Introduction — vii

SEAWHISPERS — 1
R. L. Davennor

THE LAST SINGER — 9
Aisling Wilder

BLOOD OF THE STARS — 33
S. K. Sayari

PAVANE FOR A PRINCE — 43
Christiana Matthews

NEVERENDING SUMMER — 61
Ine Gausel

THE DOE PRIESTESS — 77
S. K. Sayari

BEAUTY'S CURSE — 91
A. M. Dilsaver

THE BLEEDER'S WIFE — 119
Aisling Wilder

HARVEST — 131
Christiana matthews

THE PRICE OF PROPHECY — 151
Ine Gausel

WITCH-DRAGON — 177
S. K. Sayari

CURSED IN BLOOD — 191
Jay Rose

DEATH'S REQUIEM — 223
Ine Gausel

FEED THE SEA — 239
Aisling Wilder

HEART OF SHADOWS A. M. Dilsaver	251
WYRMS OF AVASAL S. K. Sayari	281
About the Authors	295
S. K. Sayari	297
A. M. Dilsaver	299
R. L. Davennor	301
Christiana Matthews	303
Jay Rose	305
Aisling Wilder	307
Ine Gausel	309
About the Editors	311

INTRODUCTION

To make a promise is to be bound by oath to your word—for the honourable, at least. But many are not honourable. Especially not in this book. In the face of love, lust, envy, fear, anger, and deception, binding words are easily cast aside.

The driving force behind this anthology was to explore what we fondly call 'our happy dark hearts.' After all, while hope and heroes and happy endings are all lovely things to read about, not everyone is a hero. Not everyone makes the 'right' choice. Not everyone can hope for happiness.

Now, the characters we created aren't necessarily villains, but we can assure you that we, as the authors, have indeed taken lessons from some. After all, who better to learn from than the ones who never get happy endings?

The authors contributing to this anthology were asked to create gripping stories incorporating both an oath and a betrayal, not necessarily in that order. They were also tasked to weave stories that enrapture readers with fantastical elements of deliciously dark fantasy.

From tales of dryads and jinni to stories of dragons and wizards, you'll partake in a journey that will leave you ques-

INTRODUCTION

tioning characters' morals and actions, and perhaps sympathizing with their cause.

So grab your cloak and lantern, turn the page, and descend into the depths of darkness with us.

S. K. SAYARI
2020

INTRODUCTION

THE PATH OF DARKNESS

Here Death walks among us,
And jinni lose their hearts.
Hearts are cursed in blood,
And princes play their parts.

The witch-dragon approaches;
The sirens lay in wait;
A bounty hunter reels at
The twist in her own fate.

A hidden song is calling—
We'll dance into the night.
The shadows keep us warm,
And the Darkness brings us light.

Loved ones haunt our dreams
While we bury our old ghosts,
Trading brand new love
For the one we needed most.

Blood drips from the walls
And the moon is out of sight;
You won't know who to trust
When the Scourge rains from the skies.

Strength of will is tested
As new promises are forged,
But bonds are meant to be broken—
Dear reader, you've been warned.

A. M. DILSAVER
2021

SEAWHISPERS

R. L. DAVENNOR

R. L. DAVENNOR

Music - https://soundcloud.com/rldavennor/seawhispers

by the sea
lived a witch
alone
but content
she weathered
storms
she weathered
torment
with no ears
to hear
she heard them
speak
the dead
buried
the living
shriek

Waves caressed Agathe's toes like soft sheets of silk. The tiny grains of sand were gentle against her tired skin, ebbing and flowing with the lull of the tide. She closed her eyes, relishing the breeze enveloping her where the ocean couldn't, and exhaled before beginning her song. The melody started quiet and low—a stark contrast to the sirens' resounding laments that had echoed along these shores for centuries—but despite the competition, Agathe sang it anyway.

Her world had gone silent years ago, even the music, but she had never stopped singing. Agathe didn't have a choice; if she refused to give life to the lyrics, the songs within her writhed and thrashed like eels, desperate to get out and be heard. Luckily for them both, music was a thing she enjoyed—a distraction. And the sirens liked it too.

They began to appear when Agathe reached the chorus.

Settling onto the rocks dotting the landscape, the creatures watched her, their glowing eyes shining like beacons. One might mistake a siren for a beautiful maiden in passing, but certainly not when up close. Their appearance had terrified her until she'd grown to know them. With sallow skin, thinning hair, and bony frames, the sirens quite resembled Agathe in her old age. The only beautiful thing about any of them was their voices—Agathe's ragged and low, the sirens' ethereal and other-worldly. Their razor-sharp teeth glittered in the morning sunlight, reflecting on the surface of the waves.

Blood dripped down their chins when they smiled.

The sirens had feasted well last night. A ship had fallen victim to the brutal storm that raged until dawn, and Agathe had counted more than a dozen corpses littering the waves before they were devoured one by one. The waters lapping at her feet were tinged red, but rather than signaling an end, it was only the beginning. The sirens hadn't come to listen to her song or keep her company.

Not today.

Agathe ignored their whispers until they flooded her mind, sinking their claws in deep. She'd heard nothing but the sirens' voices for nearly two decades, and as much as the creatures brought her comfort, in moments like this, it was enough to drive a person mad. The sirens' matriarch, Ligeia, spoke loudest.

Defeated, Agathe halted her melody and frowned. "I'd really like to finish my song." Though she couldn't hear her own voice, a faint rattling in her skull informed her she spoke aloud.

Ligeia shook her head, eyes narrowing into slits. *Young must feed.*

"They had all night to feed."

Not enough. Need more.

Agathe clenched her fists. The sirens had multiplied in recent months, their hunger never sated no matter how many corpses the sea offered, and the newborns were the most ravenous of them all. It worried her.

"How many?" she asked, referring to the number of bodies that had washed ashore in the night. They may have escaped the sirens' clutches once, but they wouldn't a second time, not with Agathe around to fetch them. Refusal wasn't an option. If she tried, the sirens' whispers would flood her mind until she truly did lose it.

Ligeia raised a trio of bony fingers.

Three. These days, it was a struggle for Agathe to lift even one of the waterlogged corpses. Her hunchback was getting worse with each passing year, and it didn't help that her bad leg acted up any chance it got. She hadn't needed to rely on a cane thus far and wasn't about to start now.

Agathe smiled. "I'd best get to work, then."

Ligeia hissed something in her mother tongue before slipping beneath the waves. One by one her sisters followed and Agathe was once again alone. She should have been accustomed to it now, after decades of solitude.

She wasn't.

Absently rubbing the place where a ring should've sat, Agathe began limping her way from the surf, each step placed deliberately and carefully. Her joints protested, but she welcomed this over the aches that liked to settle in her heart and mind. Physical pain was tangible—and with the right poultices, fixable—unlike the invisible wounds inflicted by *him*.

No, she reminded herself. *Matthias is dead.*

If she kept saying it, maybe one day she'd actually believe it.

Progress was slow, but Agathe eventually made it back to her modest dwelling. A long-abandoned lighthouse acted as a shield for what was essentially a shack in comparison, but it was functional, and it was home. Once through the door of the smaller house, she eyed the array of herbs and bottles along the far wall. A poultice to soothe her joints was more than tempting, but there wasn't time. Not with corpses awaiting her attention.

Agathe turned instead toward her sled. A modest creation, she'd fashioned it out of twine and driftwood to aid in dragging the dead sailors back out to sea. Once upon a time, she'd been able to shoulder the bodies with nothing but her own strength, the same strength that had seen her through heartbreak. She smiled, envisioning her younger self swimming and singing among sirens. Vibrant, fierce, and beautiful, she'd been a sight to behold.

"Hells," she said aloud, "I *still* am."

She now sported wispy grey hair, sagging and wrinkled skin, and a misshapen frame, but Agathe's eyes were still bright, and she was still walking this earth. Like the rocks dotting the cliffside, she'd weathered countless storms without incident, unshaken and unbroken.

After wrapping the sled's rope around her waist and ensuring she possessed her dagger, Agathe set off.

There was only one place where corpses washed up. Her work may have been hard, but it at least kept the bodies from fouling the beach. Without her hearing, the fresh, salty air was even more precious, and Agathe would keel over before allowing anything to ruin her peace. Certainly not filthy *men*. Even alive, they always reeked to high heaven. The scent of death was almost preferable.

The cove wasn't far. Surrounded by jagged rocks, the shallows meant the sirens couldn't swim here, and the narrow inlets were the perfect width for human bodies. It was a sanctuary of sorts, a cathedral if the ocean possessed one, complete with hymns and prayers from the sailors begging for death. Occasionally, but rarely, the ones that ended up here were still alive.

Today, though, the corpses lay lifeless. Agathe exhaled—less work for her. She wasn't opposed to slitting throats but would hate to get more blood on her robes when previous stains still lingered. Approaching the first body, she kicked it gingerly, grimacing not at his bruised and bloated face, but at the *smell*. It didn't matter that she'd been doing this for decades; there simply was no getting used to it.

She worked as quickly as her tired bones would allow. After positioning the sled behind the dead man's head, Agathe yanked his arms to pull him the rest of the way. Dragging the loaded sled from the beach and into the tide always took longest—she swore the sand worked against her. But once she made it to the shallows, the ocean took it from there. Agathe walked alongside the floating sled and its cargo, guiding it through the inlet while enjoying the tide caressing her lower half.

Faster, hurry!

Agathe shot Ligeia a pointed glare. The siren matriarch and her sisters waited just beyond the cove, prepared to pounce the moment their prize was within reach.

"I'll get there when I get there." Agathe kept her pace steady, grateful the tide swayed in her favor.

Ligeia was upon the corpse the instant Agathe shoved her sled into the open sea. It made no difference to the sirens that the body had already started to decompose; they tore into the flesh as if starving. Crimson leaked into the waters around them. Clotted and thick, the blood gathered in clumps, releasing a putrid scent that forced Agathe to hold her breath.

She didn't stay to watch the carnage and yanked her sled free at the first opportunity. Gathering the second corpse went quicker and expended less effort, given the smaller man was missing a leg. The sirens finished the remains before Agathe had fully turned away, and Ligeia wasted no time demanding the third.

He proved a challenge. Tall and dense, Agathe's sled could barely accommodate his frame, and she exhausted herself getting him aboard. She doubled over, resting her hands on her knees while she caught her breath, and took the opportunity to study him. His skin was cool to the touch, but not nearly as frigid as the others. He possessed all his limbs. Even his clothing appeared in relatively good condition—soaked and torn, but not tattered. That wasn't what caught her attention.

He was staring at her.

He was *alive*.

His widened eyes as blue as the waves, he spoke words she couldn't hear. He didn't seem capable of movement apart from his head, and Agathe wondered if he was truly as whole as she'd thought. *Please*, he begged again and again—beyond that, she didn't bother to read his cracked and parched lips.

He wanted her to save him.

Agathe scoffed before reaching for her knife. He was hardly the first pathetic soul to beg for his life, and he wouldn't be the last. For some reason, they all saw her as a savior, foolishly unaware they spoke to Death itself. Dropping to her knees, she rested the blade against his throat. One slice and it would be over.

But as she tensed to do so, on the sailor's hand a second piece of metal glinted in the fading sunlight.

A wedding band.

The sight took her back forty years. The ring was nearly identical to the one Agathe had placed upon Matthias's finger all those years ago: plain and unassuming. If she closed her eyes, she could hear his laugh intermingled with the flowing tide, followed by the vow he'd whispered into her ear.

"*Always and only you.*"

If only he'd been telling the truth.

Agathe glanced at the still-living sailor. She could—*should*—be merciful.

She didn't want to be.

Sheathing her blade, Agathe turned toward the tide. Despite struggling so much with the loading, dragging him into the surf was surprisingly easy, as was delivering him to be devoured.

No doubt hearing the man's cries, Ligeia gave Agathe a toothy, bloody grin. *Fresh?*

"Fresh."

She stayed to watch him die.

Once the sirens had eaten their fill and disappeared beneath the crimson surf, Agathe made her way back to shore. She secured the sled's rope around her waist, humming various pitches until the correct one resonated in her skull, and started toward home.

She finished her song with a smile.

passing ships
come and go
never
stay long
beware the
waves
beware their
songs
the sirens
at play
they'll lure you
down
whispering
words of love
until you
drown

THE LAST SINGER

AISLING WILDER

*S*eya looked out from under the trees that sheltered the Sourcespring, their branches covering the deep pool in a canopy of green. The sun beamed above, its light reflected by the glass-calm lake surrounding the island. Everything was so still this morn. Too still. At the island's edge, the water mirrored with perfect clarity the trees that curved from its banks, each branch and leaf looking back upon itself. It was as if she stood between twin worlds. There was not a sound around her. Neither birdsong nor rustle of animal nor whisper of wind. It was as if the island, the lake, and the world beyond were holding their breath. Waiting. Waiting for her to act.

"Enough!"

Sovereign Iker slammed his palm on the stone table, sending small, carved figurines flying in every direction. One—hooded, hands raised—went clattering across the maps and charts and then rolled to an awkward stop right in front of Seya, one of its arms breaking off in the process. She stared down at the tiny, one-armed mage, a familiar fist of dread clenching around her heart.

The rest of the council fell silent as their sovereign pushed himself to his feet. Nylah—

Sovereign's Champion—stood, offering her hand, but Iker waved her off and so she sat back down, her frown echoed on the rest of the visages in the room.

Seya did not need Song to read what lay behind each. The Sovereign was ill, aged before his time by the ravages of war, grey and withered with a disease that neither magic nor medicine, Song nor sage could cure. He was the last of his line, with no heir to follow. His death without naming a successor would leave Lurandia leaderless while the world was ending. Nine generations of enmity and hate had left the people of the Three

Lands starving, the realm wasted. Plague and drought, vestiges of dark magic, had devastated what war had not already taken. Lurandia was the last unbroken hold, the last land whole, the only hope. The other kings were long dead, their heirs divided, their lands broken into smaller and smaller domains ruled by warlords and dark mages, and these in constant conflict—when they were not pitted together against Lurandia itself. Which they now were. Under siege for nigh on three years now, the country's stores were almost empty, its cities full of refugees who had fled from border towns and farms where no more food could grow.

Iker had not started the war. Like his mother, and his mother's father before her, he had proffered peace. Once or twice, he had even succeeded. Seya recalled time upon time in these very chambers, meetings between heads of state from Vrenia and Annerid, accord upon accord signed and swiftly broken.

With a grimace of pain, Iker finally rose to his feet.

"Enough." He declared again, his voice firm, its deep timbre belying his illness. "It is past time for debate. We have already attempted every course of action you suggest, thrice over." His gaze traversed the room, lingering on each member of the council as he spoke. "The war has ravaged the Three Lands beyond repair. Our armies still repel those of Vrenia and Annerid, 'tis true—but they cannot hold much longer. Plague has already begun to take our people all along the edges of the kingdom; it takes our soldiers. Already, drought moves inland. Our magic is failing."

His gaze stopped then. His eyes—once blue, now grey with illness—grew dark as they met her own.

"Councillor Seya."

Seya did not stand, although her inaction bought sideways glances from the others. She was too tired, and besides, her true station did not require her to stand for any sovereign. She was a Singer, and the last of her kind.

Once, long long ago, Singers had held the Three Lands in perfect harmony, soothing any dissonance. Once, Singers had flourished, with eighteen glorious Choruses in nine illustrious Halls. Once, they had gathered the prodigies—children with the Song inborn—from the length and breadth of every land, had trained those children in schools renowned throughout the Three Lands. Once, the refrains, sung in perfect pitch and radiant resonance, reverberated across the lands, year after year, voice after voice. No longer. Now the Songs were soured, the melodies broken, the refrains lost. Forgotten.

"Sire?"

"It is time."

IT WAS TIME. *Loosing a long breath, Seya drew another, from deep within her core. Then a second, and a third. With the fourth she let forth sound—a low hum, closing her eyes and reaching out with her spirit for the strands of life and strife around her. With the fifth, she found the Source; with the sixth she breathed it in, its shimmering waves filling her, matching its resonance to her own. With the seventh, she began to walk deosil around the pool, eyes closed so she could see the dissonance as with the eighth she drew it forth: strands of black, shimmering with echoes of copper, silver, and gold, arching toward her from everywhere at once. From the trees and stones of the island, from the lake beyond, and further still. With the ninth breath, her hum changed to Song, and she raised her arms, up and out, reaching further. Beyond the lake, to the three great rivers, coaxing, drawing, pulling as her Song grew louder still.*

ALMOST AS ONE, the rest of the council turned to look at her, their disquiet palpable. Seya let loose a sigh she had been holding for too long and shook her head. "I still do not know if it is right."

"Perhaps not." Iker leaned forward, trembling hands splayed out on the map before him. "But it must be done. For the sake of all the lands."

Nylah looked from one to the other before turning toward Seya, her voice full of trepidation. "What must be done?"

Seya did not answer. Instead, she stood, gathered up the figurine in one hand, and walked around the table, stopping just opposite Iker. "I have failed. Failed the land. Failed the Song."

"Not yet." Iker smiled at her—then turned to the rest. "I am dying." He held up his hand at the vocalisations of dismay. "Do not protest. You all know it to be true. It is time." He repeated the phrase, then turned again to Seya, his tone changing to one of ritual and authority.

"Seya of Kings Isle. I, Sovereign Iker Aberel, last of my line, do now name thee Sovereign, and all thy line after thee, until such time thou or they should name another. As it is said, so let it be done."

She had expected someone to gasp or shout. But no. Every voice in the room was silent, every eye staring as Iker moved slowly around the table to sit with a grateful sigh into the chair she herself had not so long ago abandoned. Seya waited until he was settled and then she, too, sat gently into the Sovereign's seat, the furs that draped it still warm from the heat of Sovereign— Councillor Iker's recent habitation.

She took a calming breath as every eye drifted from Iker back to her. In each face she read varying degrees of apprehension. Understandable. Her now-former office, that of Arch-Archivist, had commanded little respect and even less attention. Coupled with her grey-streaked hair, apparent middle age, and lengthy time spent quietly attending and chronicling council meetings—long before any of the other councillors were promoted to their stations—this had had the intended effect: none of them had taken much note of her.

Until now.

Seya leaned in and placed a pale finger in the very centre of the map laid out before her, where a small circle was inked in blue. Giving resonance to her voice so none of the Council of Nine would mistake her next words, she spoke.

"You all know it is from Lough Argia the three great rivers—the Lura, the Vre, and the Anner—spring forth. It is from these waters all music was born. Both high and low. You know this also."

She took the one-armed mage figurine. "What you do not know, because only Singers know, is that here"—she placed the figurine in the very centre of the blue-inked lake—"is an island, sacred to Singers. It is called Iturria, and in the centre of the island is the Sourcespring."

"The what?" Nylah again, her brow furrowed further.

"The Sourcespring. The spring is the Source, and the Source is life. It is light also, and love. It is what gave the waters Song, and they in turn gave the Song to Singers and the Singers gave it to the world."

"But all the Singers are gone."

"No." Iker's deep voice reverberated around the walls. "Not all."

"Indeed." Seya looked again to Iker, then to Nylah. "The Last Singer stands before you."

The room erupted into exclamations of disbelief, even dismay. Seya raised her hand, but even then it took a few moments for the council to quiet. In the silence that followed, it was the Keeper of Stores who spoke first, his dark eyes clouded.

"Surely the Singers are a story only. One told to soothe children. When we are grown, we learn better the ways of the world. No one can sing away the troubles that haunt man. No one can sing away hatred, nor defeat a warlord or dark mage with a Song."

Seya smiled. "But I say to you, I am a Singer, and have sung those very Songs. I am a Singer, and the last of my kind. I have been such long before you were born, and Source willing, I will remain so after you are dead."

Seya waited a moment, to allow them time for thought, then continued. "Singers live very long lives—lives connected to the Song, and the Song to waters, and the waters to the Source. As long as the Source remains, Singers remain. And the Source"—again she tapped the map, lifting the little figurine up and putting it back down again, bringing them back to the point at hand—"is here."

Murmurs and grumblings filled the room, and then a voice, louder than the rest. The Exarch and Provider of Providence, his intonation honied with the long habit of homilies.

"The Source has no earthly station. It cannot be located, for it is and is not within and without all things."

"As always, Exarch, your words remove all meaning from what you say," Seya snapped. Her patience, long tested, was wearing thin. "The Source is a thing in a place, and I know this, for I have been there. I have seen it."

She did not say what else she had done. Further knowledge —of the sound and of the taste and the feel of the Source—was hers and hers alone. Once, it had been shared with others. No longer. She shook her head and turned back to the council, taking a breath to continue before being interrupted again, this time by the stern and frowning Lady of Legions.

"But why then, are there no other Singers? If they—if you— cannot die?"

"I did not say we cannot die. I said we live long. But we can die, and we can be killed. And the reason the world remains at war, Lady Legion, is because we have been killed. And not merely killed, but decimated."

Seya stood, and walked across the chamber toward the western window. "It began slowly. So slow, so subtle, that none noted it. In each generation, fewer and fewer Singers were born. When we did note it, we thought perhaps we simply had not found them, or that it was a shift that would right itself again. But it did not. And then, what Singers were left began to disappear."

She pulled back the heavy curtain, her gaze taking in the citadel and the rest of the island below before wandering further, across the River Torring and to the west. Her mind ranged across the lesser rivers and plains, over the hills toward the Great Lura, and the Sourcespring. Too far to see from where she now stood, but she could hear its Song, though faint.

"You are all too young to know what it was like. To live in peace. To be allowed to flourish, and to move freely throughout the Three Lands. To learn. To love. To sing." She shook her head and turned back from the window to the room, carrying on.

"When we finally realised what was happening, it was too late. All but twelve Singers were dead or missing, and all those here in Lurandia. Of the other Choruses not a note remained. The Halls were abandoned. No new Singers had been born anywhere in three generations. And then began the first war."

The Master of Ships scoffed—then looked around and saw no one else laughing. He gulped, then looked to Seya, a tremor in his voice. "You are saying that you witnessed the First War?"

"I did. And the Second, and the Third. After the Fourth, there were only six of us left. After the Fifth we stopped singing against the dissonance, for the cacophony was too great. That was when we realised the Sourcespring was waning. The Song flowed less and less with each passing year. We tried to get back to it, but we were too few, and the power of the enemy too great. We retreated then, back over the Three Rivers, here to Kings Isle. Concentrating our power on protecting Lurandia from what we feared would come. After the Sixth War, three of us lost our voices singing against the discord and died not long after. After the Seventh, there were only two of us left. And now we are in the Ninth War. And it is only myself who sings."

When the first strand touched her outstretched arms, the pain of it arched through her, like the piercing of a hundred thorns. She winced but did not falter—her Song constant, melodious with each intake and outgive of air, no space now between the notes. A second strand followed fast upon the first, then a third, each tendril spiralling around her outstretched arms, tighter and tighter, slicing into her skin as she bound them to her. As each was pinioned, she listened, hearing what notes were needed, and so willing the winding until every strand thrummed in echo, their oscillation sending shimmering resonance back along each filament, back to whence they came and back again to her, and forth and back, note upon note.

Once more, the room fell silent. Seya felt she could almost see their thoughts, such was the disquiet on their faces. Then Tian, the Master Mage, spoke for the first time that evening.

"What, then, is the thing that must be done? I do not assume you and now-Councillor Iker only spoke of your naming, Sovereign."

Seya nodded, turning from the window and walking once more to her chair, resting her hand on the back of it.

"I, Seya of Kings Isle, Sovereign of Lurandia and Last Singer, command that from this day forth, Lurandia shall be ruled by Singers. Here our existence shall be secret no more. I command that Seekers be sent forth to every land, searching anew for those children who may yet have the Song inborn. I command that any child so gifted be brought here under guard, and with great haste. I further command that Kings Isle be henceforth known as Song Holme, and this castle as Singer's Keep." She paused, looking to each councillor, meeting and holding every gaze, as she continued. "Lady of Legions, I command our armies be called back from the borders to guard the citadel. Place our legions in secure encampments at a distance no greater than a hundred leagues from the citadel."

Penah, Lady of Legions, nodded, her lips a tight line as Seya turned to the round-bellied merchant in the next chair.

"Rhain, Keeper of Stores, I command you ensure the stores and coffers of the kingdom are counted then placed under guard; thereafter, all citizens of Lurandia must be given food and fresh water, rationed to last as long as they may whilst keeping as many alive for as long as possible."

She looked then to the white-haired and long-bearded Elcin.

"Chief of Colleges, I command your schools gather all the knowledge they can as swiftly as possible—in whatever form it may be—and bring all back here, to the Athenaeum. Every Song, story, poem, and saga; every name; every word; every record and number, is to be copied and put to memory by as many scribes and oracles as can fit within the walls."

The scholar bowed his head slightly, his eyes dark with thought as Seya focused on Tian, who was now pale and staring in shock.

"Master Mage. I command that you gather to the citadel your most loyal mages. Bid them prepare to defend all the land and people behind the outermost walls for as long as they can. I command also that you work your strongest spells upon the Keep, safeguarding it with all the power you may hold."

She then looked to the two councillors in the last seats. Mail, and Nylah.

"Master of Ships, you will ready your swiftest craft, small enough to be sailed by two, and stocked with supplies for a three-day journey down the Torring. Champion Nylah, at first light on the morrow, you will meet me outside the gates and escort me to the river. We sail at dawn for the Source."

So saying, she stood, and without a look behind, strode from the council chambers. As soon as the guard shut the door after her, the room behind became a storm of voices, as she knew it would. Great change always birthed great consternation. But although they might question, or argue, they would obey. They must. Each had taken a sacred oath, upon their lifeblood, to obey the word of the Sovereign. This was the reasoning behind Iker's naming of her. Her word—the word of a Singer—must be law, and her laws must be followed. It was the only way to save the Three Lands from what might come should she fail.

HER ARMS GREW TIRED, *trembling as more strands latched and wound around them, as she fastened and tensed them, turning and tuning, discordance to harmony, again and again—and still she reached for more. She must gather it all. Beyond the lake, beyond the great rivers, she reached, pulling strands wherever she found them. Where armies gathered, she took; where men argued, she took; where they fitfully slept, she took. Where plague reigned, she took; where drought worried, she took. Within and around her, the discord grew. And still, she Sang; and still, she walked; and still, she pulled and turned and changed, each strand reluctantly releasing the blackness that tarnished its tone, each note resolving, one by one. And still she sought out more, gathering the sounds of hate, of fear, of jealousy, of envy, and of rage—she coaxed all into the Song, listening, singing, changing, healing, until she could take no more. She was already so burdened, so weighted. It was so hard. Too hard. For a moment her breath faltered, and the burgeoning harmony soured.*

Seya moved swiftly through the halls and up the stairs to her tower. Singer's Tower, she decided it would hitherto be known. Changing the names would take time, she knew. But names were important. The change needed to begin now if it was to last. All Songs, please let it last.

Reaching her chambers, she strode into her library, threw her cloak across a settee, and collapsed with a sigh into a chair at the table. Taking up the greater part of the room, its surface was covered with stacks of books, piles of parchment, ink, quills, lamps, and half-burnt candles. Her head slumped into her hands, and she allowed herself, for the first time that morning, to truly feel the doubt and uncertainty that had haunted her since she'd first spoken to Iker of her plan three nights gone. She could not show any sign of her misgivings to the council, or to anyone ever again. She was a Singer. The last. The only. She must act the part, always . And their plan would work. It must. The Sovereign—former Sovereign—had agreed. It was the only way.

Shoving away candles and ink, she wiped her eyes and gathered the nearest parchment, smoothing out the wide, wrinkled page. Time to continue from where she'd left off. Singing to the page all she knew of the Source, all the Songs: the melodies and modes, the harmonies, motives, scales, phrasings, pitches, keys, modulations, notes, rhythms, and refrains. Songs on the page would never be the same as Songs sung, but it was the only way to save them. For the future. A future she might never see, but she would not leave the Songs in her to fade and die. They must live on. She closed her eyes, took a breath into her core—and began to sing.

Some time later, she woke to a soft knock at her chamber door. Woolly-headed, she stumbled to her feet, smoothed her dress, and turned to face the door.

"Enter."

Much to her surprise, her voice was weak and rough, her

throat chafed, sound barely able to leave her lips. The knock came again, more insistent. They had not heard. Shaking her head, she paused, then took a breath and tried again, reaching for resonance.

"Enter."

There. This time it came at her call. Thank the Source. But how long until it would not?

The door opened, and in walked Nylah. The young woman shut the door behind her, then turned and bowed, one hand on the pommel of the sword at her side. "Sovereign."

"Champion?"

"Forgive me, sire, but dawn approaches. Your servants are without, some bearing fruit and bread, and others to dress you and help you pack for the journey."

Seya nodded, then looked back around to the table, which—again to her surprise—was covered with page upon page of freshly inked parchment. She must have finished sometime in the night. She lifted the topmost page, checking the final note was right, as she did not recall the singing of it, and then realised the young woman was still awaiting an answer.

"Very well. I will eat, yes, and would have you join me. Bid them to enter with food. But as to the rest, I shall dress myself, and I have already packed."

The young warrior nodded, opening the chamber door to speak with the waiting servants. Moments later, she returned with two servants bearing trays of the aforementioned food and drink. They walked to the table and began to clear the parchments to make room.

"No!" Seya shouted without meaning to; the servants jumped and stepped back, looking frightened. She shook her head, taking up the pages and placing them beside stacks and stacks of the same, all along shelves she had cleared for the purpose.

"I do not want these disturbed." She frowned and turned

back, annoyed at herself for the loss of control and for feeling the need to explain. "Carry on."

The servants bowed and laid out the trays then, at a wave of Nylah's hand, left the room. The Champion pulled out a chair and with another bow, smiled at Seya.

"Sovereign?"

With a nod, Seya sat down, realising then how hungry she was as her stomach gave a growl that was more than a little musical. She had ripped off a good chunk of bread and slathered on a great helping of butter and jam before she saw that the Champion was still standing. Waiting.

"Sit. Eat. Please."

With a nod, the warrior sat and began to eat with obvious hunger. Seya smiled, and they shared their meal in silence, Nylah finishing first, then seeming to wait again.

Seya raised a brow. "Is there something else?"

Her Champion took a breath to speak, then stopped herself, shaking her head and frowning down at her plate.

"Say your piece, Champion. You may speak freely."

Nylah frowned. "May I ask, Sovereign, why is it only now you wish to travel to the Sourcespring? Why have you not gone before?"

Seya smiled. She'd wondered when that question would arise, and was glad it was this young woman to have asked it.

"You may ask, Champion, and I shall tell you. Until now, no one knew I was the Last Singer. I could not reveal the truth, because my Songs for Lurandia were not complete, and I could not risk leaving the land unsung, should anything happen to me."

The young woman looked puzzled. "Unsung?"

Seya nodded. "A land unsung is a land unprotected. Even Tian with his mages cannot hear the Song of the land, cannot find the harmonies and sing it back, do not know the notes to sing. I have spent the last century singing to the land, infusing every stone, every speck of earth and breath of wind, every drop of water and blade of grass with Songs of peace and protection, of serenity and salvation, beginning with this very tower, out to the Keep and the city beyond, and as far as I could into the lands surrounding, all on my own. The Songs will hold, even should all other magic fail, even should the kingdom fall. I could not leave until the last note was sung."

Nylah sat back slowly, understanding blooming across her features. "This is why Iker named you. Why you gave the council those commands."

Seya smiled. "Yes. The city shall stand. The Songs I have sung will hold it safe for as long as the land itself remains. Now it shall be a shelter for Singers, should more rise, and for the Song itself, forevermore."

The young warrior fell silent, her face dark with thought. She took a sip of cider, then looked up once more. "But why the urgency? Why leave Lurandia now, when you have only just been named? Surely you are more needed here, as Singer and Sovereign, to continue your protection of the land?"

Seya sat back, considering the woman across from her. How much to tell her? Nylah gazed back, a surprising innocence in her eyes, warrior though she was. Innocence and honesty. Seya supposed she should know the truth. She was the Sovereign's Champion after all. Her personal guard. More—the warrior was sworn to defend her to the death.

"That protection has cost me, Champion—and cost me dearly. Singing so much for so long and so often is a strain. My voice is fading, and I do not know for how much longer I may give rise to the refrains needed. To sing harmony back into the world, one must find the right resonance, draw the discord to one's own self and hold it, to then heal it. It is...trying. Even when the Singers were more, few could undertake such a task. And none alone."

Nylah nodded, frowning as Seya went on.

"When the war was more distant, and Lurandia still free of struggle and strife, I could hear the Source, feel its Song and gather strength from it as needed. But now the dissonance is too great, the Sourcespring too distant and faded. It cannot come to me, so I must travel to it, and there—immersed in its intonation—I will draw strength to sing once more to the world."

Seya sighed. The Source would renew her Song, and her Song would renew the lands. She nodded, as much to herself as to the young woman; she took a last sip of cider, pushed the tray to one side, then stood and walked to her wardrobe, laying out the clothes for the journey.

Nylah stood as if pulled from thought, and then bowed. "Thank you, sire. I shall make ready and await you with steeds and stores in the courtyard."

Seya nodded absently as she pulled out two fur-lined cloaks and compared them. "Very well. I will be down shortly."

Her Champion moved to the door—then paused once more. "Sovereign...forgive me for asking one thing more, but can you show me?"

"Show you what?" Seya looked up.

"Show me...something of the Song?" A childlike hope played across the younger woman's features. "I mean no disrespect, please understand. As a child, I was told stories of the Singers long ago, who held the Three Lands safe in the bosom of their Song. How those Songs could move men and mountains alike, such was their power."

Seya smiled. It had been so long since she had been asked such a question. Iker had always known what she was and known, too, that it was her power that had kept Lurandia so long from the worst ravages of war. No one else in the Council of Nine had dared ask last night, out of fear or pride or both, she did not know. And yet here was one who dared.

Nylah smiled in return, an expression that lit her entire face.

Seya considered the young woman before her. She had never had much time for those of the warrior class. All her long life she had considered the ability to fight and to know the methods of battle a base, if necessary, skillset. Her own talents—the ability to sing, to know the notes, to see the strands of life and hear the music they made, and to control it all—were far more useful. After all, when Singers held sway, there was no need to fight. No space for discord. For that was what fighting was. Discordance. Cacophony. No harmony in it. And yet in Nylah's face, Seya saw now there was beauty and grace in the way the warrior held herself. Like a cat, resting, but ready and willing to pounce.

She acquiesced. "I will show you. Just a little now, as I am tired, and as I said, my voice is not what it once was. Still...."

So saying, she searched the room and, spying a candelabrum atop the mantlepiece, closed her eyes, took a low, deep breath, and loosed it as a hum. Reaching out with the Sight of Song, she found a single strand, grasped it to her, and wrapped it around her fingertips. Not too taut for so light a task. She sent the opposite end thrumming toward the candelabrum and changed her humming to words, singing the Song of Fire, sending the notes in harmony to each wick, lifting the melody to a quickening crescendo—and the candles burst into flame. Behind her, she heard the warrior gasp as she finished the Song, let go the strand, and opened her eyes once again.

SHOCK REVERBERATED *through her as the sour notes clashed against the rest. Fighting to keep her voice steady, she found the loosening strands and wound them tighter, until the harmony settled again—then yet another loosened, another wrong note souring the whole. No. Once more she found it, once more she wound it, once more the Song rang true, but now she knew. She could hold no more. Every fibre of*

her being shook with the effort of keeping what she had. So she pulled back, concentrating only on healing the strands she bore. She turned her steps inward, spiralling in toward the Sourcespring, drawing the strands with her, weaving them, round and round, keeping each clear and separate from the rest, yet all part of the whole, her voice soaring in healing Song above it all.

~

"But I do not understand." Nylah shook her head. "I've read the old stories, and *The Book of Names*. They give no mention of Singers coming to Lurandia. They all state that the Singers died off throughout the Three Lands long before the First War."

They had been sailing for two-and-a-half days without incident, keeping to the centre of the Torring, the middling river that flowed from Lough Argia southeasterly past Kings Isle—now Song Holme—and on into the Southern Sea. The guards that had accompanied them had disembarked at Torringside—the last town before the lake—on the shores of the smaller Lough Torring, after much reassurance from Nylah and further insistence from Seya herself. They would undertake the rest of the journey alone.

Seya nodded. "Yes. The stories and books do not mention Singers in Lurandia because I willed it thus."

Nylah frowned, but after a moment, nodded. "You did not wish to be remembered."

Seya looked to the warrior and smiled. "Precisely. It had become obvious that someone—or many someones, I still do not know—wanted the Singers not simply dead, but eradicated completely. I decided the best prospect for our survival —for my own and the world's—would be to let them believe they had succeeded. Once I was the last, and a generation or two had passed, it was simple enough to change the records and let myself be forgotten, by all save the Sovereigns of

Lurandia. The task fell to each Sovereign to keep The Last Singer secret and safe within the bounds of Kings Isle, and in return—"

"In return, you kept the discord of war from the land." Nylah finished for her.

Seya nodded. "A vow I have kept. But a task in which I have failed."

She sighed and looked out across the water as they passed yet another abandoned village. There had been more of them as the river veered west. Drought and plague were already stalking these lands and moving further inland with each passing day. It was eerie to see no children running along the shores, no farmers in fields, nor fishermen in other boats. Only the river, the reeds, the water birds and insects, and the odd jumping fish accompanied their journey.

As the day wore on Nylah grew silent, one hand on the tiller, the other on the bowline. Like most Lurandians, she was an expert sailor. The nation's common second name was *Land of Rivers*, and all children born and raised in the land knew their way around water and boats from birth. The past two days had been pleasant, or would have been, had it not been for the urgency of Seya's impending task. She found the young warrior's company easy enough. They spoke of their upbringings, how Nylah had been a fisherman's daughter, had taught herself sword-and battle-craft long before she found a knight to sponsor her, and so went from page, to knight, to Champion, then to Sovereign's Champion, far more swiftly than most. Her calling, she named it—which made Seya smile.

For her part, Seya told the young warrior of her own origins. The daughter of a smallholding lord, she was found at the age of three to have the Song inborn and was then taken to join the Chorus in the nearest Great Hall in Vrenia.

Nylah looked surprised at that. "You're not Lurandian, then?"

"No." Seya smiled. "I'm Vrenian by birth. Near Olnda, in the north. Sorry to disappoint."

The young woman shook her head. "Not disappointed. Just surprised. Sovereign."

"You must remember, when I was young, the Three Lands were not at war. They were as one, and their Sovereigns allies. Besides, Singers give up allegiance to land and liege once they take the Song."

"I see." Nylah frowned in thought and fell silent for a time.

The day wore into evening, the river carrying them on and on. As the sun set behind the western mountains, the young woman spoke again.

"'Tis only a short way now, Sovereign, to the lough."

Seya nodded, her gaze drifting, half dreaming, once more toward the shore now cloaked in mist. She could hear the Sourcesong louder now, and the sound lit a light of hope within her—then she gasped awake to a thump, and a jolt.

"We've run aground." A tight-lipped Nylah was already gathering in the sail. "I'm sorry, Sovereign, but we'll have to wade from here."

"Where are we?" Seya blinked, looking around.

"It's difficult to say, sire." The young warrior gestured, and Seya stood to find the boat surrounded by mist, through which loomed the ghostly stalks of nearby reeds.

"How long did I sleep?"

"Half the night. It is morning now. I let you rest, Sovereign, as you seemed tired. The journey was quiet, and I knew the way. We're in the source of the river now, where it meets the lough. Only it's shallower than it should be. And I'm not certain where to go from here."

Seya squinted, peering through the mist, but she could not see more than a few yards in any direction. The mist swallowed the dawn light, and it was impossible to know which way to go, much less how they were going to get there. She looked over to find Nylah watching her. Waiting.

Seya nodded. "Let me listen."

～

T<small>IRED</small>. *She was so tired. How long had she been walking? How long singing, how long holding the strands? She did not know. But she must go on. Round and round, in and out, with each pass building the Song. Her bones ached now, each step agony, and her arms—she could no longer feel her arms. She could only feel the thousand strands, only hear the constant, thundering chorus. More than half were healed now. Harmony began to surpass discord. Soon. Soon the melody would reach its end, soon she could let go the Song—perfect and pure—into the Sourcespring, filling it, freeing it, helping it to flow once again. Whole and new. Soon. She breathed in, air filling lungs, and out, Song leaving lips. Soon. Strand upon strand. Soon. She was almost there.*

～

"A<small>LMOST THERE</small>." Seya spoke, eyes closed, from where she was carried in Nylah's arms. They had waded this way for what seemed like hours through the mist, Seya listening, Nylah carrying her. The mist was so heavy at times it drowned out even the Source and she had to have the young warrior stop and hold perfectly still until she could hear it again. But it was louder now. And was the mist clearing?

"There!" Yes. She opened her eyes. Not a hundred yards away. The island. Iturria, covered in low trees that curved up from shore like the leafy arms of dryads, beckoning, welcoming.

"I will walk from here."

"Sire." Nylah nodded, and put Seya down into murky water that reached only to her knees. The shallowness of the lake was troubling. It used to be so deep. No matter. Soon she would clear the Sourcespring, find the discord and change it, free the lands from the bonds that held them, right the wrongs, and the Song and the waters would flow again. Then Singers would be born anew, and the Three Lands would heal.

She smiled to Nylah and began to wade toward the shore, the young warrior following close behind. The mist curled away as they neared the island—so much so that by the time they were out of the water and onto the sand, it had cleared completely. As if the island had expected her. Wanted her there.

Seya turned to her companion who had freed herself from pack and shield and was now stringing her longbow.

"I must begin. I do not know how long this will take, nor entirely what it may entail."

The young woman nodded. "No matter, sire. I am your champion. I shall guard you, guide you, lend you whatever skill and strength I may have."

"Thank you, but all I need now is for you to wait as I do what must be done."

"As you wish." Nylah looked at her, suddenly serious. "May I ask what it is you are going to do?"

"You may." Seya nodded. "I am going to sing. To heal the lands, renew the Source, and end the war."

The young woman bowed low. "Then I wish you well, Sovereign. May your Song be true."

Seya smiled, to hear the old blessing. It was right. She gave Nylah one last nod, then headed into the trees, seeking the Source.

～

Seya gasped as the music built and built, until it was near more than she could hold, the rhythm ringing through her bones, the Song falling from her lips and rising toward perfection, each strand she held now shimmering, soaring, into one shining, heavenly crescendo. Her feet, bare, curled into the moss around the pool as she circled inward, faster and faster, lifting her arms, her voice pure and sweet, holding the notes high as she turned toward the Sourcespring—it turned toward her, reaching, needing the Song, thirsting for it. Yes. She took the last step, and stopped, facing the water. One final breath, one last long note—and then something struck her in the back. The strands, held so perfectly, jolted; the clarion chorus wavered.

Pain bloomed then, or fire, she was not certain. She opened her eyes and looked down, surprised to see the bloodied head of an arrow protruding from her breast. She tried to breathe, tried to hold the last note, but her breath failed. The Song faltered. Fled. And then she fell, face down into the pool, her lifeblood joining the stale water. The strands of discord, freed from her grasp, plunged in after, a tangled cacophony of chaos—clashing, crashing, sinking. Down with her into the dark.

∾

THE WOMAN who had for a long time been called Nylah knelt on the sand as she unstrung her bow. It had been a good shot. Clean, she'd made certain. There'd been no need to make the Singer suffer. And no orders to. She'd been Vrenian after all, like herself. She stood up, shrugged on pack and quiver, and took one last look around the island. Curious, how silent it was, now the singing was gone.

That Song had been beautiful. Sad, and heart-achingly lovely. As she'd listened, she swore she'd been able to hear more than just the one voice. It was eerie. No one should hold that kind of power. She'd done the Three Lands a favour. Now Vrenia would prevail, and soon there would be one land, with no Singers to interfere.

She nodded to herself. Better get back to the boat. As she waded away, she looked back and was surprised to see the island shrouded in mist again. Yet this time the mist seemed to be full of shadows. Reaching, twisting shadows that swallowed all light, all sound. Shadows that were moving with purpose toward the shore. Toward her.

Fear curled into her throat as she rushed into the water, but where before it had been waist high, now it grew deeper, and deeper still, until she wasn't wading, but swimming, and then something cold curled around her outstretched arm, and another something around her waist, tearing her with sudden force up and out of the water. She screamed—or tried to—as the cold that held her curled tighter and tighter, crushing the breath from her lungs. Her heart pounded hard as she kicked and struggled—but the cold only held on, crushing her in its icy arms. She fought to see what had her as her vision blurred to red, but all she could see was shadow. Darkness.

She felt pain then, all across her skin, as if a thousand bees stung at once—and then felt only an oddly pleasant sensation. She couldn't think what it reminded her of. For some reason, to her mind came an image of a babe, suckling at its mother's breast. She dully wondered why, as her heartbeat faltered. Faded.

And then she was falling, to land against something wet. Cold. Sand. The island's shore.

She stared, cheek down on the sand, across where the lake should have been. Except now there was no lake. Instead, she lay dying at the edge of an impossible abyss, itself infested with swarming, twisting shadows; shadows that branched out across the Three Lands, dark strands that hummed with terrible hunger as they reached: wanting, drinking, taking.

Leaving only silence.

BLOOD OF THE STARS

S. K. SAYARI

*N*adine sat stiffly in her chair, pecking at the food on her plate: braised duck, charred vegetables, and some sort of disgusting, mushy greens. Celestials didn't even need to consume food; the very act of eating was pointless.

Brynna, on the other hand, daintily placed a vegetable in her mouth with her fork, smiling at the Sol Elf who sat across from her. He wore a crown of thorns and roses, his auburn hair braided and his ears tapered at the tips. Brynna sharply contrasted his Elven features—her hair as dark as a raven's feathers, skin as pale as pearls, and lips a soft pink. When Brynna's plate was spotless, the Elf offered her a hand and she took it with pink cheeks and a slight giggle, letting him lead her to the center of the ballroom. Many other pairs were already waltzing, and Brynna and the Elf joined them, swaying to the lilting melody.

Nadine resisted the urge to gag. Filthy Elves, all they ever did was fight each other. Their power waxed and waned with the Sun and Moon's cycle, but during the last Eclipse—when both Elf races had been at the height of their power—they'd slaughtered each other. Now, during The Lady of the Sky's Feast of Millennial Peace, they behaved.

But for how long?

She rolled her eyes and crossed her arms. The Sol and Luna Elves would cause some sort of commotion during the seven-day, seven-night feast. There was no doubt about it.

A small-nosed Luna Elf with rouge-painted cheeks approached Nadine, bashfully rubbing the back of his neck. If he dared to ask her, the Keeper of the Sun, to dance—

"Would you like to—?"

"*No.*" Base creatures deserved nothing but her hatred.

The Elf's shoulders drooped, and he nodded before making his way to his next target, a straw-haired she-Elf.

"You don't need to be so surly," murmured Nadine's mother.

To Nadine, her mother was the very image of beauty and grace. The stars shone in her eyes, and her skin radiated light itself; a crown inlaid with azure jewels rested on her silvery hair.

The Lady of the Sky clicked her tongue. "You should enjoy yourself."

"Ah, yes, enjoy myself in the company of savages," muttered Nadine.

"You always were such a grumpy child. Brynna's the nice one."

"And you always were such an overbearing parent."

Nadine and her mother locked gazes, and they burst into laughter.

"I like it when it's just us. You, me, and Brynna," said Nadine, her voice sounding smaller than usual. "I don't want things to change. Ever."

The Lady of the Sky smiled, the gesture reaching her eyes, the stars within them twinkling brightly.

"Then so it shall be."

~

NADINE SAT IN HER CHAMBERS, running the teeth of a wooden comb through her pearly hair. Each strand had to be brushed smooth or it would irritate her. She was relieved to have a short break from the ball—thankfully, it was almost over with. There were only two days and three nights left. So far, the Elves had been pleasant enough. They hadn't begun fighting with one another...yet.

Shouting erupted outside, and Nadine leaped to her feet. Bounding toward her door, she opened it to see a red-faced Brynna, tears streaking her face, storming out of their mother's chambers.

Nadine reached out for her sister's arm as she passed but

hesitated. Never, since they had been created of stardust, had Brynna fought with their mother.

Gingerly stepping toward their mother's chambers, Nadine peeked inside. For the first time in millennia, the Lady of the Sky looked tired. The stars within her eyes were dull, and lines creased the skin underneath her eyes and around her mouth.

"What was that about?" asked Nadine.

"It is nothing, my child. Come; sit with me."

Nadine plopped down onto the bed, cuddling into her mother's side. "What's wrong, Mother?"

"Are you happy, my dear Nadine?"

"Of course, Mother! Why do you ask?"

The Lady of the Sky sighed. "It is nothing. I hope I am the mother you both deserve, regardless of how strict I am with you in your duties. The Sun and Moon *must* rise and fall each day and night. If you were to be lax in your duties, the Elves would suffer."

Nadine chewed at her lip. The Elves of each race leeched their energy from the Moon and Sun. If one race were to absorb more light and become more powerful, they would destroy the other. Not that she cared whether they lived or not. She only cared to make her mother happy.

The Lady of the Sky sniffled. "I just hope you know that I love you."

Nadine nodded and wrapped her arms around her mother. "I know, Mother. I know, and I love you too."

∼

The metallic smell of blood caught Nadine's attention as she walked through the Sky Temple on the seventh night of the feast. She muttered a curse and grabbed her golden sunstaff, pursing her lips. The Elves must have finally broken out in a fight, and now she would have to clean up their mess. Nadine shook her head. Mother should have known better than to host this ball.

She followed the scent, which grew stronger with each step. Water flowed freely through deep grooves in the opalescent stone, cascading down the edges of the temple and turning to fine mist in the air. Gnarled trees reached up for the clouds above, their leaves a perpetual waxy jade. The stone, cool and smooth against Nadine's feet, was riddled with spongy moss.

The crimson stain in the moss near Mother's chambers took Nadine's breath away and set her heart racing. Her fingers shook as she took one step forward, then another, until she reached the door.

Inside, her mother lay face down in a pool of blood.

Nadine's vision swam, and she crumbled to the floor. Was the world spinning, or was she spinning? Or was it both?

It couldn't be possible. It *had* to be false.

Screams pierced her ears, yet they seemed distant and otherworldly. Nadine didn't realize she was being shaken until fingers dug into her shoulders like a snake biting into flesh.

"—dine. Nadine! Calm down!"

Nadine looked up, her vision blurred with tears, to see a watery Brynna with a furrowed brow. Brynna wiped away Nadine's tears, hushing her and stroking her cheeks.

"How are you so calm?" whispered Nadine. She shuddered at her sister's touch, icy cold.

Brynna blinked. "I'm very upset right now. But it's not the time to panic. We must—"

"Find who did this!" Fire ripped through Nadine's gut, spreading to her limbs, scorching her shattered heart. It was the Elves. They had done this.

It had to be them.

"We must make sure everyone else is safe," said Brynna, stroking Nadine's hair.

"Who cares about the Elves? They're the ones who did this!"

Nadine's chest twinged with pain. It was as if Brynna didn't care for their mother at all. Nadine narrowed her eyes, clenching her fists. "Did you know anything about this? Did you?"

"Nadine, you *must* be calm."

With a shaky breath, Nadine bit down on her tongue until she tasted blood. Swallowing, she looked up at Brynna, unable to keep hot tears from spilling forth.

"We must promise to find Mother's killer. No matter what it takes! Promise me, Brynna."

Brynna opened her mouth, hesitating. "I—I don't know—"

"Brynna!"

"I swear," muttered Brynna.

Nadine nodded and rose to her feet, wobbling. "Now that our mother is dead…" she whispered, her voice growing louder as each word was spoken. "Now that she is gone, I will reign over the Sky Temple."

"I will not object to that," said Brynna, lowering her head.

Nadine swallowed again. Could she ever fill her mother's position as Lady of the Sky? Doubt crept through her body, sending shivers up her spine.

"As long as you grant me one wish," murmured Brynna.

Nadine blinked. A wish? "And what is that?"

"I want to live below…with the Elves."

Bile rose in Nadine's throat. "Absolutely *not*."

Brynna's pallid cheeks turned even more ashen, her lips trembling. "Why? Can you not give me at least this? Is this about duty? Because—"

"Duty?" hissed Nadine. "No, this isn't about duty—the Elves can rot for all I care. This is about *us*. You and me. We are all each other has left now that Mother is gone. Did you really think I'd grant you such a preposterous wish?"

Brynna closed her eyes. "Fine. Have it your way." With a huff, she turned and left, leaving Nadine to attend to the body.

∾

BURROWING her head into her sheets, Nadine let the tears she'd been holding flow freely. She had spent the whole day kicking each and every Elf out of the Sky Temple, raking the rooms to make sure not a single wretch remained. Now, after hours of tossing and turning in her bed, she still couldn't sleep.

She wished she could hold her breath until she stopped breathing. The loss of her mother had broken her spirit, numbed her body. She remembered the stagnant stars in her mother's glassy eyes, and wept.

But she had to live. She had to find who'd killed her mother.

A slight rustle froze her, fear tickling her fingertips like spiders biting into her skin. Muffled footsteps padded closer—the footsteps of someone trying very hard to not be noticed. Nadine tensed in her bedding. An Elf assassin. She would destroy it.

A vice-like grip suddenly wrapped around Nadine's mouth, muting her cry. Nadine thrashed, her foot hitting flesh. The grip on her hair loosened, and Nadine leaped out of her bed and at the intruder. Wrapped in a cloak and armed with a knife, the assassin hissed as their bodies collided.

She grappled with the dark figure, wrestling for the knife. A knee to their stomach was all it took for her assailant to double over, wheezing. Nadine snatched the weapon and ripped their cloak off. She almost screamed in shock, the knife slipping from her grasp. It clattered in the silence, deafening to her ears.

Brynna!

Her sister's expression was like stone—unyielding, unwavering. She stepped toward Nadine, her eyes flickering toward the knife.

Nadine's breath came quicker, and she followed her sister's gaze. The weapon was well within reach, but she would leave her side vulnerable if she lunged for it. She didn't know what Brynna was capable of at this point.

"What the damned are you doing?" she hissed.

Brynna opened her mouth, darkness flashing across her eyes, but then she stepped back. Sweat beaded her forehead, her eyes swimming with hesitation. "You don't understand. Neither did Mother! That's...that's why...."

"Treacherous swine," snarled Nadine as realization sank in. "I'll have your head!"

Resolve set Brynna's expression back to stone, and she jerked, taking a step forward. "My head? You don't even—"

"You murdered your mother, tried to murder your own sister...so you could be with a *filthy Elf*?" The very thought threatened to drive Nadine mad.

"I've never felt this way about anyone or anything before! I love him!"

Pathetic. Absolutely pathetic. "That's your excuse? You love that Elf more than me? More than your *own mother*?"

"She wasn't our mother! She created us, gave us no will, and forced us to obey her," insisted Brynna, her voice hoarse.

Nadine screeched and leaped toward the knife. Brynna did the same, but Nadine was faster; snatching the weapon, she whipped her arm outward. Brynna gasped and stumbled back, and Nadine sprinted at her. Again the two wrestled, the knife slipping from Nadine's grasp. Brynna went for it, and Nadine took the chance to wrap her hand around her sister's throat, smashing her head down onto stone.

Dazed, Brynna uttered a garbled cry for help, but Nadine did not stop. She scrambled for the knife and slammed it down into Brynna's heart. The Moon Keeper's mouth twisted into a grimace, her body jerking and eyes rolling into the back of her head—then she lay still.

Nadine's mouth went dry, the musty stench of death permeating her senses. A sob wracked her body as she unfurled her hand from Brynna's neck. How had it come to this? How had she killed her own sister?

"I'm sorry. Brynna, I'm sorry. Wake up, please. Don't leave me like Mother did. Who will help me keep the Elves under control if you can't sing to the Moon?"

Brynna stayed silent, her eyes glassy and unseeing. Nadine brought trembling hands to her mouth and whimpered. What had she done?

Bile surged from the pit of her stomach, her vision throbbing red. The Elves were to blame. This was their fault. Brynna's death, their mother's death....

All of it.

Panting, Nadine rose, the bloody knife still within her grasp. Trudging through the Sky Temple, she made her way to the sanctum.

She raised her hands, taking a moment to clear her throat. When she began to sing, her voice was harsh and choppy, unlike the smooth, sweet notes she usually produced. The Sun responded to her anger and grief, its light vibrating with intensity, blinding her. Then, with a trembling breath, she slashed her arms downward, almost screaming her song. The Sun pulsed, then fell, colliding with the Realm of Elves. As the light grew, expanding, flames licking up to the Sky Temple itself, Nadine raised her arms to the sky once more.

She would burn, and the world would burn with her.

When the Moon betrayed the Sun,
All became Undone.

PAVANE FOR A PRINCE

CHRISTIANA MATTHEWS

*L*ights blazed from every public room in the palace, but the ballroom outshone them all. Crystal chandeliers magnified the glow of a hundred candles, and light flared from silver sconces around the walls.

Prince Aubrey Serrar, heir to the tiny principality of Serrarn Isle, put up his hand to shield his eyes from the glare and made his way through the bejewelled, perfumed, and chattering throng to the adjacent card room—which, if equally noisy, at least promised something stronger to drink. Not that wine would make him feel any better. He pushed a hand through his dark hair and winced. Great Goddess, his head felt as if it were about to fall off!

"Aubrey?" Before he could reach that comparative sanctuary, a soft hand touched his arm and the anxious face of his betrothed appeared at his side. "What ails you? You don't look at all well."

Elayna, as always, glowed with health. Her cheeks were faintly flushed, her blue eyes sparkled, and her fine, flaxen hair, coming loose from its ribbons, clustered in ringlets about her elegant neck.

He laid a hand over hers and summoned a smile. "It's nothing. I'm tired, that's all."

"Will you dance with me? People expect it, you know, at a betrothal ball." Her smile was a little hesitant.

The hammers began beating at his brow ridge again. He had loved to dance, once. Now…now it was the most exquisite torture he knew. A craving that consumed him, crowding out all other thoughts and the faint pricking of conscience. But perhaps…perhaps just this once he could resist the call, the damnable insistent call which drew him away from the palace. It had drawn him, night after night, for…gods, he couldn't even remember how long.

Surely he could resist, for once, if he was any sort of man. He owed Elayna one dance at least on the night they announced their engagement.

"Of course," he started to say, but at the sight of the swaying dancers the familiar need arose, tightening his muscles and clawing at his stomach. Sweat broke out on his brow and his hands began to shake uncontrollably.

"Aubrey?" Elayna's voice held the seeds of panic. "Perhaps you should lie down. I think you need a physician."

"No!" The world's greatest healer would be unable to help him, to cure the canker which ate at his soul.

Several guests glanced at them curiously. He removed her hand and stepped away from her, lowering his voice. "I can't, Elayna. I'm sorry, I'm so very sorry, but…but I've just remembered I have to speak to my father."

Leaving her alone, frowning and confused in the middle of the ballroom, he cravenly fled. The call was building in his blood, in his soul, taunting him, pulling him, drawing him away, out of the gates of the palace, down to the stables, and deep into the forest.

The next hour passed as if in a dream or a drug-fueled haze. He could recall nothing of the ride. He didn't even remember going to the stables; he never did. But somehow there he was, mounted on his favourite dun gelding with a tall russet hound at his side, miles away from the ball, his family, Elayna, and everything and everyone he should care about. Still did care about, in some tiny, rebellious corner of his mind. Some part of him recognized the wrongness of this. Some flicker of his own identity still struggled to break free, but each time he made this trek the whispering magic overcame it a little more.

He slid to the ground, trembling with a familiar mixture of exhaustion, dread, and guilt—of shameful anticipation. Several times he'd thought he heard somebody following, but a cursory glance behind revealed no one, and the pull had become so strong he could barely think of anything else.

A small hillock, covered with brilliant green moss, appeared in a perfectly circular clearing among the trees. By now activating the spell was automatic; he spoke the words without thinking:

"*Open, bright hill, green hill, in the name of the dancing hind,*
Allow the young man entrance, with his horse and his hound behind."

And heard, with a shiver of horror, a dulcet voice add to the formula:

"*And also allow his lady, for her own peace of mind.*"

Elayna! Elayna had followed him. He tried to turn and expel her, but the otherworld enchantment had him firmly in its grip and he could only move forward. Forward, through the veil and into the faery realm.

Behind him, Elayna gasped in astonishment, and he recalled —almost fondly—how he'd reacted to his first sight of the Faery Hall beneath the hollow hill. Nothing in his father's palace or any citadel of man could compare to it. Gold, silver, copper, bronze, and all manner of precious stones were lavishly employed, but the effect was not garish. The skill and artistry on display would make any craftsman weep with envy and with joy.

Jewel-studded silver or gold also adorned the exquisite inhabitants, encircling their arms, wrists, and necks or hanging from their ears. More gems glittered in their hair, and their multi-coloured raiment shimmered with the sheen of silk and the lustre of golden cloth. The air, far from being musty as one might expect from an underground cavern, was redolent of lilies, honeysuckle, and rose.

How much was real and how much was illusion Aubrey could not have said, but that was immaterial. All that mattered was the music, the glorious, transcendent music, and the dance. As the faery folk led the horses and the dog away, a slender, sylph-like creature wearing celadon and emerald green drifted toward him, both hands extended in invitation. He shivered, wanting to refuse, to turn away. But he couldn't. Even with Elayna watching, he couldn't deny the need.

First, the faery woman led him into a galliard, stately yet lively, then the Queen's Almaine and a succession of circle and country dances, followed by an indecent but exhilarating exercise called a 'waltz,' and finally—mercifully—a slow and elegant pavane. At the end of it he collapsed onto a long settee, chest heaving and perspiration sheening his brow, his breath coming in gasps. His green-clad companion had disappeared, but several others took her place, chivvying him, plying him with fans, urging him to continue. With an effort, ignoring his aching feet, burning calves, and pounding heart, he pushed them away and stumbled over to Elayna, still standing wide-eyed against the wall.

"Get out of here!" he said urgently, gripping her by the shoulders. "You shouldn't be here, Elayna. This place is evil—it eats you. Devours you. Why in the Lady's name did you follow me?"

She didn't try to escape his hold; just regarded him with troubled blue eyes. "I wanted to find out what was wrong. How long has this been going on, Aubrey?"

"I don't know. A few weeks…a couple of months maybe. What does it matter? Please, Elayna, beloved, you have to leave!"

She ignored him. "You've been ill for almost a year. When did it start, or do you not even know?" Her frown deepened at his flustered response. "You don't, do you? You're befuddled by their enchantments. No wonder you're always bone-tired if this is how you've been spending your nights." She gave a short, incredulous laugh. "And to think I feared a more traditional rival. A mistress, a courtesan—even a common whore. Or do they offer those services too?'

He flushed, dropped his hands, and looked away. It had, in fact, begun with a seduction, a chance encounter in a tavern with a bewitching raven-haired creature in a filmy, blood-red gown. His flesh quivered at the memory. He didn't have extensive experience in the arts of love but was reasonably certain that even the most high-flying courtesan could learn a thing or two from the succubus who'd first lured him inside the hill. Soft, skillful hands, warm, luscious lips, and a tongue far more flexible than any human woman's.

But the pyrotechnic sex, he had soon discovered, was but a precursor to the real objective—to addict him to the dance. For no woman's touch, not even the faery woman's, roused in him the exultant frisson of desire that was the faery dance. It did not, he thought bitterly, bode well for his marriage bed. Providing he made it as far as his wedding.

"Aubrey." Long, slender hands—some dark-skinned, some pale, some tawny—wound about his waist and tangled in his hair. "Come away, Aubrey. Come to us; dance with us. We need you."

He tried to pull away, but they were much too strong. Even one of them could throw him around like a child's toy, for all their seeming frailty. He followed them back onto the floor, stumbling with exhaustion, and felt his heart leap and almost stop when he saw a tall, elegant male bow to Elayna and lead her out as well.

"No!" Sheer terror for his betrothed gave him the strength to tear himself from their grasp. "Let her go!" He tried to shove the creature away, but it was like pushing against solid brick.

The man—if you could call him that, with his pointed ears and ruby eyes—subjected Aubrey to a long, deliberate, and vaguely insulting scrutiny. "From the dance? Certainly, although such an enchanting creature would surely perform with beauty and grace. But from this hall? I think not."

Aubrey's spine tried to burst from his skin and wrap itself around his throat. "You can't keep her here! This is my future wife! She must come home with me to her rooms in the palace."

The faery smiled cruelly, displaying white teeth set between long, pointed canines. "Very well; I'll make you a bargain. The woman stays here tonight, just for a single night, and when you return on the morrow…we'll see if you still desire to remove her."

Aubrey thought of stories he'd heard, of people emerging from a night beneath the hollow hill to find that years had passed in the outer world. He shook his head and the faery, correctly divining his alarm, reassured him.

"Time will flow the same, both within the hill and without. Nor will her virtue be compromised. Make your choice on the morrow, mortal man, or forfeit both your lives now."

Aubrey swallowed. They'd never proposed violence before, but then he supposed they hadn't needed to. This was the first time he'd ever dared to deny or defy them.

"If you harm her—if you so much as touch her—I swear I'll find a way to kill you." His voice shook from a combination of anger and fear.

Again, that smile. "You have my word, Prince. Your lady is our honoured guest, and I promise we'll treat her as such. She'll know none of the delights that you have. You realize, do you not, that my kind never lie?"

Aubrey nodded, although the assurance failed to calm him. They might not lie outright, but they could twist and obscure the truth better than any courtier or politician. At last he said, looking not at the faery but at Elayna, "Wait for me, beloved. I promise to return and do whatever I must to bring you home again."

Elayna's lip trembled and tears stood in her eyes, but he knew she had too much courage and pride to indulge in useless protest. He rode away with a heavy heart.

∼

As always, Aubrey entered the palace via a side door. Moving stealthily and pausing at intervals to check that the way was clear, he ascended to his room on the third floor via a servant's stairway. Even at this hour he had to take care to avoid the occasional maid, but over time he'd learned the safest, least-used route.

He didn't bother to undress, just wrenched off his boots—another skill he'd had to learn since this craziness had begun; it used to take his manservant half an hour to ease the moulded leather over his calves without marking that glossy perfection—and threw himself into bed fully clothed. Another hairline crack had appeared in the ceiling, and the resident spider had moved her web to the far corner. It had amused him, once, tracking the battle between spider and servants, the first seeking to maintain her webs, the second to destroy them. Now it just served as a reminder of the impermanence of life, of happiness, of joy.

Oh, gods, what if he lost her? What if he could never hold her again, his lovely Elayna? Never hear her sweet voice or look into her blue, blue eyes. Never dance with her, laugh with her. Or tell her how much he loved her.

All night he tossed and squirmed upon the down coverlet, unable to sleep. How long had it been since he'd slept through a night? He couldn't remember. Restful slumber, boundless energy, and a tranquil life...all those things belonged in the faery-free past, the time before the hollow hill had claimed him. Staring with aching eyes at the ceiling, the chandelier, the panelled walls, and the heavy, carved wardrobes, his gaze eventually wandered across the room to the green velvet drapes. Elayna had declared her intention of changing them once this room became theirs instead of just his. Once they were wed. She'd thought green to be an unlucky colour.

Perhaps she was right. What trick, what subterfuge might the inhabitants of the hill use to make him renounce his beloved? Nothing came to mind, but he knew from bitter experience that their imagination and their capacity for cruelty far exceeded his. They must have something planned, though—else, why had they sent him home?

∼

MORNING, they'd said, but hadn't specified the hour. He left the palace at dawn, bleary-eyed but for once clear-headed, replaying the faery lord's promise and trying to find the kinks and tricks in it. How did they treat honoured guests? He should have tried to pin them down and get more information. She wouldn't experience the things he had, they'd said, but he had no doubt that their repertoire of delights was beyond extensive. Thoughts of that creature doing to Elayna even half of the things his succubus had done to him kept scrolling through his mind, making his heart jump like a frightened hare and his bowels coil in pythonesque knots.

By the time he'd reached the hill's entrance both the horse and he were lathered in sweat— one from exhaustion, the other from apprehension. Only the dog appeared unaffected; she'd simply enjoyed the run.

The words, this time, suffered no modification.

"Open, bright hill, green hill, in the name of the dancing hind,
Allow the young man entrance, with his horse and his hound behind."

Elayna waited as promised in the centre of the hall, the faery host crowding around her. And at her side, his eyes wide with wonder and a welcoming smile on his lips, stood Aubrey's youngest brother.

Fear tightened Aubrey's throat and gripped his heart with cold fingers. "Byron, what are you doing here? How did you find your way into the hill?"

The boy laughed merrily, unconscious of the danger. "I'd just gone to bed last night when I heard something at the window, as though a stone had been thrown. I looked out and saw Elayna. She beckoned me, so I went down and followed her here. Have you ever seen anything more beautiful, Aubrey?"

Aubrey glanced at Elayna, who shook her head.

"It wasn't Elayna, Byron. It was one of *them*, wearing a glamour." He glared at the leader of the host. "Wasn't it? You didn't have time to entice my brother as you did me, so you used illusion and trickery. Send him home now!"

A golden-haired vision in violet laughed shrilly. "No, Prince, we can't do that. We promised you a bargain, and this young man is our bargaining chip. If you wish to leave with the woman, you must forfeit the boy—and vice versa."

Aubrey shook his head. "No. I won't choose. I can't. Take me and let them both go."

Golden-hair made a moue of mock sorrow. "But you're very nearly used up, and we need some fresh blood. I must say, you've done quite well. Not many of our conquests last the best part of a year. That may have been because we allowed you to leave through the day, to recover. I doubt that will be necessary with either of these two, though. They're young, fresh. We can play all day and dance all night, and they'll still last for months before they fade away."

As he continued to shake his head in denial, she added coldly, "Let me make it simple for you. Choose, or we kill you all. Which might, admittedly, relieve you of a burden…but imagine the sorrow it would bring to your family. And hers."

Aubrey closed his eyes, fighting panic. Byron was but fourteen years old, on the cusp of manhood. He was fit and agile and strong, but to be forced to dance night after night—as Aubrey was certain would happen—would eventually kill him.

But the same was true of Elayna.

"Choose," repeated the faery. "And know that whichever one you take with you, the other must remain with us forever."

He took a deep breath and announced his decision.

THE DAY they'd chosen for their wedding dawned bright, clear, and in every way perfect but one.

Elayna smoothed her white dress and gazed with tear-filled, unseeing eyes at the posy of red and white roses she carried. Red, the colour of blood and of death, and white, the colour of mourning. She listened to the priestess intone the funeral rites in a fog of near desperation, wondering if the pain would ever end, how she could summon the strength to go on.

For the Fae, in their cold, uncaring, magnificent hall, had in the end claimed not one victim, but two.

A handsome, dark-haired, dark-eyed man approached, and her heart contracted painfully at the sight. He looked so very much like Aubrey. All three brothers had shared those hawk-nosed, angular features, that slender yet well-muscled frame. Only Byron had varied the pattern, having level brows rather than arched, and hazel eyes instead of brown.

"You have my deepest condolences, Lady Elayna," said Rupert, the middle prince. No, now the only prince, and the heir. "I can't believe he is truly gone. The accident..." His voice broke for a moment, then he brought himself back under control. "The accident was so unforeseen. Bizarre, really. Such a little hill; anyone would have thought the horse could negotiate it with ease." He hesitated, as if about to say more, then shook his head and patted Elayna's shoulder. "Utterly bizarre. The dun must have ploughed into the rise at full tilt, they said. I can't understand why Aubrey wouldn't have even attempted to turn him aside."

"I can," muttered Elayna, without thinking.

"What?" Rupert looked puzzled. "What did you say?"

She shook her head and looked away. "Nothing. It was nothing." How could she explain? They'd all think she was mad. Sometimes she thought so herself.

"And the way the horse fell on the dog," continued Rupert, trying, despite her discomfort, to unravel the mystery surrounding his brother's passing. Striving to make sense of it. "The way all three suffered broken necks, dying instantly. It was so very odd."

Elayna nodded. Her eyes remained dry, but her nose prickled, and the bones of her face ached with unshed tears. "Oh, Rupert," she whispered, "what am I going to do? I don't know how to continue without him."

He gathered her to him and hugged her, murmuring broken words of comfort, and for a moment she relaxed against him. But he sounded so much like Aubrey it hurt. Gods, he even smelled like Aubrey!

She took a deep breath and pushed away from him. "You should go and speak to your father. He needs you now more than ever."

Rupert's mother, the princess, had died a year ago from a fever, and now from a loving family of five they were reduced to two princes. Two lonely and bewildered men.

Rupert nodded, gave her shoulder a final pat, and moved away, murmuring under his breath, "So bizarre."

Elayna watched him go while her family, friends, and neighbours sought to comfort her. All thought the circumstances of Prince Aubrey's death were strange indeed, especially coming so soon after the disappearance and presumed death of Prince Byron.

For her own peace of mind, Elayna tried to believe at first that it had truly been an accident, but doubts kept creeping in. Peace of mind. The phrase reminded her of the rhyme she'd used to gain entrance to the palace under the hill and she went over those unbelievable events again in her mind—as she had done every day and every night since. Especially the promise Aubrey had made to her as he rode away, leaving her there.

And finally, she thought of young Byron, alone among alien strangers.

~

NOBODY WAS GREATLY SURPRISED WHEN, shortly after the funeral, Lady Elayna also went missing. Rupert, scouring the countryside as part of the search party, kept repeating the word 'bizarre' to himself like a litany. Elayna had always been so level-headed —but then, so had Aubrey until almost a year ago. Over the past twelve moons Rupert had watched his outgoing, cheerful brother become progressively more reserved, morose, and prone to jumping at shadows.

Then Byron had disappeared, and Elayna had seemingly caught the infection as well. It had been, thought Rupert— moving carefully through the forest and scanning his surroundings for any sign of the vanished lady—like living with a pair of unhappy ghosts.

Even in the throes of his illness, whatever it was, Aubrey had still demonstrated his love for Elayna—until the forest had claimed his youngest brother, after which he'd seemed unable even to look at her. Or she at him. Then had come the accident that had killed Aubrey and made Rupert the reluctant heir. He shook his head again. The entire sequence of events was just absurd.

Like his father, Elayna's parents, and the rest of the court, he fully expected to find a body, not a living woman. Watching her withdraw more and more over the past month, it had seemed obvious to him that she found it difficult to contemplate life without Aubrey. He'd be unsurprised if she'd opted to take her own life. Strange that he'd found no trace yet, though, after two days of searching. The island wasn't that large. Even stranger, her horse had vanished as well, and so had Byron's favourite steed. So many mysteries piled one upon the other made Rupert's skin twitch.

Lost in his musings, he didn't notice the clearing until the hill loomed in front of him. It seemed to spring up out of nowhere. Rupert drew the rein with a startled oath, making his mare rear beneath him. He leaned forward to pat her neck, uttering senseless, soothing endearments, and looked around in puzzlement. He knew every inch of Serrarn Isle, and neither the clearing nor the hill were a part of it. Mystified but not yet alarmed, he dismounted and approached.

"They won't let you in, you know. Not after your brother reneged on his promise. A shame, because you're even better-looking than he was. But there it is." The voice was rich, warm, and honey-smooth, like the very finest mead.

He spun around. A woman stood draped against a nearby tree, her green silk gown and nut-brown hair blending so well with the surrounding woodland that she seemed to be part of it.

Anger made his voice sharp. "What do you know about my brother? Are you talking about Aubrey or Byron? And who are you?"

A trill of laughter answered him. "Names. Your kind put so much stock in names. You can call me Esmerelda, if you like. As for your brothers, I knew both of them, very well indeed." A smile played about her cherry-red lips but failed to reach her eyes.

A half-dozen furious strides and he'd pinned her arms behind her with one hand, holding his knife to her throat with the other. "Talk, Witch. I want answers! Who won't let me in where, and what's this talk of a broken promise?"

She tried to lean away from the iron blade, peeling her lips back from her teeth to reveal pointed canines. "Put that thing away, unless you want the boy to suffer."

Shock made him lower and almost drop the knife. "What boy? Do you mean Byron's alive?"

The woman's emerald robes parted to reveal other shades of green as she swayed away from the tree; celadon, pale mint, and apple. "He is. In there." She jerked her head toward the mossy hill. "If you put away the blood metal and dance with me, I'll answer all your questions."

Rupert knew the stories. He understood what kind of mounds could swallow people whole, and what kind of sylph-like women would shy away from the touch of cold iron. He rammed his knife into its sheath and glared at her. "I don't dance, except with a sword. How about you tell me what I want to know, or I'll sheath the iron in your throat. Where's my little brother? And what do you know about Aubrey's death?"

Casting a disdainful glance at the covered knife, she settled herself in a flurry of green silk on the grass and patted the ground beside her. "At least let's be comfortable. It's a long tale."

He did as she asked and listened in stunned disbelief to her account of Prince Aubrey's enchantment, Elayna's intrusion into the hollow hill, and the faery band's subsequent abduction of Byron.

"Your brother chose his woman, as we thought he would. But he didn't adhere to the agreement. Three times during the next two moons he came back to the hill, seeking entrance. Seeking to reclaim his brother. Thrice he recited the rhyme, and thrice the door remained closed to him. So he tried to force entry—and you know the result. We snapped his fool neck for him, and his horse and his hound as well."

Rupert shook his head. "How could you believe that he wouldn't try? How could anybody accept such a…a deceitful bargain? No wonder he and Elayna drifted about looking heartbroken." He looked up. "I'll offer you a trade. Take me and let my brother go."

Esmerelda shook her head and rose to her feet in a billow of graduated green silk, rowanberry lips curved in a mocking smile. "It's too late for that. The boy is lost. So, too, will the woman, if you don't find her soon. I can help you search, pretty man, if you'll only dance with me." She glanced at the scabbard at his hip, barely concealing a shudder. "There's a saying among your people, I believe. 'Never give a sword to a man who cannot dance.' Let's see if there's any truth to it. Join me in a pavane; there's really nothing to it."

She reached down and drew a long, red nail along his cheek. Blood welled in its wake, and she sucked it from her fingertip, slow and sensuous, then licked her lips for emphasis.

Grasping his hands and pulling him up beside her, she started to hum a slow, haunting melody evocative of harps and violins. Her cold, calm beauty made Rupert think of another aphorism: 'Never trust your heart to a man who cannot cry.' Or woman either, he supposed. The only emotion she'd shown, other than contempt, was fear of his knife and his sword. He tried to snatch his hand away, but her grip was surprisingly strong. So was her perfume, a combination of musk, floral, and spice that drowned his senses and weakened his resolve.

Almost against his will, she led him through the dance steps, measured and deliberate to begin with, then adding dips and little hops. Leading him in a circle around the fairy hill.

Could a woman ravish a man? Perhaps a faery could. The indignity of the thought gave him the strength to pull away from her embrace and grope for his sword.

"Stupid man," she spat as the raised blade gathered sunlight, and gestured behind them toward the faery hill. "You might deny me my desire, but yours was already forfeit. Your brother broke his oath to us—and we collect on our debts. *Always.*"

The green mound shivered and became transparent to reveal the faery host parading through the complicated forms of a lively galliard, his younger brother among them. Rupert screamed Byron's name and threw himself at the hill, but the barrier, although translucent, remained solid. In a desperate attempt to lever it open he thrust forward with his sword; the barrier gripped the blade and held it fast.

Esmerelda spun away, laughing, and as she disappeared inside the Faery Hall, Rupert saw a fair-haired, blank-faced female dancer, shorter than the others, twirl and leap across the floor. *No! It couldn't be*! He abandoned his effort to retrieve the sword and threw himself at the mound, beating at it with his fists and raining curses on it, to no avail. The Hall and the dancers vanished, and the hill became once more just a mossy green mound, a sword hilt now protruding from its sod.

Rupert's shoulders slumped in defeat. He didn't know the charm, and force would not avail. At last, with his knuckles scraped and bleeding and his throat so raw he could barely manage a whisper, he rose and turned to go. As he did so, something stabbed through the sole of his stout leather boot.

Looking down, he saw what it was. A thorn from a wilting posy of red and white roses.

NEVERENDING SUMMER

INE GAUSEL

Warm, autumn-brown eyes met Mirdoll's. The elf in front of him let his robe fall to his elbows, showing off more of his pale and slender body. A small blush always appeared on his face when he undressed, even though they'd done this twice a week for three months. Phoebus—that name fit him so well—bit his lip and tucked a few strands of fire-red hair behind his ear. An obvious attempt at seduction, the elf still too young to have learned subtlety.

Mirdoll saw Phoebus's lips move, but it took a moment of silence for him to realize he'd been spoken to. He straightened his back, suddenly aware of his own posture. Taking the paintbrush out of his mouth, he answered, "What?"

"You're staring," Phoebus repeated. The robe slid off his arms and down to the floor, leaving the young elf completely naked.

"Can't help myself. You look absolutely ravishing."

Phoebus giggled but said nothing more before he began to recreate the pose he'd held the last time they'd met. He used his hands to frame his face as if in the middle of caressing his own cheek. Those beautiful brown eyes went to the ceiling, staring longingly at nothing. Then he lifted his left foot just a little, which Mirdoll had told him to do, to give the painting some dynamism.

Mirdoll looked to his painting. Phoebus had posed correctly—unfortunately leaving Mirdoll with no valid reason to approach and correct the stance, to touch the elf's warm skin and inhale the smell of lavender. Phoebus always smelled of lavender.

He dipped the brush into the paint, and the evening's first brushstroke landed on the canvas. Mirdoll's gaze went back and forth between his model and the picture. He wanted to—needed to—paint every scar, beauty mark, and freckle.

"Mirdoll?" Phoebus asked after a ten-minute silence. "What do you think about when you look at me?"

When Mirdoll lifted his head to look at the gorgeous man once again, his muse was no longer holding the pose. Phoebus tilted his head to the side.

"I think about how beautiful you are," Mirdoll answered. It was the truth, but he also thought about long, warm summer days. He thought about beating hearts and heavy breathing. About empty words and broken promises. "You remind me of someone I knew when I was younger."

"Younger? Aren't you still young?" Phoebus pointed out.

Mirdoll caught himself. He did appear young, though he was more than twice the age of the man before him.

"A lover?" Phoebus toed the distance between them, sitting down beside him.

"I'm not done painting," Mirdoll stated, hoping Phoebus would return to his pose. Instead, his muse leaned over him to peek at the canvas.

"So that's what I look like from the front." Phoebus grabbed a lock of his own hair to compare the color to the one in the painting—Mirdoll had worked hard to make it completely indistinguishable.

"Yes, Phoebus, that is what"—he quickly grabbed the elf's hand, inches from touching the wet paint—"you look like." He let out a deep sigh. "It's not dry yet. Please, pose for five more minutes. I'm only missing a few details."

"Answer my question first," Phoebus said, softly pushing his nose against Mirdoll's. "Was he your lover? The man I remind you of."

"Yes. He was."

"What was his name?" The way Phoebus smiled told Mirdoll that he was only teasing him. The playfulness was another reminder of the love he'd once known. The love he had lost.

"His name was Get-back-up-there-and-pose." Mirdoll

forced a chuckle as he gently tried to push the elf away so he would do as he was told.

Tender lips met Mirdoll's for a chaste kiss before Phoebus stood up and went back to looking like an angelic statue. Mirdoll felt guilty for wanting more than that single kiss, for the lust he felt at the pit of his stomach. Phoebus confused him. Made him doubt. He pushed the feeling to the back of his mind as he continued to paint.

He remembered the first time he'd met Phoebus, how he'd had to look at him twice—how he'd hoped that red hair and freckled face had belonged to someone else. He was the mirror image of his past love, and the young elf had made Mirdoll's heart beat anew. That was why he'd had to paint him: to not lose sight of such perfection once again. To keep *him* close. For a second chance.

Just as Phoebus started to become impatient, and perhaps a bit tired, Mirdoll finished the piece by adding the beauty mark that enhanced Phoebus's cheekbones, right beneath his left eye. Mirdoll smiled, happy to finally be done.

"Phoebus, come here. Tell me what you think."

The young man put his robe on before he came running. He smiled brightly as he laid eyes upon the artwork.

"You made me look absolutely stunning. Thank you, Mirdoll." He folded his hands, admiring his own beauty. "I look a little bit like my father," he added with a chuckle. A small pause, and his demeanor suddenly turned serious. "On that note.... Would you like to come over for dinner one day? I'd love for you to meet my parents."

Mirdoll's body stiffened as he realized it was over. It had gone too far. His heart hammered beneath his ribs as he understood what he had to do. This desire would be nothing but a distraction from his real goal. There was too much at stake. He couldn't let Phoebus infect his life—the boy was an imposter, nothing more.

"I'd love to see Darion again," he said quietly.

"What?" Phoebus said, about to turn around.

Mirdoll glimpsed a smile on the naive elf's lips. It swiftly disappeared as the bullet pierced his head. The pistol deafened Mirdoll for a second, leaving a ringing sound in his ears.

"I'm sorry," he said as he lowered the gun.

He noticed the wounded man struggle for his breath, even though he lay still, his blood pooling on the floor. Mirdoll fell to his knees. Phoebus's eyes didn't follow his movement—he was still alive, but not present.

"I can't fall in love with you. You're not him," Mirdoll said, a twinge of guilt tugging at his heart. Turning the pistol in his hand, getting ready to strike with the butt, he spoke to the dying man one last time. "I'd give anything to be as beautiful as you, Phoebus. Beauty means happiness; only ugly people suffer. Leave this world knowing that I have shared with you the only lesson life has taught me."

Those autumn-brown eyes met his one last time, right before he slammed the cold metal into Phoebus's head.

Mirdoll sat in silence for a moment. He could barely breathe as he listened for someone outside the tenement. Voices. Screaming. Running. The door being knocked down. But there was no sound. Had no one heard the gunshot?

As he realized that no one would barge in and arrest him, his heart started hammering for a completely different reason. Phoebus was dead. What was he supposed to do now? Another chance at love lost—the last bridge set ablaze.

He cursed under his breath at his own stupidity. Tears rolled down his cheeks as he mumbled to himself, "Think, Doll. Think...."

An idea.

His mourning ended as he got to his feet. Grabbing the canvas by the edges as to not smear any of the paint, he headed over to a full-length mirror in the corner of the room. After putting the painting against the wall, he looked into his own pale-sapphire eyes—the only authentic part of his body right now.

A glance at the painting was all he needed. When he looked again into the mirror, Phoebus stared back. Not all hope was lost; rather, it seemed like his impulsivity could lead him down a similar path to the one he had been frantically searching for. Darion would hold him again. Not as a lover this time, but as a son.

~

Twenty years earlier

TWO HUGE HANDS *covered his eyes. A shadow had approached from behind, then blinded him. The lavender scent filled his nostrils, and he smiled. A nibble on his earlobe made his knees crumble as desire consumed his thoughts.*

Darion breathed into his ear, "I love you, Doll."

"Forever?" Mirdoll asked, his heart beating so hard he thought maybe Darion could hear the drumming sound.

"Forever and always. To the ends of the Eternal Chaos itself, and back. No one will ever come between us." Gently, Darion removed his hands.

Mirdoll turned around, looking straight into the golden-brown eyes of his beloved. He reached for the fiery hair that hung in front of Darion's face, pushing it behind his ear to get a better view of his beautifully freckled features.

It was without a doubt Darion's attractiveness that had drawn Mirdoll to him at first, the thought of them as the most perfect couple —both of them the epitome of beauty, sculpted and handsome. Anyone who passed them on the street would either want to be them or be with them. But even after he had conquered Darion's affections, and the unobtainable had been obtained, Mirdoll's heart had refused to let go.

No one had ever made him feel so safe just by holding him or made him feel so incredibly loved just by kissing his cheek.
Darion would be his.
Forever.

～

THE CONSTABLE LED him down a long hallway.

"I hope you understand the severity of what you've done, young man," he said, his face stern. "Your parents have been worried sick."

"Yes, officer," Mirdoll answered meekly. He'd kept away for a week, to make it look like Phoebus had run away. It would make any differences in behavior seem less suspicious—they'd just be happy that he was back.

When they reached the end of the corridor, the constable opened the door leading out of the station.

Mirdoll's gaze went straight to Darion's, and before he'd realized what was happening, he was surrounded by strong arms. He hugged his beloved back. It had been such a long time. Years had passed, but his embrace still felt the same. Pure bliss surged through Mirdoll's body. The hug ended too quickly for his taste, but when Darion pulled away and their eyes met once more, he forgot his discontent.

"We've been so worried. You can't just run off like that," his love said, brows meeting in a frown. "What were you thinking?" Warm hands touched Mirdoll's cheeks, caressing lightly.

Mirdoll didn't answer. He had Phoebus's appearance, not his voice.

"My dear. I'm so happy you're alright," a woman's voice called out. "Oh, Phoebus, my boy."

Smaller arms clung to him, and that was when he remembered. That temptress and thief—the elf woman who had seduced his Darion. He had never laid eyes on her; Darion had only told Mirdoll that he'd met her, how great she was, and had even dared speak her cursed name. A name Mirdoll wouldn't give her the satisfaction of ever uttering in either thought or word. This was the first time he'd seen her blonde hair. Her pink lips. Her beautiful green eyes. He was certain her eyes were the feature that had lured Darion to her. Those eyes had smiled at his beloved, and he had been unable to resist.

Mirdoll had to pull away from her; the embrace made him doubt himself.

She looked surprised. "What's wrong, love?"

The softness of her voice. The way she spoke that word. *Love*. That was how she spoke to Darion.

That voice had stolen everything from him. Everything was wrong. She seemed so oblivious to the crime she'd committed against him.

"Are you okay, Son?" Darion spoke this time.

That dark voice seemed so familiar, yet there was a strangeness to it. Mirdoll gazed at Darion once more, for a moment hoping the man he loved would recognize him through his magical disguise. He wanted Darion to look into the fake brown eyes and see the pale blue ones of someone who had never stopped loving him.

"Let's go home, eh? You need some rest." Darion gave the woman an apologetic look before putting one strong arm over Mirdoll's shoulders. Mirdoll basked in the feeling of Darion's touch, however fatherly it was. He felt protected and loved.

The carriage ride felt like it lasted forever. No one spoke, only glances were exchanged. The woman tried to smile at him, but he turned away every time. He didn't want to look at her, scared of noticing how perfect she actually was.

Walking into the mansion, Darion ordered his kitchen staff to prepare Phoebus's favorite dish. Apparently, he wanted them all to have a nice family dinner. Mirdoll was then ordered to go take a bath before the meal. Finding the bathroom took some time, but in the end, he lay soaking in the tub.

He closed his eyes and let the water consume him. Sinking into the dark depths of his own mind, he wondered—for the hundredth time—how he wanted this to play out. Getting that woman out of the picture, that was what he wished for. Back to the blissful days where Darion lusted only for him, that was where he wanted to go. Mirdoll felt a sting behind his eyes, and he wondered if it was possible to cry whilst underwater.

∼

THIS COULDN'T BE RIGHT—IT *was supposed to be a perfect summer day. Just the two of them, sitting in the meadow of tall grass and colorful flowers. The sun would shine upon them, highlight their hair. Make them squint as they looked at each other. Warm their cheeks. Then they'd embrace, and Darion would place small kisses down his neck, bruising his flawless skin.*

It was all completely wrong.

"A shapeshifter? Mirdoll, are you serious?" Darion yelled at him. Never had he heard such heartbreak in his beloved's voice. "You can't keep that a secret from someone."

Mirdoll's whole body shook as he held himself, trying to compensate for the touch Darion now starved him of. How could he have been so careless as to drink that concoction Darion had given him? The funny smell should have been a sign. He should have known.

His glowing fair skin had turned the treacherous deep blue he'd been born with. His hair was now black instead of the blond that had turned Darion's head the first time they'd met. Looking like his true self, he felt naked and exposed.

His beloved could never love anyone so flawed. So ugly.

"Dar, it doesn't matter. I'm still me, I'm the same. Nothing has to change," Mirdoll tried to reassure him, but even he could hear the uncertainty in his voice.

As he walked closer, Darion moved away.

"You lied to me. You made me believe you were an elf."

"You told me I was beautiful inside and out!"

"That is not the point. Doll..." Darion trailed off. For a silent moment, his gaze lingered on Mirdoll, and tears formed in the corners of his eyes.

"Who told you?" Mirdoll asked, breaking the silence between them. He had to know who had set his beloved against him. "Who made you doubt me?"

Darion seemed to think. Then he opened his mouth, and Mirdoll's heart sank. "You did. No one is this perfect."

∼

MIRDOLL'S HEAD resurfaced as he sat up. Water dripped onto his pale skin—Phoebus's skin. He was certain a life lived as Darion's son was not an option; that was not the love he searched for. Nor was killing Darion's woman and taking her place—Darion's love would still not belong to him.

Mirdoll would have to reveal himself. Maybe Darion would be happy to see him again? Maybe he'd regretted marrying that woman and would want him back? Mirdoll smiled at the thought.

He imagined Darion laying eyes on him again after such a long time. Without hesitation, he'd turn from the woman to pull Mirdoll into a loving embrace. In a moment, Darion would realize the love he thought he felt for that whore had never been real, and that anger had clouded his judgment all those years ago. They'd kiss, and Mirdoll would once again have conquered Darion's love.

He stepped out of the tub, got dressed, then headed out into the hallway. A few turns around corners and peeks into a couple of rooms later, he was lost. Darion's mansion was so huge it felt like a labyrinth. He opened another door and looked into the darkness. No one was there either. Mirdoll sighed as he closed the door. Turning around, he almost walked straight into one of the servants.

"Looking for something, Master Phoebus?"

Mirdoll nodded, at first hoping he could avoid speaking. If the servants remembered their young master's voice too well, it could pose a problem. But he knew he would have to tell the servant what he was looking for in the end, so he cleared his throat before saying, "Father."

"He is in his study. Naturally. You'll see him at dinner." The servant smiled.

"Bring me to him, please," Mirdoll said quietly.

"He would probably not like to be disturbed, Master—"

"Please."

The servant was still reluctant but ushered him along anyway. After what seemed like a five-minute walk, they stopped outside a door identical to all the others. The servant knocked rhythmically, as if he was delivering a secret watchword.

"Sir, Master Phoebus would like to speak with you."

A faint sound came from the other side of the door, and the servant opened it for Mirdoll to enter. After treading over the threshold, the door was closed behind him. Now, he was all alone with Darion, who was sitting in a large leather chair with his hands full of papers.

"Son." Darion's voice was as dark and smooth as ever. He got up and approached Mirdoll. His arms wrapped around him and held him close. "I'm so glad you're safe. I was so worried. You mean everything to me."

And just like that, Mirdoll changed his mind. His beloved was holding him so close, keeping him so warm. He wanted Darion to hold *him* like that, but there was no guarantee that he would, and now that Mirdoll—in a strange way—had what he wanted, he did not want to risk losing it that quickly. One day, he would find a perfect moment to tell his love who he really was, but for now he just wanted to enjoy the attention. He relaxed into the hug, savoring the moment and the smell of lavender that surrounded him.

∼

MIRDOLL WOULD HAVE RECOGNIZED that gorgeous face anywhere. Darion stood only steps away, studying a bottle of perfume. He approached the man he hadn't seen in weeks. Oh, how he had missed the warmth from those golden-brown eyes gazing at him through the bed's mesh canopy. The electricity that had sparked between them every time they touched. He'd been so lonely without Darion's arms holding him close.

"You don't need any perfume, Dar. You always smell great." Mirdoll smiled.

Darion jumped, a little startled.

"Doll. Hi. It's not for me." Was Darion trying to hide the pink bottle in his hand? "What are you doing here?"

"I was just passing through when I saw you." A quick glance at the perfume Darion was holding, then Mirdoll turned his gaze back to the beautiful man before him. "You remembered that I prefer floral scents." Mirdoll giggled. "You don't have to buy me anything, Dar. I forgive you."

"Forgive me?" Darion lifted his brow.

"Yes. For overreacting. I love you, and I want to be with you."

His beloved looked away from him. "Doll.... I've found someone else."

That made Mirdoll pause. It had just been a few weeks, and Darion was already buying gifts for someone else? What could this person have that Mirdoll didn't? His heart started to race as he silently panicked. What was he lacking? What could he be lacking? Except true elf ancestry.

"Just an infatuation, I'm sure," Mirdoll said, keeping his perfect composure. "Describe him to me, I'll give you what you're lusting for."

Darion scoffed. "Why would you assume such a thing? Beauty is not the only thing I care about. You could look like her all you want, but you still wouldn't be her."

"Dar—" Mirdoll began, but Darion interrupted.

"I've realized that all you have ever done is make me feel inferior. You've held me to an impossible standard, and I'm tired of you only acknowledging my looks. You're so shallow. When I'm with Mirabell, I can be myself—I can be imperfect."

⁓

FIVE WEEKS PASSED. Most days it rained, which meant the family stayed inside the mansion. Mirdoll didn't mind; it gave him the opportunity to spend time with Darion. Some days they played chess or backgammon, other days they just sat beside each other and read.

Darion laughed with him and smiled when they had fun together, even though he seemed worried that his son had turned mute. It had been hard not to speak; there was so much Mirdoll wanted to tell Darion. He wanted to tell him about how he'd followed his dream to become a painter, and that he carried a small vial of lavender oil next to his heart everywhere he went, because nothing inspired him more than the thought of his beloved.

The woman barely left them alone on those rainy days, and sometimes Mirdoll found it hard to hide his contempt for her. Nothing dampened his mood more than seeing her kiss *his* man, and seeing Darion smile at her right after. Had his beloved forgotten how good they'd had it without her?

When the sun shone again on day thirty-seven, the woman finally decided to spend the afternoon in town. Mirdoll joined Darion outside to wave her off as the horses trotted away.

"Now that we're alone, how do you think we should spend the day?" Darion asked. "What about croquet?"

Mirdoll nodded, then pointed to his clothes to hint that he wanted to dress for the occasion. Darion seemed to understand, giving him a smile.

"Sure. I'll set it up," his beloved said before leaving for the garden.

When he got to Phoebus's bedroom, Mirdoll's whole body started to shiver. This was his best chance to reveal who he really was, now that they were alone—and would be for several hours. His heart hammered beneath his ribs, and even though he sweated, his body felt cold.

It was now or never.

Walking toward the garden, Mirdoll played out every scenario he could imagine in his mind. He imagined Darion mad, sad, neutral, and happy. He tried to plan what the first thing he said should be. Nothing felt right.

When he reached the door leading out to the green-grassed lawn surrounded by all sorts of beautifully colored flowers, he looked around, making sure he was alone. Certain that no one could see him, he changed. The red hair that had once belonged to Phoebus turned a bright, golden color. His eyes returned to their natural pale blue, and his skin darkened slightly. He still looked elven, just like when he and Darion had first met.

He headed outside with all the confidence he could muster. Darion didn't notice him at first, still busy setting up the croquet course. Mirdoll stopped a few steps away, unable to keep from smiling at the sight of the happy man in front of him.

"Darion," he said.

"Yes?" Darion answered, not turning to look at first.

Then his shoulders stiffened, and for the first time in twenty years, Darion's brown eyes met Mirdoll's blue ones. "Doll?" he whispered in obvious disbelief. He looked like he wanted to ask a million questions at once. In the end, all he said was, "How did you find me?"

"It wasn't that difficult," Mirdoll answered, hoping to avoid going into details. "I've missed you, Dar."

"I've missed you too, Doll. But why are you still pretending to be someone you're not?" Darion walked over and gently touched Mirdoll's golden hair, then his pointy elven ears. "This isn't you."

"It's the me you fell in love with, Dar. The me you promised to love forever," Mirdoll retorted, a sudden bitter taste in his mouth. "You promised."

"You are not entitled to my love. You lied to me. Broke my trust. Do you think love can withstand deceit just because it was promised to you?"

"Everything we experienced together, everything I said, was not a lie—that was real, and it was love. Does it matter what I look like?" Mirdoll could not resist holding Darion's face between his hands, caressing those soft cheeks with his thumbs.

"I don't care what you look like. I care that I never knew who you really were, and that you, in your search for perfection, lost your individuality. You were never truly yourself when we were together; therefore, I made no promise to *you*. You don't exist." Taking ahold of Mirdoll's wrists, Darion pried the hands from his face.

"Make the promise to the real me then."

Again, he changed. Blond hair turned black, and his skin went from fair to blue. His face became his own. Only his eyes stayed the same—the eyes he'd always looked upon Darion with.

Darion studied him in silence. The world seemed to complete a full turn around the sun before he spoke up again. "It's too late, Doll. I have a life of my own, and it's about time that you get one yourself. You'll find someone who can love you better than I can. Just...be yourself from the beginning, okay?"

The world had circled the sun in vain. Moments later, it

shattered. For five whole weeks, Mirdoll had watched Darion treat someone else the way he'd promised he would treat him. He had watched the love of his life kiss and caress someone else the way he had kissed and caressed him. Deep down, he'd known Darion was happy with the person he'd chosen, but it crushed Mirdoll to admit it to himself.

"Doll, please leave. My son will be down here any second now. I don't want him to meet you," Darion said, looking away.

"Of course, Dar." Mirdoll swallowed. "I still love you. I'd do anything to make you happy."

"I appreciate it."

Darion turned his back to Mirdoll and continued preparing the course. Mirdoll turned away, too, walking slowly back to the door. A sudden awareness of one of the croquet clubs lying in the grass made him think. Phoebus wasn't here anymore. In a few minutes, Darion would notice. He'd go upstairs and find no one. Later, he would realize that his son had never been found and that he'd been the victim of another lie. Darion would not be happy; his heart would be broken, and he would grieve.

The thought that Darion, in the end, would feel anger and resentment toward him—instead of the small fraction of love he was certain was still there—made Mirdoll nauseous. Unable to breathe. He'd rather it all ended here, where there still was some understanding between them.

He silently picked up the club. It was heavier than he'd thought. It weighed on his heart and conscience, yet he felt it the better option.

Walking slowly back toward Darion, he lifted the club up over his head.

THE DOE PRIESTESS

S. K. SAYARI

*D*eath often came too soon for those who did not deserve it.

Desmond lowered himself to one knee at his sister's bedside. Queen Daymira's head lolled to the side—her cheeks pallid and sunken, the whites of her eyes riddled with red, her lips cracked. Matted auburn hair, dull and stringy, clung to her forehead, and the musty stench of death wafted from her body as her breath rattled in her chest. Desmond gritted his teeth, pushing away the tightness in his chest. He would save his sister, no matter the price. She had been his stalwart companion, his friend, his confidant, for so many years. She deserved to be healthy and happy.

Taking comfort in the thin scroll within his grasp, Desmond ran his thumb along the crackly parchment. "Daya, I received a message. It must be her. She's coming…she has to be coming. To save you."

Only a guttural groan left his sister's lips. She raised a shaking hand, lowered it, then raised it once more. With his free hand, Desmond took it—it was as if she had dipped her hand into a river of ice. His lips quivered. Would the Doe Priestess be strong enough to save someone on the cusp of death? He squeezed his sister's hand tightly. He couldn't afford to have doubts now.

Desmond had tried everything. Herbal medicine, healing magics, and even animal sacrifices. Said to be kindred to the Lady of the Spirits, the Doe Priestess was rumoured to ward away evil with her very presence, bless those she found worthy, and give life itself to those she wished. She had been but a legend to Desmond until he had ordered his servants to scour the continent for her. And scoured they had, lest they wished to return empty-handed to his wrath.

The Lady of the Spirits…if he only had her powers, he could save his sister himself. But while the Doe Priestess had proven to be real, the Lady of the Spirits had never truly been seen by man.

"Look, Sister. Look. Let's open the scroll together." Desmond let go of Daya's hand, and it fell limp onto the crisp, lilac sheets she lay in. He quickly broke the golden wax seal on the scroll, unfurling the paper. "'I shall arrive on the first morn of Shorasmonth to see to the Queen of Marsommer.' That's what the Doe Priestess wrote, Sister. She'll be here tomorrow. She's a priestess, so she has to heal you. She has to...."

Desmond locked gazes with his sister, but it was as if she had no presence in her body—she looked past him with milky irises, far away into the distance. The sight made his heart squeeze with sadness. Rising, he bent over and placed a gentle kiss on her cheek.

"All will be well, Daya. I shall do anything—everything—to keep you alive."

Anything?

The voice whispered within Desmond's ears, and he jumped. What was this sorcery? He looked from side to side, but saw no other person, no other creature within the chambers. He licked his lips, nodding.

"Y-yes. Anything." He frowned then, not knowing why he was speaking to a voice most likely in his head. It sounded... strange, sending prickles of worry throughout him.

Is that so? said the voice with a chuckle. *You know what you are?*

"W-what?"

A liar.

～

Rasha walked along the path of one of the many courtyards of Castle Marsommer, letting her fingers graze the petals and leaves of the wildflowers that grew on the trellises. They twisted and writhed around the wood, finding ways to bloom even in the crowded environment they grew in. Cerulean, indigo, periwinkle, and cerise...the colours all so vibrant. So full of *life*.

It was detestable.

Humans clung to life more strongly than a hawk did to its prey. Letting go was the hardest part for them. It had been apparent in the way the castle nobles had invited her in, all hoping to receive her blessings. As if blessings could ward away death. No, Rasha did not offer blessings to battle death—she courted it.

The humans looked to her as kin of the Lady of the Spirits. Rasha scoffed. They were right, in a sense. But they were also wrong. The Lady of the Spirits didn't exist. Even the name they had given her—the Doe Priestess—was false. Rasha was no priestess.

But the little humans didn't need to know that.

She longed for her home, where the barren trees twisted and writhed, where the mire bubbled, and where soot coated the earth like a blanket. But home was far away from the world of man. She sighed. She had no choice but to enter the land of the living for even the darkest of creatures needed to feed.

Feeding was easy in the mortal realm; no one suspected a so-called healer. And 'healing' was easy when she had accumulated so many souls over the years. But it was the thrill of the game that Rasha loved most. Give them hope, then steal it all away. Rasha licked her lips. Her game with the Prince of Marsommer was just beginning.

The clicking of boots on stone shook her out of her thoughts. She turned, raising an eyebrow as she did so. A servant stood a distance away, eyes lowered to the ground, cheeks alight with pink. Rasha slipped on a sweet smile and stepped toward the servant.

"Yes?"

"Lady Priestess. Will you come see the prince now?"

"Of course," Rasha said. "Lead the way."

She stroked the petal of a snow-white lily as she left, and it shrivelled, crumbling to ash.

∽

The Doe Priestess, a dark-haired woman wearing a gilded crown mimicking the antlers of a deer, walked into the chambers with a smile on her lips. She curtsied, and Desmond wondered how her neck didn't break under the weight of her crown.

"I am Rasha," said the Doe Priestess. "How can I serve you, Prince of Marsommer?"

"You must attend to my sister. Please, come here."

Rasha nodded and stepped toward the bed. She hovered her hand over Queen Daymira's head, her brow wrinkling and her lips curling into a dainty scowl.

"I cannot help one whose soul is lost."

"What do you mean?" Desmond barked. "I demand you heal her! I don't care if she's dying, or dead—you are the Doe Priestess, and you *will* heal her!"

"Do you truly think you can cheat death?" Rasha whispered. "You can stave off the symptoms, but you cannot avoid it."

Desmond jerked with fear that the priestess would be unable to help. "I will do anything. Anything!"

"Very well, then. Perhaps there is a way to save your sister...."

"W-what? What is it?"

Rasha's lips curled into a smile, eerie and sinister, and Desmond shivered. "A soul for a soul."

"What?" Desmond tilted his head to the side. A soul...for a soul? Was this woman speaking of a sacrifice? He had already tried sacrifices. Unless she meant...

"A soul for—"

"I heard you, damn it all!" said Desmond, his voice quivering. He shook his head, pushing away the truth of her words, wanting to stay ignorant.

"Your sister's soul is leaving her body. If you want it to stay, you must offer up compensation to the Lady of the Dead."

"The...Lady of the Dead?" Desmond shivered once more. He had always known that the Lady of the Spirits watched over men, but he had never heard of this title.

"Have you never heard of her?" crooned the Doe Priestess. "She reigns over the Realm of the Dead."

Desmond narrowed his eyes. The Lady of the Spirits, the Lady of the Dead, the Doe Priestess...too many women who bore more power over his predicament than he liked. "And who are you to her?"

Rasha laughed, throwing her head back, but offered no answer. Desmond clenched his fists, frustration bubbling in his chest. How dare this priestess laugh during such a dark time!

"I asked—"

"She will choose a soul to take in return, should you wish to proceed," Rasha interrupted. "You have no say in the matter. If you do not comply, the Lady of the Dead will return the favour to you fivefold."

"Lives are aplenty in Marsommer," growled Desmond. He would sacrifice anything, anyone—

"And what if she asks for yours?" whispered the Doe Priestess.

Desmond hesitated. Would he sacrifice his own life for Daya's? Part of him wished he didn't know the true, secret answer to that question. He licked his lips and nodded, answering in the way he thought he should. "Then I shall...give it."

He would gladly give his life for his sister's, he assured himself. Anything to save the sweet soul that suffered. Anything....

You know the truth, Desmond of Marsommer. You know how heavy her life weighs in comparison to your own.

The Doe Priestess's lips curled into a smile, soft yet malevolent.

"I-I must think on the matter." Desmond stiffly nodded, eager to have the priestess out of his sister's chambers. "You may leave now."

Rasha lowered her head and backed out of the room, curtsying before she closed the door. Desmond turned to his sister, chewing at his lip.

Daya would die a thousand times before she took another's life to help herself. Yet...what she didn't know wouldn't hurt her. He placed his hand on Daya's forehead and she closed her eyes, falling into a restless slumber.

The priestess's words rung in his ears: *A soul for a soul.* He would sacrifice anyone to save Daya. But when he thought of losing his own soul, his heart beat haphazardly with fear. He didn't want to die, not for anyone, no matter how precious they were to him.

He would pay the price of guilt, but nothing more.

∽

THE PRINCE TAPPED his fingers on his thighs as he watched Rasha. She stood in front of him, a smirk upturning her lips. Humans tended to amuse her, and this one was no different.

"You will bring me the flaxen-haired maid who labours in the kitchens from dawn to dusk. She will sate the Lady of the Dead's appetite for your sister's soul."

"How do you know all of this? Is this Dead Lady speaking to you?"

Rasha raised her chin, holding back her laughter. What a fool! "What will it be?"

The prince's jaw twitched. He rose and marched out of the

chamber. Rasha smirked, turning her attention to the Queen of Marsommer. She raised her hand to the queen's forehead, pushing away stray locks of hair, and inhaled deeply.

"Your soul smells so sweet, dear Queen. All pure souls are absolutely *delicious*. You'll be mine, one day...."

At the thudding of footsteps, Rasha stepped away from the woman's bed, lacing her fingers together. She wouldn't want to set the prince's mind to unease when her meal was so close.

The prince slammed open the chamber doors, storming in with a sobbing, flaxen-haired woman. He dragged her by her hair to Rasha's side, throwing her to the ground.

"Do as you swore."

"I swore nothing," murmured Rasha, bending down. She caressed the maid's cheek, offering her a honeyed smile. "What is your name, my sweet?"

"L-Lora," whispered the maid, her body trembling more fiercely than a rabbit being hunted by a wolf.

"Well, dear Lora," said Rasha, "I want you to close your eyes and think of your happiest memories. Will you do that for me?"

Lora nodded, closing her eyes, her breathing ragged. She twitched as Rasha leaned forward and kissed her forehead. When Rasha broke the kiss, Lora's eyes fluttered and she sagged to the ground, her expression peaceful. Her skin turned grey, crumbling to fine ash.

Rasha held her breath, rising and stepping toward the queen's bed. The prince started as Rasha bent down, pressing her lips to the woman's clammy forehead. She breathed out, and the queen convulsed.

"Daya!" shouted the prince, shoving Rasha to the side.

Rasha grimaced in annoyance, smoothing her skirts as the prince took his sister into his arms, cradling her.

"Daya, say something...."

"D-Des..." the queen whispered, her eyes slowly opening.

They were soft and full of light, her cheeks flooding with colour, her lips reddening.

The prince sobbed, lowering the queen to the bed, where she looked at Rasha, her eyes muddled with confusion. He turned to Rasha, bowing low. "Thank you, Lady Priestess."

"Priestess?" asked the queen.

"She simply healed you with her magic," said the prince in a smooth voice. Rasha raised an eyebrow but conceded, bowing her head.

"Dear Queen, do enjoy your health."

The queen's lips curled down with confusion, her forehead wrinkling. Rasha suppressed a giggle and turned, sweeping out of the chamber. Nobles and servants alike bowed down to her—as they should—as she left Castle Marsommer.

∽

DESMOND SQUEEZED Daymira's hand as the two walked arm in arm through the gardens. The soothing lullaby of the castle bard rang through the trees, settling over the flowers like a sweet blanket. Daymira raised her face to the sky and Desmond did the same, basking in the soft heat of the summer sun.

"I cannot ever thank you enough for saving me, my dear brother."

"Of course, Daya. I swore an oath, after all, back when we were children."

"What oath was that?"

"I swore that you would be safe. And I swear now that no one will ever take your life from you. We are going to live long, happy lives. Together."

Liar, liar, burn in fire....

Desmond winced at the voice. It had persisted for weeks, constantly nagging at him. He wished he could destroy it, but he didn't know where it came from.

Daymira laughed. "I hope so, Des. I am simply grateful to be here, living life with you."

Desmond coughed, a fit wracking his body, then smiled at Daymira. A twinge pierced his chest, and he clutched his shirt, smiling through the pain. The coughing had started a few days ago, but he was sure it would pass in the coming days. "All will be well."

⁓

WITH A ROAR, Desmond threw the herbal medicine to the ground. Everything tasted like ash, everything smelled like vomit, and nothing healed him. Bitterness coated his tongue and pierced his heart. He took no pleasure in the light of the sun, in the smell of the flowers, in the company of his sister. The very sight of her sent spikes of irritation through him. *She* was healthy, but what about him?

"Daya, what was this vile concoction? Are you trying to poison me?"

Daymira shook her head, her frown deep as hurt crossed her features. "Brother, nonsense! I am simply trying to *help* you. Can you not see that?"

Desmond hacked into his hand, his chest twisting, his bones aching. "I don't have much time. Summon the Doe Priestess!"

"Y-yes, Brother.... I shall do so with haste." Daymira's voice broke as she lowered her head, sweeping out of the room.

Desmond's heart twisted, but he pushed the guilt aside. He had no time for *feelings*. He had to save himself before he suffered a gruesome death at the hands of his illness.

Virtue lasts only so long, dearest Desmond of Marsommer, said the voice.

"Silence!" shouted Desmond. He placed his head in his hands, sobs racking his body. "Why me? Why has this happened to me?"

He sniffled, wiping at his nose. Whenever he thought of the end of his life, he quivered and whimpered. He didn't want to die, not like this. Had this happened because he had saved his sister? Bile rose in his throat, threatening to choke him. Was this the price for cheating death?

If so, then he refused to pay it.

～

DESMOND COUGHED IN HIS BED, his hand coming away from his mouth crimson. He whimpered, wiping away the blood on his sheets. "Sister, when is the priestess coming? I must know!"

"She should be here by now," whispered Daymira, her brow knotted with worry. Desmond sighed, the exhalation turning into another cough.

At a knock on the door, his heart skipped in his chest. The Doe Priestess entered, a smile playing at her rouge lips.

"You," breathed Desmond, his breaths ragged and tasting rancid in his mouth. "Heal me."

The Doe Priestess walked over to Desmond, a wicked light in her eyes. "I cannot. If you wish to be saved, you must offer me a life for yours."

"What?" asked Daymira. "What do you mean, a life must be offered? Des, what is this woman talking about?"

"Silence, Daya!" Desmond wiped at his forehead, his hand trembling, and turned his attention back to the Doe Priestess. "Tell me. Who is it?"

The Doe Priestess licked her lips. "The Lady of the Dead calls for one she yearns for—one who has escaped her grasp. She calls for the Queen of Marsommer!"

Queen Daymira wrung her hands. "What is this madness?"

"You must make your choice. Either you die, or your beloved sister does, my prince." The Doe Priestess curtsied, her eyes brimming with excitement and malice. Desmond cringed at her visible enjoyment of his predicament.

All shall be revealed....

"Daya, I saved you. I saved your life. Now...for me.... Save me now."

Daymira opened her mouth, her lips trembling like blossoms in the wind. "I..."

"Daya! I'm going to die if you don't help me!"

"I don't want to die either!" Daymira shook her head, clutching her head. "I can't die, I just got my life back! Don't ask this of me, Brother, please...."

Desmond clenched his fist, working his jaw. He had saved his sister, only for her to betray him. A bitter taste settled on the roof of his mouth.

"Then I shall die," he said.

The Doe Priestess blinked and raised an eyebrow. "How noble of—"

"But not today," the Prince of Marsommer interrupted.

If Daymira's death was the key to his survival, then so be it—he would sacrifice her. Her life belonged to him; it had ever since he had saved her. He didn't deserve to die here and now. The queen furrowed her brow, her lips parting in surprise.

"Today, my sister will die."

The Doe Priestess threw back her head and cackled. She raised her hands once more, her nails elongating, her hair turning white as fresh snow, the whites of her eyes blackening. Queen Daymira screamed, clutching her skirts as she rose, aiming for the door—but Desmond stopped her, gripping her arm, his fingers digging into her skin.

"Get back here," he snarled. "I won't die. Not today. Not ever!"

"Treachery!" screamed Daymira. "I curse you, Desmond! I curse you to a life in Hell!"

Desmond grimaced, tendrils of pain piercing his chest. He

coughed, letting go of his sister, who bolted for the door, but the Doe Priestess—or whatever that woman was—was faster. She wrapped her hand around Daymira's throat, and Daymira convulsed, writhing. Her skin greyed, and her movements slowed until she exploded to fine ash.

"So *delicious*," growled the priestess, her voice a multitudinous cacophony.

"Heal me now," pleaded Desmond, his own voice hoarse.

The priestess grinned, revealing pearly, tapered teeth. She stalked to Desmond, raising a clawed hand, running her nail along the length of his jaw. Desmond shivered, his strength returning to him. Yet the more vigour he felt, the more his vision blurred. Metallicity settled on his tongue like a thick film, leaving him gagging. "What's…"

"Your sister cursed you," whispered the Doe Priestess. "And cursed you shall be, to a lifeless existence in Hell."

Desmond arched and raised his hands for the priestess. "Help…me.…"

The voice laughed in his head, a guttural, dark sound, and Desmond's mouth contorted into a grimace, realizing the voice was *Rasha's*. Hot tears rolled down Desmond's cheeks, and he reached out for someone, anyone, to save him.

The priestess stepped away, grinning, and Desmond's skin turned as grey as a rabbit's fur. His fingers began to crumble, and he screamed. The last thing he saw was the Doe Priestess… or perhaps, the Lady of the Dead herself.

"Welcome to eternal Hell."

BEAUTY'S CURSE

A. M. DILSAVER

Don't go into the forest.

A warning Derrick had heard his entire life. Unreasonable, given the sheer number of tall pines that surrounded the kingdom of Groschier, effectively cutting them off from the rest of the world. Ancient, looming black trunks formed a maze around him, with needles so sharp they could poke an eye out. Derrick pushed one of the dangerous branches out of his way as Rivi passed between the narrow trunks, the horse's hooves muted by snow-covered needles on the muddy ground.

There's a monster at the heart of the forest.

Demoni, they called it. A beast of nightmare and madness that preyed on the Groschier queens, drawn by their youthful beauty, their flawless grace. For years, Derrick had thought it little more than a bedtime story designed to scare reckless young princes, to keep them from wandering too far from the formidable stone walls of the castle.

But they had all seen the box. Left in Queen Lilith's bedroom, elegantly carved and sitting primly on her nightstand. Empty, an omen of what it would hold in one year's time—the queen's heart.

His mother's heart.

Derrick had been traipsing through these woods for months with no sign of the monster, but he could feel it. An invisible darkness lurking in the trees. A menacing presence that hovered at the back of his neck. A sense of something dreadfully wrong.

And yet...nothing.

Rivi whinnied softly, tossing his head as he picked up on Derrick's tension. Derrick tried to loosen his shoulders, easing out a tense breath, but he couldn't relax. Not when his mother's life hung in the balance. He had to find the monster and kill it before it claimed her heart as well. He had to be the one to break the curse. Eight generations of queens had fallen, killed exactly one year after they'd received the box, their hearts ripped from their chests. Queen Lilith would not be the ninth.

Only a week remained, the year whittled down a month at a time as Derrick forged into the forest over and over, while his mother withered away before his eyes. Every time he returned to the castle, she seemed to have aged another ten years, her eyes slowly leaking their light, the rosy hue of her cheeks faded and sallow.

Rivi snorted and veered sharply to the left, though Derrick saw nothing untoward. Just a pile of wood from a fallen...

Not random wood—a structure. Built halfway into a slope in the ground, the door stood a good head shorter than Derrick's six-foot height. Though dilapidated, the brown brick chipped and crumbling, some semblance of the hovel's original charm shone through the sagging shutters and lopsided chimney. Window boxes even hung below dirt-encrusted panes, though any plants had long since withered to dust.

Derrick dismounted and tossed Rivi's reins loosely over a tree branch as he approached the structure. The horse shuffled uncomfortably, but the trees remained as silent and unrelenting as before. Derrick doubted that whatever monster lurked in these woods lived in a forgotten little hovel on the side of a hill.

The door swung open on creaking hinges, exposing the darkness beyond. Stale air rushed out, tinged with the bitter tang of ice and death. Not the overwhelming stench of a decaying body, but the haunting chill of the forgotten. Derrick ducked through the doorframe and discovered a room bigger than he had anticipated, a long rectangle that burrowed into the hillside.

Nothing moved. The cottage lay still, laced with cobwebs and frozen memories. As his eyes grew accustomed to the dark, Derrick picked out shapes—the short slope of a chair, the tall angles of a stovepipe, the gaunt hollow of a firepit. And beds. An entire wall of beds.

They weren't empty.

Derrick sucked in a breath, every instinct telling him not to look. To get out of this hovel, where death tainted the air and coated his lungs. But he had to know.

Breathe out.

Step forward.

The body that lay on the first bed was almost unrecognizable as human. Two legs, two arms, a lumpy head, but the skin resembled leather that had been twisted into shape and melted over the bones with heat and horror. Mouth open in a silent scream, frozen in everlasting terror. And the chest...

Derrick clamped a hand over his mouth. While the rest of the body appeared mostly intact—right down to the scraggly nest of hair that had once been a beard—the chest had been ripped open, a gaping hole surrounded by petrified flesh and shredded skin. The heart was missing, torn clean from the body.

Fighting the urge to vomit, Derrick stumbled to the next bed, then the next. Six bodies. Six mummified corpses. Hearts missing, dead so long they no longer smelled of decay.

Fear trickled down his spine like the cobwebs that tickled the back of his neck. Six bodies.

Seven beds.

Spinning so abruptly that he almost knocked over a chair, Derrick staggered for the door, collapsing to his knees in the muddy snow. He sucked in deep gulps of air, welcoming the bitter cold that burned his throat and scrubbed away the wrongness of the cottage.

He had thought the monster only killed Groschier's queens, but those...*things*...in the cottage—men?—had definitely not been queens. Again he thought of the box by his mother's bed, imagined it holding her heart, pictured her body twisted and mutilated like these corpses. Tears speckled the snow, mixing with the grime on dirt-stained hands. Anger churned in his gut, burning away his tears, strengthening his resolve. He forced his legs to move, worn boots scratching gouges in the earth as he heaved himself up. If he could not find the monster here, he would return to the castle, defend his mother there at all costs. No one knew how the beast got in, only that every queen was found dead after the allotted year. Derrick refused to let that happen.

But first, he would take care of that death hole. Retrieving his flint from Rivi's saddlebag, Derrick strode purposefully back toward the dilapidated dwelling. He didn't even need to gather firewood; the hovel was full of dusty furniture that would blaze nicely, obliterating the ghastly remains. He tossed a flaming pine branch inside and glared into the wreckage, as if daring the demoni to come out and fight him right then and there.

Rivi whinnied anxiously, breaking Derrick out of his trance.

"I'm coming." Wearily, Derrick made his way back to the horse and mounted, clicking his tongue as he turned Rivi away from the cottage. The air had grown colder as the sun sank lower, its amber rays blending into the flames behind him until the snow reflected the same deep ochre.

They had barely traipsed a hundred yards when the trees ended so abruptly that Rivi stopped short. Derrick looked around in awe. The clearing curved unnaturally, as if some ancient hand had reached down and pushed the trees back to form a perfect circle. A stone casket covered by a dome of glass rested on a plinth in the center. Nothing moved, not even Rivi, the forest devoid of all sounds, silence resting heavily on snow-laced branches.

He dismounted quietly, afraid to disrupt the surreal silence, and tossed Rivi's reins over a tree branch. It did not feel right to bring a horse into the somehow sacred clearing. Even the amber rays that slipped through the branches of the pines stopped short before reaching the strange coffin, as if unwilling to disturb what lay beneath.

A chill seeped through Derrick's skin, latched onto his

bones, but he forced himself to walk forward. He needed to see, needed to know what lay inside. As he approached the bizarre sarcophagus, his heavy boots crunched through dead briars, twisted brown fingers that tugged at his pants, urging him to go back. A sense of foreboding slithered through his gut, the feeling of something dangerous lacing the air. This was not natural. This was not supposed to be here. This—

Was the most beautiful thing he had ever seen.

Thick glass covered the coffin, etched with symbols Derrick could not hope to identify. A girl about his age lay inside, still as death, as if she had merely been frozen in time, trapped in eternal youth. Her presence simultaneously filled him with fear and awe. As much as instinct warned him to run as far away as possible, another voice urged him to stay, to wake her up, to take her home. His hand pressed against the lid, and it slid back with an almost imperceptible hiss.

If the girl had been beautiful through the glass, she was breathtaking now—her lips so full and red they looked as if they'd been painted with blood, her skin so perfectly smooth and pale she resembled the delicate china dolls his cousins played with. Thick, black hair framed her head in a dark halo, a perfect contrast to her pure white gown. The girl possessed a fearful perfection that made Derrick lean closer even as he tried to turn away.

Closer, a voice whispered in his head, a silent urging, a desperate need. His eyes widened in horror as he found himself obeying, those red lips looming closer, beckoning sweetly. Fear cooled his bones even as desire heated his blood, and he could not stop now, did not want to stop. He loved her already, he was sure of it, and a chaotic swirl of emotions swept through him as his lips touched hers.

A gasp, a fluttering of lashes, and the girl slowly turned to look at him with eyes dark as kohl. Derrick reeled back in horror, both at what he had done and at the supernatural chill that lingered on his lips.

"My lady!" Derrick fell to his knees in a display of obeisance, the thorny branches poking through his pants. "I did not mean to disturb you." He bowed his head with a trembling fear, half-expecting to feel the tang of steel against his neck.

"Where am I?"

He looked up at the sound of her voice, impossibly small in the vastness of the forest. "You don't know?"

She sat up, dried rose petals gathering in a crumbling array in her lap. "I...it feels like a dream." Her eyes blinked in wide-eyed innocence, no trace of anger at the kiss. Or perhaps she did not even realize he had done it.

Derrick stood slowly, not wishing to scare her. Guilt twisted his stomach, and yet a warm feeling still flowed through him, drawing him toward her, urging him to kiss her again even while his stomach revolted at the thought. Disgust welled in him—disgust at himself? Or at the thought of touching those deathly cold lips again?

He squeezed his fists together until the skin around his knuckles split in the winter air. The pain centered him, kept him focused. "The monster, it did this to you?"

She blinked, and for a second Derrick imagined he saw an amused flicker in those coal-black eyes, the corner of her perfectly formed lips twitching in humor.

"I...I don't know," she replied softly, and he found himself falling, falling deep into those eyes. Eyes that filled him with terror and desire, revulsion and longing.

"Who are you?" he asked gently. "Where did you come from?"

"I am Evangelline," she replied, voice light and singsong and not of this world.

"Evangelline," he repeated, the name a caress on his tongue.

His foot slipped forward half a step, as if compelled by something outside himself.

"Are you from Veranmoor?" she asked.

He frowned at the name, distant and familiar, a warning in the back of his mind. Another kingdom? His heart jolted as he remembered that other kingdoms existed, that *his* kingdom existed. Reality came crashing back—a burning cottage, a monster in the woods, his mother's curse...

"No, my kingdom is Groschier."

Evangelline stretched out one slender arm, ghost-white in the near-darkness, reaching for him. "Help me down?"

He moved forward at once, nearly tripping in his haste to reach out, to touch those dainty fingers, to feel the warmth of her—

"You're freezing!"

She slid off the coffin gracefully, the silk folds of her dress shimmering like liquid. The dried flower petals fluttered to the ground, and he noticed she wore tiny black slippers, not nearly sturdy enough for an extended trek in the forest.

Ripping his cloak off, Derrick gingerly wrapped it around her shoulders. The rich fabric fell around her in thick grey folds, suddenly looking like little more than a potato sack on such otherworldly beauty.

"Would you...take me with you?" she asked haltingly, staring up at him with such irresistible sweetness that he had to clench his fists to keep from kissing her again.

"Yes. Of course." He stepped back, out of the briars, and offered his hand. Evangelline took it and he shivered at the touch of ice on his palm. How he longed to wrap his arms around her, to share his warmth, to bring this beauty back to life.

Rivi shook his head, stamping a hoof restlessly at the edge of the clearing as they approached. Evangelline extended a hand, so small and delicate that Derrick almost jerked it back, afraid of the horse's testy nature. To his surprise, the stallion froze, not moving a muscle as Evangelline stroked his sturdy neck.

"Good creature," she crooned, and Derrick's body shuddered at her voice. The sound reached inside him, erasing his worries, until she filled his mind completely.

"I'll take you to my castle," Derrick murmured as he watched her stroke Rivi's mane with a moon-white hand.

And then she was stroking him, her palm caressing the curve of his cheek, eyes dark and hungry as they flicked down to his mouth. Her lips parted slightly, danger lurking behind the outline of her teeth, but Derrick leaned forward anyway, already craving the kiss.

A shriek pierced the air, making them all freeze, and a shadow of irritation skimmed over Evangelline's face.

Derrick yanked out his sword, scanning the trees for the source of the scream. The echo lingered in the air, a buzzing in his head, but he saw nothing. It sounded again, its ungodly tenor reverberating off the trees, filling his very marrow with ice. Nothing he'd ever heard screamed like that.

Nothing human.

He turned to Evangelline. "Take Rivi," he urged as the need to protect her washed over him. "Get away from here."

He lifted her up onto the saddle as if she weighed nothing, the white folds of her skirt fluttering around him like angel wings.

"Be safe, my prince," she said, then turned Rivi away with a delicate flick of the wrist.

Another scream shattered the night, and Derrick turned back toward the coffin, sword brandished with both hands. This was it—the moment he'd spent the last year chasing. Today he would slay the demoni and save his mother from the curse, free his kingdom once and for all.

The monster appeared on the other side of the clearing, stepping out of the trees on two legs. It stood shorter than

Derrick had expected—smaller, but no less malicious. Evil seeped off the creature in almost visible waves, its body a horrible amalgam of man and beast. Twisted black skin covered every inch of the demoni's frame, its hands and feet tapering into vicious claws. Deep yellow eyes dropped to the empty coffin, and the demoni shrieked in fury.

Derrick held his ground as the monster barreled toward him in a flurry of black limbs and hatred. He sidestepped and slashed his sword as the demoni lunged, but the creature barely seemed to notice the gash in its side, or the thick black liquid oozing out. It lunged again—quicker this time—and the sword twisted out of Derrick's hand as the beast pinned him to the ground. He gasped against the sudden weight that crushed him, the burn of angry claws slicing his shoulder, and opened his eyes to a mouthful of teeth. Derrick managed to get one hand around the beast's throat, forcing the elongated canines to stop an inch from his face.

Growling, the demoni's mouth opened wider, flecks of saliva burning Derrick's cheeks and forehead. He locked his elbow, fingers struggling to hold their purchase on tar-black skin that flaked under his hand and desperately tried to free his pinned arm. Pain radiated with the movement, a burning that sank deep into his bones as the monster's claws sank in further. Relief and desperation flooded through him as his fingers brushed the dagger strapped to his thigh. He jabbed the weapon blindly, relieved to feel the blade connect with something solid.

Howling in rage and pain, the demoni lurched sideways, giving Derrick enough leverage to slither away. He scrabbled to his feet, snatching his sword just in time to block the monster's lunge. The demoni fell back, anger and pain combining into a lethal fury that rent the night in another eerie scream.

Derrick didn't give it time to attack again. Raising the sword with both hands, he swung, severing the monster's head in one swipe. The dark mound rolled across the ground, staining the snow with a tar-like fluid that hissed against the cold. Panting heavily, Derrick stared down at the mutilated corpse, its twisted limbs twitching sporadically before finally stilling in the black-flecked snow. The monster in the heart of the forest...a creature of death and nightmares...and yet, somehow humanoid.

Ragged breath stilling in his chest, Derrick realized the creature resembled the corpses he'd seen in the cottage—the same twisted flesh, the same scraggly substance that might have once been hair. The only difference was the chest, still intact.

An image of the seventh bed flashed in his mind. Had this creature been responsible for those deaths? Or had they all been demoni? Maybe they—

"Derrick?"

He spun around, yanking his sword back up before Evangelline's voice registered in his mind. She approached on Rivi, a black horse carrying a white rider, and he threw up a hand to stop her.

"Don't—you don't want to see."

Her dark eyes peered curiously around him as if she *did* want to see, but she obediently pulled Rivi to a stop, her perfectly smooth forehead creasing into a furrow of worry. "You are well?"

Derrick looked down at clothes that sported multiple tears, his bright-red blood mingling with the demoni's black. His shoulder burned, the two-inch claw marks causing a hissing pain that shot all the way down to his fingers, but he barely felt it as realization dawned.

Holy crimson moon, he'd just ended the curse. The monster at the heart of the forest was dead.

A shaky laugh echoed through the wintry forest. "It's over," he whispered, almost collapsing to his knees in relief.

Instead, he pushed his feet forward, his sword cutting a line in the muddy snow as he dragged it behind him, exhaustion pulling at his bones. As he reached Rivi, Derrick sheathed the weapon and looked up at Evangelline. The light had all but disappeared at this point, but her smile radiated with a glow of its own.

"You saved me," she crooned. One pale finger reached out to drag a soft, chilling line down his cheek. "My prince."

Derrick suppressed a shiver and gently pulled her hand away from his face, cupping it in his palms to warm it. Something tugged at him—a nudge in the back of his mind, a reminder of danger. But the monster was dead and he could not seem to pull himself away from the perfect symmetry of Evangelline's face. The petite nose that tilted up slightly, the way her ears came to a gentle point, the shadows swirling in her eyes.

How he loved those eyes. How he loved her.

"Marry me," he breathed, the words out before his brain even registered what he'd said. Yet when it did, he couldn't bear to call them back. Not when this gorgeous creature stared at him with such open adoration, her laugh cracking like ice crystals in the trees.

"Of course," she said. As if there were no other man in the world, no one else she would rather be with.

The thought sent a heady warmth through Derrick, his chest swelling with elation as he pulled himself up into the saddle behind her, wincing at the fire that erupted along his collarbone and down his arm.

Evangelline turned to smile at him, a brilliant flash of teeth even whiter than her skin, and Derrick forgot the pain. He waited, breathless, to see if she would kiss him. A strange feeling gripped his stomach, as if simultaneously elated and terrified, but she only blinked those liquid eyes and leaned back against his chest, lacing her ice-cold fingers in her lap.

Derrick circled his arms around her to take the reins, clicking his tongue at Rivi. The horse needed no encouragement, jumping immediately into a canter that would take them home.

"You are happy?" Evangelline asked, lightly tracing the veins on one of his hands. "This is what you came for, to slay the monster?"

A smile tugged at Derrick's lips. "Yes. To break the curse."

"Curse?"

"In Groschier—my kingdom. All the queens die." He blinked against a fresh wave of pain. "The monster kills them."

"Why?"

He shook his head, then stopped at the surge of dizziness. "No one knows. They say it feeds on their beauty."

"Perhaps your kings should choose uglier brides."

Derrick blinked against the bluntness of her words, but he couldn't deny the ring of truth. Would that have made a difference? He thought of the portraits lining the wall in the great hall, a somber reminder of the generations before his mother. Eight queens, all impossibly beautiful, all found with their hearts ripped out.

"And you came alone?" Evangelline's voice nudged him out of his thoughts. "A single prince to slay something so powerful?"

"Well…" Derrick stopped. He didn't want to tell her that he *hadn't* come alone. That every time he set out, a contingent of soldiers accompanied him. And every time he neared the heart of the forest, they turned back in fear, unwilling to press further, even for their queen. In the beginning Derrick had tried forcing them, ordering them, shaming them. He'd watched in bewilderment as each one—brave men, trusted soldiers—wilted into trembling fools, overcome with inexplicable fear. More than one had passed out from the sheer terror of something they could not see.

"She's my mother," he finished simply.

They plodded in silence for several minutes. Derrick shivered in the frigid air without his cloak. His adrenaline and exultation faded, replaced with fatigue and an aching cold. His shoulder throbbed, and he forced himself to keep talking in an effort to stay alert.

"Where did you say you were from?"

"Veranmoor," she replied.

That word again, a niggle in the back of his mind, something he couldn't quite place. A haze clouded his mind, making it difficult to concentrate.

"How did you come to be in the woods?"

She sighed, her breath a tiny cloud in the air. "I was...left there. For the monster."

Derrick blanched. His hands squeezed the reins, as if wringing the neck of whoever had done this unspeakable thing. "Why?"

He felt her shrug against his chest. "Perhaps your people were right. That the monster is attracted by beauty. My people thought so as well. Thought they could get something in return."

"Did they?"

"I don't know. I woke up to you."

Derrick's mind reeled, and not just from the pain that had now spread to his chest. The idea that someone could be so callous, so cruel, turned his stomach. He would make it home, tend to his injuries, see to his mother...then he would track down those people and avenge Evangelline.

He just needed to remember where Veranmoor was.

He leaned forward, a sudden thought occurring. "How did you..." He closed his eyes against a wave of nausea. "How did you know I was a prince?"

Evangelline laughed, a tinkling sound hovering in the dark, pattering down his spine like spider legs. "They all are."

"They?" Derrick tried to ask, but his vision swam and his body slipped sideways, a darkness deeper than the forest surrounding him on all sides. The fall seemed to last an eternity, wrapped up in a single second. The next thing he knew, he tasted dirt, and Evangelline hovered over him, concern wrinkling her pretty forehead.

"You *are* hurt," she accused, red lips pushed out in a pout, darkness hissing around her eyes.

"It's fine," he wheezed, but he could barely breathe against the burning in his shoulder now, his skin beaded with sweat even as he shivered from the cold.

"Let me look."

Hard fingers prodded at him, forcing him to sit up, and he was surprised to see a fire blazing a few yards away. How long had he been unconscious?

With surprising strength for such a small creature, Evangelline helped him stand, moving him in front of the orange flames. Derrick tried to protest as she inspected his arm, wanting to shield her innocent eyes from the foul consequence of his battle with the demoni. But she was already tugging at his cloak, peeling away his vest and shirt next, her fingers like pinpricks of ice that raised goosebumps on the exposed flesh of his arms and torso.

"It's bad," she said simply, and Derrick bit his tongue to keep from telling her she could work on her bedside manner.

"Just a scratch," he bit out through clenched teeth, but a headache pounded at the base of his skull, blurring the edges of his vision, and everywhere the demoni's claws had cut him burned with a heat he'd never felt before.

"It will get infected," Evangelline lectured.

Derrick wanted to smile at such an angelic face trying to appear admonishing, but her next words stopped him cold.

"I've never met anyone who survived a demoni attack."

He tried to think back to all the rumors and legends he'd heard growing up. Few had seen the demoni up close, and even fewer bodies had been recovered. Those who survived an attack had only lived long enough to breathe whispers of black skin and pointed teeth before they went mad, running from the castle to disappear back into the forest, never to be seen again.

"Well, how many have you seen?" Derrick asked, more to distract himself than anything. He couldn't picture her as more than eighteen, no matter how many years she had slept in the forest.

"Enough." Her dark eyes flicked up to his, the admonishment clear this time. "Usually the monster just rips them apart, but a demoni's claws also contain venom. You'll be dead in a week if not treated."

His mind whirled, her words—spoken in that deceptively sweet voice—like a slap to the face. A week. They were still days away from his castle.

"I'll need to suck out the venom."

"I don't think that actually wor—"

But her mouth already latched onto his skin like a leech, lips pressed flush against the worst of the wound. His stomach rolled to think of her perfect face anywhere near a demoni's venom, but her fingernails pressed painfully into the soft underside of his arm as she squeezed his bicep in an ice-cold grip.

Wrong. This is wrong....

The burning in his wound intensified, sharp fingers of pain reaching, spreading across his arm and torso. He screamed, overcome with the sudden urge to shove her away—or cut off the arm altogether.

Sleep, a voice whispered. The same voice that had urged him to kiss Evangelline in the coffin. A voice that was nowhere and everywhere at once. A voice that demanded to be obeyed.

The pain faded, retracting to a dull ache, and a sleepy kind of calm washed over him. Derrick fought against the darkness, struggling to remain conscious. Something bad was happening —had already happened—and he didn't want to leave Evangelline alone. A numbness both welcome and terrifying had replaced the ache in his shoulder, and he strained to move his fingers.

Sleep.

Evangelline raised her head and smiled, blood smeared across her swollen lips. The fire cast strange shadows over her eyes and teeth, making her look almost inhuman.

"Feel better, my love?" She looked up at him sweetly, her eyes two pools of obsidian. Darkness leaked from them, curling around her temples in tiny swirls of black, but when Derrick blinked, the image was gone.

He nodded, too tired to reply, and let the movement carry him all the way to the ground.

He slept.

~

Relief filled Derrick at the first glimpse of the castle turrets through the trees, pushing back some of the pain that had beat at the base of his skull every day for the last week. At least he no longer wanted to cut his arm off, though it did throb with unnecessary pain. He'd been in too much of a hurry to let Evangelline tend to his wound today, and a painful burning sensation replaced the numbness that had made the last week bearable.

King Vlad met them almost as soon as they stepped inside the castle walls. He looked older than Derrick remembered, as if he too had aged along with the queen. Deep lines creased his face, and his beard was almost entirely grey.

"Derrick, where have you been? Don't you realize how long —are you injured?" The king interrupted himself as he noticed the makeshift sling around Derrick's arm.

Gripping his elbow with one hand to still the pain in his shoulder, Derrick looked proudly into his father's eyes. "I killed it."

The king's eyes widened, blue like Derrick's, and tinged with hope. "The…you…?"

"I killed it," Derrick repeated with pride and a weariness that could sink ships. "The demoni is dead."

King Vlad's face broke into a smile, and though it could not ease the wrinkles and sleep deprivation that sullied his skin, the king's face practically glowed. "My boy…" He clapped Derrick on the back, then turned to a servant nearby. "Disband the army! My son has defeated the monster!"

"Father, there's something else." Derrick's eyes sparkled with delight, pain temporarily forgotten as he took Evangelline's tiny hand in his, holding it out to the king. "This is Evangelline. She is to be my wife."

Surprise flashed through King Vlad's eyes, his brow furrowed, as if he were trying to work something out.

When he didn't immediately reach out, Evangelline took the king's hand in her own and smiled. "A pleasure to meet you, dear king," she said in that alluring voice Derrick found irresistible.

King Vlad's face instantly relaxed, frown replaced by a dazed sort of grin. "Fair maiden," he murmured, bowing to place a whiskery kiss against her snow-white hand. "Welcome to my kingdom. I will have a room set up for you at once."

"Where is Mother?" Even knowing she was safe now, Derrick's throat still felt too tight.

"Who?" King Vlad's eyes, still hazy, flicked back to Derrick, then he blinked and straightened abruptly. "Your mother is resting."

"I must see her, tell her the news. Evangelline, you—"

"I'll be fine," she said softly, running a hand down Derrick's arm. "I'll see you shortly."

He shivered and brushed a kiss against her cheek before hurrying to his mother's room. Guards lined the hallway, posted at every stairwell, every doorway, dutifully guarding every possible entrance. Each clapped a hand over their heart in obeisance as Derrick passed, and he nodded back, not bothering to tell them their service was no longer needed. Urgency propelled him to the queen's bedchamber, where ten guards formed a barrier outside the door. Derrick dismissed all but two, hoping for a little more privacy. After all, no monster would be stalking the halls tonight.

Derrick knocked softly on the queen's door. When no one answered, one of the guards opened it with an apologetic grimace.

"She doesn't get up much these days, Your Highness."

Chest tightening, Derrick stepped inside and had to wait a few moments to let his eyes adjust to the darkness. "Mother?"

The lump on the bed stirred but did not speak—barely even a lump, at that. Derrick felt his throat constrict at how thin she had grown. How long had it been—a month? Two? He had stayed out longer than usual, but he couldn't have been gone more than a few weeks. How had she faded this much already, a mere shadow of the radiant queen she had once been?

Crossing to the window, he pulled back the drapes to let in the late afternoon sun. Orange rays spilled across the room, and Derrick winced. His head throbbed so fiercely now that even the soft light felt like an axe being driven through his skull. His stomach rolled—from hunger or pain, he did not know—but he ignored it as he idly watched the swirls of dust that flickered and twirled in the amber light.

"Derrick?" His mother's voice, once lilting and beautiful, now sounded frail and weak.

Derrick rushed to her side and slipped one hand under her own. "Mother. I didn't know you were awake."

The gaunt face that stared at him could barely be recognized as his mother, her green eyes faded, cheeks hollow. Once considered the most beautiful woman in the land, Queen Lilith resembled a half-starved corpse left to rot in an opulent bedroom.

The mummified remains from the cottage flashed through his mind, but he pushed them away. No. Not his mother. She was safe now.

"My son."

Tears blurred Derrick's eyes and he squeezed her hand, careful not to bruise the paper-thin skin.

She reached up to brush matted strands of brown hair off his sweat-damp forehead. "Your hair got long," she murmured, stroking his cheek before letting her arm fall heavily back to the bed.

"Mother, I killed it." He leaned forward, so she'd be sure to hear him. "I killed the monster."

Queen Lilith's face contorted—not in relief but in agitation. "I've been trying..." Her voice trailed off as she struggled to move beneath the covers. "Trying to give it back."

Her head lurched to the left, movements jerky, eyes rolling. She must have deteriorated more than Derrick had thought, but it was okay now. She would get better. The curse was broken. They could all live happily ever after.

"Mother, it's okay." He put a comforting hand on her arm, urging her to be still. "Did you hear me? The demoni is dead, Mother. You're safe. And I found someone—the most beautiful girl in the whole world. You must meet—"

The queen moaned, head twitching back and forth. Her arm strained against Derrick's grip, and he realized she was trying to point to something. He followed her gaze to the bedside table, his face darkening as he spotted the crimson-stained box, now so dark it looked black.

"Why do you still have that?" he snapped, the headache flaring behind his eyes as he picked it up.

"I...I tried to get rid of it," she moaned. "It always comes back."

Derrick frowned at the dark wood, the elegant swirls decorating the side. An otherwise pretty relic, if not for the wickedness of its presence. "What do you mean it always comes back?"

Queen Lilith thrashed again, distraught. "I tried...I wanted to give it back. You have to believe me!" Her voice rose into a shriek, as if pleading with someone far away.

"Tried to give what back?" Derrick asked, a horrible sense of foreboding curtailing his hope. "The box?"

"No... The mirror..."

"Mother, there's no mirror here."

Derrick shook his head in frustration and guilt. She had gone mad, wasted away from months of worry, years of living in terror. And all because of that blasted curse. All because of this stupid box. He hurled it across the room, watching in satisfaction as it shattered against the plaster, falling to the floor in a shower of splinters. He stared at it for several seconds, his headache flaring with renewed vigor. When he heard a sharp knocking sound, it took several seconds to realize it came from the door and not his head.

Crossing the room, he yanked the door open to find Evangelline waiting in the hallway. She had changed, now clad in a dress the color of blood, her ebony hair twisted on top of her head in a tight bun, an apple blossom tucked into the dark strands. She held a basket of apples, their shiny red skins blending with her bodice. When she smiled, her entire face lit up, erasing any concerns Derrick had felt moments ago.

"Evangelline." His voice slurred slightly, the pain in his shoulder and head making him feel cross-eyed. "What're you doing here?"

"I brought a snack. You must be starving." She held up the basket. "I know I am."

He stepped aside, allowing her to enter, and nodded to the two guards in the hallway. They each held up an apple, nodding back.

Evangelline lingered near the door, her eyes fixed on the queen's bed. Eyes that seemed too dark somehow, too full around the pupils, that exquisite darkness leaking out again. Oh, how he loved her, would do anything for her, would protect and save her just as he had done for his kingdom.

"Mother," he said softly, returning to her side. "There's someone I would like you to meet."

The queen's eyes widened, but not in joy. A frail hand clasped Derrick's as she whispered, "You should have left her in the forest."

He frowned. "What are you—"

A light touch on his shoulder, Evangelline's warm breath on his neck, and then a sharp pain exploded behind his eyes, merging with the headache at the base of his skull. His shoulders tensed, fingers curling awkwardly as his legs buckled beneath him.

"What's—what's happening?" he stammered, collapsing against the side of the bed.

"I'm helping," Evangelline said sweetly, as if talking to a small child. "It's been six days since you fought that demoni." She glanced at Queen Lilith. "Such a brave fighter he was, too. But I'm afraid the poison has reached his heart." She turned back to Derrick. "Your body is attempting to complete the change. It won't be long now."

He brought a shaky hand up to his neck. His fingers came back bloody, and he stared at Evangelline's mouth, wondering if he was hallucinating the blood staining her pale skin, the tiny black veins winding a pattern across her temples.

"Ch-change?" His legs buckled completely now, his bloodstained hand dragging a crimson smear across the duvet as he sank to the floor.

Queen Lilith made a sound—a cry? a sob?—but Derrick barely registered it, captivated by Evangelline's hypnotic stare.

"Yes, my love," she crooned, stepping toward him with a bloody smile. "You are one of my demoni now."

"No... Guards...."

"The guards are not coming. Not after eating my apples." Evangelline flashed him a wicked grin.

Let go, another voice whispered, echoing in his head, and somehow he knew that was her voice as well. Had been all along.

"The monster. Demoni...You?"

"You killed my demoni, yes." Evangelline leaned in closer to hiss in his ear. "But *I* am the real monster."

No. None of this made any sense. "I don't...understand...."

"Of course you don't, sweet prince. They never do."

Her voice was deeper than he remembered, though it still rolled over his body in a soft caress, compelling him to love her even as his mind revolted.

"But your mother does."

Evangelline spun around, the soft layers of her skirt somehow razor-sharp as they brushed against his arm.

"I have come to collect," she told the queen in a crisp tone. Brusque. Business-like. "Where is the mirror?"

Lilith turned her head in response. Derrick followed her gaze to the nightstand, but it was Evangelline who opened the drawer.

"Ahh." She let out a sigh that sent shivers racing across his skin as she turned back to the queen, her delicate, snow-white fingers wrapped around the handle of a mirror.

Derrick watched helplessly from the floor as a lancing pain shot through his feet, his toes trying to twist and curl like his fingers. He tried not to think about the creature he had fought in the forest, the way its limbs had ended in deformed claws, back hunched awkwardly, ribs exposed beneath too-tight skin.

This wasn't happening. He had killed the monster. This shouldn't be possible....

"You didn't tell him, did you?" Evangelline asked the queen, as if reading his mind.

Tears welled in Lilith's eyes but she did not reply.

Evangelline knelt beside Derrick, her skirt flaring out around her like a pool of blood. Her tongue flicked out to graze the red smear under her lips—his blood. This close he could see that the swirls near her eyes moved as if alive. The breath constricted in his chest, but something still made him wish he could lean in and kiss her.

"Have you ever wondered, Prince, why Groschier has such beautiful queens?"

He remembered her words in the forest. *Perhaps the kings should choose uglier brides*, she had said, her tone both amused and almost resentful.

Evangelline held up the mirror so he could peer into the glass. Instead of his own reflection, the glass was cloudy, almost black. "You think the monster cursed them for being beautiful. But maybe they are beautiful because the monster blessed them instead."

She pressed a finger to the glass and he wondered why he had never noticed her fingernails before, so long and sharp, almost claw-like. He wanted her to run those claws down his face, to rip the heart right out of his—

No! he screamed silently, trying to abort the thoughts, to dispel the darkness that crept into his mind.

Let go...

Ignoring the plea, Derrick watched as the glass before him rippled and a scene spread across the surface—the coffin in the forest, with Evangelline lying inside. Instead of dark, needle-sharp trees laden with snow, the branches surrounding the clearing spread bright and full with forgotten greenery, flowers of every color embracing the coffin while various forest creatures lingered nearby, as if to keep the girl company.

"She was the first sacrifice."

Evangelline's voice was soft and haunting, and Derrick realized with dread that the girl in the picture was not the one standing before him now. The girl in the coffin looked younger, her cheeks rosier, her pale hands smooth and gentle. Instinctively he knew that if she were to open her eyes, they would be a clear blue, a captivating green, a rich brown—anything but the terrifying pools of black that stared at him now.

And yet...something in those eyes called to him, to the other part of him, to the darkness that threatened to consume him, calling, calling...

"*That* is where your ancestors' beauty came from." Evangelline's words were hard now, the swirls around her eyes seeping into the dark strands of her hair. "They make a sacrifice to the monster. In return, the mirror gives them beauty—stolen beauty, but beauty nonetheless."

Derrick's mind whirled, desperate eyes struggling to see over the edge of the bed. Don't let it be true. Don't let this be true too. "Mother?"

Tears streaked Lilith's sunken cheeks. "I tried...to give it back."

"You took what you wanted. Just like they all did," Evangelline snapped, and Derrick thought of the row of paintings in the great hall, Groschier's cursed lineage. A memory surfaced in his mind, pushing past the chaos—the inscription on a plaque under one of the faces: *Veranmoor.*

"The birthplace of the first queen," he whispered, realization dawning too late. "That's where you came from? You were the first sacrifice?"

Evangelline raised an eyebrow. "Well, not me, personally. I just like the body. Still, that's impressive. They don't usually put that together."

A blinding pain flashed behind Derrick's eyes, a sharp current shooting down his spine. "They?" he managed to ask.

"The princes," she said simply, as if a centuries-old monster inhabiting a girl's body made perfect sense. "They all come. All desperate to save the new queen. Once it was even a princess."

She grinned at the memory, the dim light of the candles glinting dangerously off her teeth.

Derrick blinked back the spots in his vision. The voice in his head insisted louder now, urging him to let go, to forsake the shredded remains of his humanity. But he couldn't. Not yet. Not when another word filtered through the slivers of his sanity.

"You said *first*." He struggled to breathe through lungs that didn't want to work anymore, tucked inside a chest that tried to swell and shrink at the same time. "The *first* sacrifice."

A smirk hovered on Evangelline's lips, as if she knew his words were not meant for her.

Queen Lilith cried freely now, her body shaking in silent sobs. "I did…what I thought…I had to."

"No," Evangelline interjected. "You did what you wanted. A sacrifice for beauty. You took the mirror just like the rest. Beauty is the curse, not the mirror. Show me beauty, and I will show you death."

Derrick's reality fractured, black fingers of confusion and denial cracking the cloudy veneer of truth. His mother—his own mother…

A spasm wracked his body and he writhed on the floor, temporarily forgetting everything but the blinding pain.

Let go…

Not yet.

"Who was it?" he demanded, blood trickling from his nose, sweat plastering his hair to his forehead as he glared up at his mother.

"It doesn't matter." Evangelline waved her hand, looking bored now. "Your mother's years are up. And now I take what is mine."

She leaned over the queen, and Derrick watched in horror as she gently pushed Lilith's golden hair off her face. Time seemed to stand still, their lives hanging in the balance. Then, before he could stop her, before he could make a sound, Evangelline had thrust her hand into Queen Lilith's chest.

Derrick writhed violently as he tried to scream, desperate to control pain-laced limbs, to save his mother, but he couldn't do more than twitch and whisper as tears burned his blackening eyes.

The monster straightened, dropping a blood-stained mass into the wooden box while the queen's body lay still on the bed. Closing the lid, Evangelline turned to Derrick with fresh blood on her lips, red tongue slicking against a too-sharp canine.

Tears streamed down Derrick's face, mingling with the blood that pooled at his collarbone. "You…evil…"

And yet, even then, he could not finish the words, his ravaged mind still compelled by those dark eyes, his heart forever cursed to love her, to follow her, to protect her. At all costs.

Let go.

A command this time. Evangelline knelt beside him, her purr a heinous balm against his ears as his body succumbed to the last of the transition.

"Mirror, mirror, in my hand, who's the fairest in the land…?"

THE END

THE BLEEDER'S WIFE

AISLING WILDER

Amaya woke early, dreams of grasping shadows fading as she opened her eyes to pre-dawn light. Careful to be quiet, she stretched, then pushed herself up against the pillows, resting a moment as she rubbed the rounded hill of her belly. Not long now. She felt a heel pressing up, foot under flesh, and into her palm. She smiled.

Not long at all.

Cradling the weight of her womb, she rolled to one side then got to her feet. The babe turned once more under her touch, and she sighed, her heart overflowing with happiness. Behind her in the bed, her husband snorted and muttered something unintelligible, then rolled away from the window and drifted back into sleep.

Another smile played across her lips as she pulled on her overclothes, choosing the dark-green dress today. He liked green. "The colour of your eyes," he'd whispered, nights and nights ago.

She blushed at the thoughts that rose to her mind as she tugged on belt and shawl. Not the time. Not yet.

Soon.

Padding barefoot across the room, she scooped up her boots and opened the door, wincing as the brass handle whined in protest and the snores behind her stopped. She stopped also—breath caught, eyes closed as she listened, not daring to move—and then she heard another snore. She loosed a soft sigh and slipped out into the morning mist.

Tiny birds darted and sang among the hedgerows as she tugged on her boots, grabbed two wooden buckets, and made her way to the river. The sky grew rose-tinged in the east as she walked the short distance, and by the time she reached the rocks at the water's edge, the spray that drifted into the air—where the river plummeted into the breach—shimmered like gold.

She clambered over the rocks, lowering first one bucket,

then the other into the chilled water. Then she climbed back up to the bank, where she stopped, setting the sloshing buckets down on the grass and looking back at the water. Her gaze followed the whirling current, watching as it eddied on and on and over the edge with the roar of a thousand beasts as it fell.

Away. Into the Dark.

She closed her eyes and tipped back her head, breathing in deeply and trying to catch some scent of that fall. Her hand trailed down, resting on the rise of her abdomen as once more the babe twisted within her. As though it knew.

Of course it did. The babe was his, after all. It knew the Darkness. Darkness who had whispered secrets to her. She could still hear him. In the water. On the wind.

Canting her head to one side, leaving the buckets behind, Amaya scrambled up and over the rocks again as fast as she could, chasing the rushing water. She missed him so. Wanted to see him. Wanted to taste him. Wanted to know him again. The rocks grew larger as the river reached the edge; piled high, a barrier of boulders dragged there by the toiling hands of men long dead.

To keep them safe. Away from the breach. Away from the Dark.

Once upon a time there had been towers all along Nearbreach. Towers filled with men, ever watchful; men stoking fires, ever lit—all to keep the Darkness back.

All gone now. No more fires, no more men. The once-tall towers were mere piles of rubble, their stones added to the boulders at the river's edge, stacked higher and higher nearer the fall to discourage any who might be tempted to climb.

But she was not discouraged. She was a Bleeder's wife, after all. Chosen to live at Nearbreach Edge, to keep house and bed warm for one of the men who bled to quiet the Darkness. A Bleeder's wife was rugged and resilient, and not afraid to climb over a few boulders. Soon enough, she reached the top of the rubble, and after that, the Breach Edge—until she stood less than an arm's length away.

The sun, having risen into its short arc, lit the thundering spray of the fall in rainbow prisms of colour. The droplets rose, covering her in a crystalline mist, shimmering on her fair hair loosed from its plait by the wind that rose from the breach.

She lifted her head once more, closing her eyes and inhaling deeply.

There. The briefest whiff, mingled with the iron tang of the river and the earthy hardness of the warming rocks—there it was. The scent of Darkness itself. The aroma that was him. Within her womb the babe kicked like a wild thing; she shuddered in response and leaned in, breathing deep, lifting her nose like a dog, craving—

"Amaya! Wife! What are you doing?"

Strong arms wrapped around her, pulling her away from the edge, away from the water and the darkness. She cried out, reaching—glimpsing the shadows reaching up and out and into the torrent as she was torn away—but then she knew herself again and turned in her husband's arms, blinking up at him as she began to shiver.

Scooping her up with a frown, he carried her back down the boulder-wall, back upriver, laying her down on the soft grass beside the buckets. He tugged off his own cloak and began to rub her dry, his deep voice shaking.

"What were you thinking, standing so close? You could have been killed! And at the water's falling? You know that is Dark-Dread—it's forbidden!"

She found her voice, still trembling despite the day's growing heat.

"I know. I am sorry, Husband. I was…enchanted…by the light on the water. It drew me, and next I knew.…" She allowed herself a shudder, her eyes darting over his broad shoulders toward the river and back. "Oh, Rakin…I am sorry."

He shook his head, still frowning as he helped her to sit up in his arms. "I simply wish for your safety. You and the babe." His glance fell on her rounded belly. She smiled, gathering his large hand in her own and placing it over where the babe lay, still again.

"He's sleeping." She smiled up at her husband. "And safe."

Rakin smiled back, indulgent—a gentle giant. At times like these she felt a twinge of pity for her husband. For what he had to do. Had been bred to do. Bleeders were always big, and always men. They needed to be, for they carried more blood in their bodies than other, smaller men, and far more than women. More blood meant more to give to the breach, to quiet the Darkness and keep it from rising.

There hadn't always been Bleeders. Amaya's great-great-grandmother had recalled a story told to her when she'd been very young, by her grandmother in turn, about a time before Bleeders, before the last Darkrise. The Darkness had risen then, up and out of the breach, and begun to take—as Darkness did. The towers fell, and the men with them, their fires extinguished. Nearbreach was almost lost, and Midfall, but then the king convened a council of the wisest men in the land, and the council commanded the Darkness be fed.

A thousand men were called forth to stand at Breach Edge and bleed. And bleed they did, slicing their wrists and arms open with knives and spilling their lifeblood into the breach. Most died. But the Darkness turned from the land and sped back to the breach to feed and feed until it was sated and slept once more.

Those few who did not die were raised up, hailed as heroes, celebrated saviours of the land. And thus the Bleeders were born. They were given wives who would bear them strong children: boys who would be Bleeders and girls who would breed more of the same. They were given houses and land in Nearbreach, a store of seeds, one horse, one cow, one pig, two goats, six hens, and plenty of ale—and each was given a silver dagger in a jewelled scabbard. Every night, twenty men would walk to Breach Edge, each a league apart. Each one placed the dagger against his arm and sliced it open, feeding the breach for as long as he could stand—and the next night, twenty more would do the same, and the next, and next again, until the first were replenished and they all began again. When each Bleeder's firstborn son reached bleeding age, he, too, would be sent out along Nearbreach, to begin the same again, and so on and so on.

For the Darkness must stay sated, or it would wake once more.

Bleeders didn't tend to live long. When they bled too much and faded, or—as sometimes happened—fell whole into the breach, new Bleeders would be sent to their widows so that they might breed more Bleeder's sons. And so it would be.

Until it was not.

Amaya smiled up at her husband, patting his hand and placing her other on his arm. "Come, Husband. I am well; there is no need for worry. Help me to stand, then fetch some eggs and I will make our morning meal."

He nodded and stood, reaching out a beefy hand to help her to her feet. She gave him a soft laugh and a kiss on his cheek before gathering the water and heading back to the cottage.

Later that day, after their evening meal, Rakin took a last sip of his ale, then looked across to her.

"I think 'tis time I called the midwife. It seems to me you are very near your time, and I would that someone be here with you while I am gone."

She looked up at him and nodded. "Yes, Husband. That will be best, I think."

He stood and gathered his cloak and pack, taking down his dagger from its place above the fire and strapping it to his belt before turning back. "I will send for her then. Tell her to come this night."

THE BLEEDER'S WIFE

Again she nodded. "Thank you. I will look out for her coming."

He leaned down to kiss her, then headed to the door. "Be well, Wife."

"Bleed well, Husband." She smiled, and he was gone.

Alone, she let out a long sigh, then stood and began to clear the dishes from the table. She was not long clearing up, and once the animals were fed and locked in their stalls for the night, she carried in more wood and set about lighting the fire. She loved fire. Loved the shadows that rose to dance along the walls between the firelight.

She hummed to herself as she knelt to build the little fort of twigs and sparked the flint—a little tune: wordless, strange, and dark. She didn't know where she'd heard it first, but it had come to her with the babe. She *did* know she shouldn't be singing. Singing was forbidden in Nearbreach. And Midfall. And everywhere else, as far as she knew. But she didn't think this was really singing. Singing had words—at least in the old stories. 'Twas Songs with words that had ruined the world.

No, this wasn't singing; this was something else, and she liked it. It made her feel good. In the same way he made her feel good. She heated again, colour rising to her cheeks as he surfaced once more in her mind. She missed him. His arms around her. Dark. Powerful.

The kindling burst into flame, interrupting her thought—and a sudden sharp pain jolted from her back, arcing to wrench around her womb as her waters gushed from between her legs. She cried out and dropped the log she'd been holding; it rolled across the floor to thunk against the table leg as another pain jolted through her.

It was time.

She got to her knees as the contraction passed, but only managed to crawl a few feet before the next took her—more horrible than the last, like knives stabbing, tearing at her. She cried out again and fell to the floor, weeping, her gaze sweeping the room, seeking out shadows for comfort. There weren't enough. The sticks she had lit were burning through too quickly, the room settling into darkness again. Where was he? He'd promised. He'd whispered to her when she'd gone to him, when she'd whispered to the Dark that she was with child. He would come to her, he'd said. He'd sworn it.

The pain seemed to last forever—knifing through her as she screamed and cried—but finally, it passed enough to let her get to her knees again and grasp the log in a hand now damp with sweat. She just managed to toss it onto the fire when the next wave of pain hit. She screamed, falling again in front of the fireplace, no thought now but hope that the pain would end—and then the door burst open, and the midwife was there.

Yes.

Tutting, the older woman gathered Amaya up and helped her across to the bed. "There now, youngling, you're alright, Ezri's here."

Amaya nodded, relieved. She grasped at the woman's clothes, peering around her shoulders as she searched the corners of the room. "It hurts."

"Yes." The midwife smiled. "It does, to be sure. Never was there a time or a place when it did not. 'Tis a woman's lot, and that's the way of it. But we will make quick work of this together, you and I. And soon your babe will be born, and then won't his father be happy, hmm?"

"Yes." Amaya smiled, nodding as the woman brushed the damp hair back from her brow. "Yes. He will be happy."

She craned to see over the midwife's shoulder, searching the room—but the shadows were waning again. The fire. The fire was dying.

"The fire…" She only got the two words out before another wave hit, and she couldn't speak due to the pain.

The midwife understood, however. "Yes, dearie, don't you

worry, I'll get that fire roaring. We'll need hot water, won't we?" And when the pain passed, the woman piled more logs on the fire, filled the pot from a bucket, and set it over the flames to boil.

As the logs caught, and the flames grew, the shadows grew too, dancing in the corners of the room. Amaya closed her eyes, able to rest between the pains. He'd come now. Soon.

The stabbing pain went on and on, though, deep into the night. And still he did not come. Nor did the babe. As hour after hour crept by, the midwife looked worried—so worried that she laid out knife, needle, and thread—in case. Amaya, for her part, began to fear that day would find her before the end and he wouldn't be able to come. She grasped the older woman's hand, her own slick with sweat and shaking from exhaustion.

"Please. Let him come soon. Please, before the dawn. He has to be here."

The midwife nodded and leaned up from where she worked. "Any minute now, love. Yes. You're ready. There you go. Now push, my love. Push for me, dear!"

Amaya leaned back against the pillows, searching the room once more—and then she saw him. There, gathered in the furthest corner from the fire. Watching. Smiling.

Push.

She smiled, then screamed as she did as she was told, bearing down with all her might, once, twice, again—and then it was over, and the babe was in her arms. The midwife continued cooing and talking and working—but all she could hear, all she could see was him, closer now, his shadowy form reaching toward her as the fire flickered low.

"There you are." She smiled. She lifted the babe up, showing him to his father, and the shadow smiled back as the babe began to wail.

The midwife looked up from her clearing of what came

after. "He needs feeding, Miss, so he does. Will I show you how?"

Amaya nodded, shyly. "Yes. Please."

The older woman smiled and leaned up on the bed beside her, helping Amaya tug her dress down and talking all the while of motherhood and milk. Amaya nodded, and let the midwife talk while with her own free hand she gathered up the tangled bedclothes until she grasped the hilt of the midwife's blade.

There. She pulled it swiftly up—and sliced it quick and hard across the woman's throat.

A fount of blood gushed forth, splashing over Amaya, the babe, the bed, and the wall behind. The midwife's eyes opened wide and she tried in vain to grasp at the wound, but it was too great, and she fell—face down and blood pooling—into Amaya's lap.

Amaya looked down, frowning. "It is too much. And it spilt all over."

The babe in her arms wailed again, and so she cradled him in one arm, soothing him, while with the other she pushed and shoved the dying woman over—wincing in pain, as she herself was still sore—until the body lay face up again, exposing the bubbling wound. But the blood just ran down around the midwife's neck, soaking the bedclothes.

She looked across the room. "What should I do?"

The shadow moved then, stretching penumbral arms between flickering firelight to curl around the midwife, pulling her body up to lean so that the blood flowed freely and gathered into a pool in the hollow between her breasts.

The infant whimpered—then his perfect nostrils flared, his little lips moving, his pudgy hands flailing. Amaya nodded. "I see."

She lifted the babe, holding him close to the pooling blood, and he opened his mouth. His tiny tongue, shadow-black, flicked out to lap at the blood, cooing and whimpering as he fed.

"There now." She smiled down, then looked across the room to where the shadows were thickest. "Our son."

A shadowy arm lifted away from the body of the midwife, reaching up to caress her cheek. She closed her eyes and leaned into the caress. "I love you."

From the corner came a whisper in return; then, from the window, birdsong. The shadow bent one last lingering arm around the babe—then withdrew into the corner of the room and away, leaving the bloodless body of the midwife to flop back onto the bed.

"Hello, my son." Amaya looked down at the babe as the grey morning light filled the room. "Your father had to go. But he will return soon; never fear. Meantime, we must clean this mess, yes we must. We must make the bed anew for my husband. He will want to see you when he comes, to hold you for the first time, and to name you."

The babe hiccupped and sighed, then opened his eyes—black as a starless night—to her own, looking up at her with perfect trust and understanding as he reached his small hand to her face.

She kissed his fingers and smiled. "We must let him do so, then let him rest. Let him heal. And then, in a day or two, we will use the knife again. We'll do it better then. Not so much mess. He is large and will feed you well."

The babe cooed again as Amaya gathered him back into her arms and rocked him back and forth, humming softly a little tune: wordless, strange, discordant, and dark.

HARVEST

CHRISTIANA MATTHEWS

*P*erched in the topmost branches of one of her favourite trees, Mitera watched for many long years as dust and desperation permeated the olive grove. Olive trees are tough, but a decades-long drought had adversely affected the oil yield, which farmers like the man below her relied upon.

She peered down curiously as he set up a makeshift altar beneath a massive, thousand-year-old grandmother olive, using one of the ubiquitous granite boulders that littered the landscape. He set a small, metal bowl over a convenient hollow and filled it with a small quantity of extremely high-quality olive oil. Mitera's interest was piqued.

He was clad in threadbare, patched, and faded clothing. The soles of his leather sandals also showed patched holes, their uppers held together with bits of frayed rope. The petitioner seemed unlikely to be able to afford such largesse—the oil would have been cripplingly expensive. Mitera looked closer than she had on his previous visits. The ragged clothes had originally been of good quality; so had his footwear. So, a once-prosperous man reduced to near penury by repeated failed harvests.

"Great One," he intoned, arranging a display of leaves around and above the dish of precious oil on his altar, "Annanoe of the Harvest, hear the plea of thy subject, Dimitri. I beseech thee, please don't let my trees die! This grove is all we have, my family and I. My wife will deliver our first child soon, and I need to be able to provide for them. For all of us."

Slowly, with deliberation, he set flint to the oil, and as it smoked and popped repeated his entreaty twice more. Three times total, to catch the ear of the goddess and to summon her servant.

Mitera sorrowed with him. Day after day she'd watched him lug buckets of water from the rapidly diminishing well, seen the way his shoulders slumped, how his tread became progressively slower, more reluctant, and how readily the tears sprang to his eyes. If salt tears could have provided the grove with nourishment, Dimitri's trees would not be dying.

Now, Mitera felt the farmer's deepening despair as keenly as the rasp of a saw along her bark. Despite her mistress Annanoe's assurances that this was simply a burden humans were required to deal with and none of Mitera's fault, she couldn't help feeling responsible. She was the helper he sought, but being long past her prime, she could no longer rejuvenate his trees. Once she would have been able to easily, but now....

Mitera lifted her gaze toward the encircling granite mountains and the high pass that led to the sea. A road ran through that pass along which Dimitri's wagons had traveled in better days, delivering his pressed oil to the waiting ships and numerous overseas markets. A road they would travel again, if the goddess attended his plea—although as things currently stood, that didn't seem likely.

With a catch in his voice verging on a sob, Dimitri finished his devotions and sat back on his heels, lifting his eyes to the heavens where dwelt his goddess in splendor. That gaze drifted past Mitera's tree and paused.

"Greetings!"

She glanced around, confused. Had someone else entered the valley? Who was he talking to, and why was he looking up at her tree?

"Hello!" the hail came again.

A shiver danced along her spine. His gaze wasn't just focused on the olive tree, he was looking directly at *her*.

"H-hello. You...you can see me?" The words came haltingly. Mitera couldn't recall how long it had been since she'd last used her voice or spoken words in a human tongue.

Dimitri scratched a work-roughened hand across the dark stubble of his jaw. "You're right there. How could I not? It's not the right season for picking, you know, even for green olives. They'll still be too small and hard."

Mitera studied him. "That's as it should be. Trees need their rest, too, you know."

"I do know. I own this grove. For now, anyway, until the moneylenders repossess it. Will you come down?"

She had little choice. He could *see* her. There was nowhere to hide from a man with the sight. A normal human wouldn't be able to distinguish her from the olive tree. Mitera spun, twisted, and leaped over the arching, poorly laden branches. One hand spread flat on the ground between her splayed knees to lend her balance, she landed, catlike, at his feet. For all her countless centuries of living, she was still spry. Even if the green magic no longer came effortlessly when she beckoned.

"You're a dryad," said Dimitri.

What else would she be, with her bark-like skin and abundant grey-green hair? Did humans always state the obvious? Distant memories whispered that yes, perhaps they did. Ignoring his asinine observation, she indicated the altar. "You petition Annanoe."

Dimitri sighed heavily. "Yes. For all the good it's likely to do. My mother always said that circles of three bind the otherworld—that to contact the gods one must do so three times three. This is my third visit to the grandmother tree, and I've made my nine appeals. I've yet to see any indication that the goddess is aware of my existence, much less that she'll listen to me."

Once, Mitera herself—as the goddess's dryad handmaid—would have had enough power to grant his request after a suitable bargaining period, of course. The favour of gods always carried a price.

Dimitri collected the empty oil vessel and bowed his head to the visitor. "Well, I must return to my wife and our soon-to-be son or daughter." He fingered a short knife at his belt. "And see if I can gather something for our supper along the way, or we'll go hungry to bed yet again."

Son or daughter. An idea began to form.

"Wait!" Mitera reached out a long, brown arm to grasp his, to hold him there by her side. He looked down at the knotted, claw-like hand and curving talons clasping his elbow and tried to pull back. She tightened her grip. "I can give you what you ask for, what you need, if you grant me a boon in return."

Still focused on the strange appendage restraining him, Dimitri took some time to reply. "What kind of boon?" he asked at last.

"Your child."

"What!" He tore out of her hold, flaying his own skin and drawing blood. With a swear, he hugged the injured hand against his chest, gripping it tightly with the other and sucking air through his teeth. "You want me to sacrifice my baby? Never! Gods above, my wife would kill me if I suggested such a thing to her!"

Searching her memories, Mitera selected what she hoped was a conciliatory tone. Her voice sounded like wind soughing through old, dead leaves. "Of course not. I'm not suggesting you drive a knife into the infant's heart and feed your trees with their blood. My goddess—*our* goddess—reveres life. But this is a large island and ensuring a viable harvest, year in, year out, for such a large population stretches her resources to the limit. Therefore, she needs help. From somebody like me. I was human once, you know, before I entered her service."

Nostrils wide, eyes rimmed entirely with white, Dimitri drew in a series of short, sharp breaths and let them out again in a staccato flurry. "You're looking for a replacement."

A smile stretched her wide mouth. "You understand! Yes, yes I am."

Dimitri shook his head, slowly at first, then with increasing vigor. "No. No, I don't. I won't. I can't." His tone spiraled upward, teetered on the edge of panic.

Mitera sought a firmer voice, one that brought to mind gnarled, dry branches rasping together. "Many of the old tales speak of a firstborn son or daughter being offered up in such a bargain. How do you think I became what I am? My father went from subsistence farming to ruling a great kingdom; my siblings' territories stretched to the edges of the world. And I… I've had the satisfaction of knowing I've improved the lot of mankind. Ensured good harvests and full bellies, and provided rich, nutritious soil and fair weather for the trees, the grains, the herbs, and all of the other edible plants."

Silence.

Seconds stretched into minutes and still Dimitri said nothing. His lips and nostrils pinched closed, his brow furrowed, and he gripped his arms tightly across his chest. Then a sly look flickered across his face. "Does this bargain involve the exchange of coin?"

Mitera laughed—a dry, brittle sound. "Hardly."

"Well, let's think about this for a moment." He spoke slowly, as if the thoughts weighed him down. "My child, as a newborn, will be equally useless to both of us. I presume that if Annanoe accepts this bargain she'll have to wait until the child grows to claim them as her helper. And if I'm not to be paid in coin, I'll need them to assist me on the farm. What use is the goddess's favour if I have no labour to harvest my fecund olive trees? Allow the child to grow to adulthood before you claim them, and in the meantime, they can assist me on the farm, thus lessening the effort needed for you to make it profitable again."

Having been a farmer's daughter herself, this logic appealed to Mitera. "You make a good point. I need to speak to my goddess about it. Meet me here again at the same time tomorrow and I'll let you know what she decides."

"Well?" demanded Dimitri the next morning, seated on his now-defunct altar and twirling a broken olive branch between knobby fingers. "What's the goddess's verdict?"

Blessed Lady, the man had developed brashness overnight. Mitera descended from her tree and leaned against its trunk. "She's inclined to view your proposal with favour, as am I."

Dimitri pursed his lips and rubbed his clean-shaven chin. Perhaps he'd splurged on a barber visit after leaving her the previous day, or found the time and the motivation to use a razor. The rest of his appearance, however, remained shabby.

"Unfortunately, I've come up against a bit of a snag. My wife, Khloe. She said she'd curse you, me, and the goddess herself to the other side of Hades if we considered such a thing. She'd no more agree to give up her firstborn than cut off her own hand. In fact, she said she'd willingly give you a limb, or even two. But not her child. Never her child."

She'd been so certain he'd agree, would offer his child to the goddess as her father had offered her, so long ago. Every dryad was tasked with finding her own replacement, and Mitera had begun to think she'd finally found hers. That, after a thousand years and more of unremitting labour, she could at last go to her rest.

Disappointment rose in a black tide, threatening to thrust her out of the mortal world and transform her from substance to shadow. "Then we have nothing more to discuss. Good day to you, Dimitri of the Olive Grove."

"Hold on!" He crooked a beckoning finger. "Not so fast. Come here."

The creature's audacity knew no bounds. Mitera remained where she was. "You cannot order me around, mortal. If you wish to speak further, you will do so from there."

Dimitri gave a soft puff of sardonic laughter. "Offended you, have I? My apologies. But taking Khloe's objections into account and thinking over yesterday's conversation, I've come up with a counter-proposal." He waited.

Did he think he could force her to speak? Mitera folded her arms and dug her toes into the ground as if about to take root.

Dimitri continued to wait, but when it became increasingly evident that Mitera was prepared to remain there all day and all night, he sighed and gave in. "How about this, then. You take the youngest child instead of the eldest. That will benefit both of us, because as I said yesterday, you'll expend less energy the more helpers I have. Agreed?"

Mitera considered him. "Is your wife young and nubile?"

"Young and beautiful, inside and out." He smiled, a distant look in his eyes. "She'll be a wonderful mother. A loving mother. And I a loving, devoted husband and father."

"Many times over, I hope. So, how many child-bearing years do you suppose your Khloe has ahead of her? Fifteen, twenty?" He nodded, and Mitera smiled with a feral edge. "Good. After bearing a dozen children or more she's bound to become less attached to them, don't you think?"

The prospective father looked startled. "I...I suppose so. Maybe."

"My goddess and I have discussed this, and she said she is willing to wait. I therefore accept your proposal on her behalf. A year after your wife's courses cease to flow, you will bring your last child here and give them into the goddess's keeping. He or she will be my replacement, and for the next twenty years I'll pour all my remaining energy into reviving your grove." She moved closer, looming over him. "Now, mortal man, give me your hand."

Visibly steeling himself, he held it out. Mitera wrapped strong finger-roots around his wrist, and with her other hand pierced his palm through with a sharp and woody nail. He yelped as the blood flowed, soaking into her bark.

"Do you agree to my terms?" Her voice was stern, rasping.

"I agree." He forced the words through clenched teeth, but other than that initial cry of pain, endured without protest as she withdrew her nail and released his hand, merely cradling it against his chest and rocking slightly. Good. If his progeny inherited that stoicism, it would stand them in good stead when they entered the goddess's service. Annanoe could be a harsh mistress.

Mitera nodded. "Then it's done. She will raise them to be her helper. When they are old enough, they will serve Annanoe in my stead and I can pass to the Elysian Fields."

With a satisfied sigh she lifted her arms, floated into the air, and merged with the nearest grandmother tree.

∽

PANTHEA, trudging disconsolately through the market in her older sister's wake, didn't want to choose a bride gift for her father's soon-to-be second wife. So many vases, urns, platters, amphora, and drinking vessels to choose from. She would've dearly loved to have taken an axe or a scythe to the lot of them. She didn't want her father to take a second wife. More importantly, she didn't understand why he claimed that he *had* to marry again and bring Lymaris into their family.

Syrilda paused before a brown-and-ochre vase decorated with a key pattern and other geometric designs. Inoffensive, but busy. Panthea would have preferred the group of naked warriors, or the bearded man copulating with a goat.

"Oh, this is nice, don't you think, Thea?" Syrilda bypassed the vase and picked up a particularly hideous black-and-red dish depicting a surprised-looking octopus surrounded by clumps of limp seaweed. Scenting a sale, the merchant began to wax lyrical about the quality of his wares.

Panthea glared at him and propelled her sister onward, past

the stalls selling perfumes, jewellery, or sweetmeats. "Not unless you want to use it as a vomit receptacle. Looking at that when I'm eating would make me want to throw up. How about that one over there? Oh! Oh, Great Goddess!" She stopped, one hand to her mouth, the other clutching Syrilda's shawl.

The older girl peered at her anxiously. "What is it? What's wrong?"

"There's a woman over there in the olive tree!"

"Where? I can't see anyone. And why would somebody be climbing a tree in the middle of the market ground? You have an overactive imagination, Thea. Can you please concentrate on the bride gift? The wedding's only a week away."

"A week's not long enough," muttered Panthea.

Syrilda sighed, repositioned the brightly woven shawl around her slender brown shoulders, and quit the open market for the undercover section. "I know you disapprove, but it's not your decision. Our father is now a rich man; he can afford to support another wife and many more children. What about this? Every woman needs a mirror."

"Lymaris is vain enough already. Buy a fan or a hair comb if we absolutely *have* to offer a gift from the ten of us. Look! There she is again!" Panthea clutched her sister's arm in agitation. "She's got green hair, Rilda, the exact colour of the leaves."

"Nobody has green hair." Her sister paid for the mirror, adjusted her shawl again, and set out for home.

With a last, worried glance backward, Panthea followed. She knew she hadn't imagined the green-haired woman, even if she was commonly acknowledged to be the one among her siblings most given to fancy. The others—four boys and five more girls—were as solid and earthbound as their parents. The only other potential exception was baby Berenice, but she was barely a year old, and it was too soon to tell if she'd inherited her grandmother's troublesome gift of 'the sight.' Grandmother maintained that Dimitri, Panthea's father, had once possessed it; but he steadfastly denied it, and Panthea had certainly never seen any indication of such a thing.

Ten minutes' walk along a dusty but well-paved road brought them to an imposing villa, its brightly painted columns and red-tiled roof cheerful in the sunlight. Stands of tamarisk, oak, and chestnut shaded the grounds, and stately pines lined the driveway. Beyond the carefully tended gardens, covering the surrounding foothills and reaching almost as far as the mountain pass, grew row upon row of olive trees—Dimitri's famous orchards, which were said to produce the best oil on the island, and elsewhere. His markets had expanded beyond his home state and even further afield than the mainland to include the foreign, exotic countries at the far edges of the world.

Warned by Syrilda's reaction, Panthea didn't mention the green-haired woman to the rest of her family, but the next morning when she'd completed her chores, she slipped away to the orchards to see if she could see any other similar creatures hiding in their branches.

No sooner had she stepped on the path than the woman appeared. The same woman, and not in a tree. Standing, tall and twisted, directly in front of her.

Panthea's eyes flew wide and she took an uncertain step back. "You're real. I didn't imagine you." Her voice sounded strained.

The green-haired, woman-shaped, half-tree sighed and closed her eyes. "You should have had no room for doubt if your father had been honest with you. You share his gift, child, and he and I are old acquaintances. Why didn't he tell you about me? Does he not love you? He promised once that he would. You and all of your siblings."

Panthea gaped at her. "Of course he loves me. Papa puts family above everything."

"Yet it seems he's tired of your mother and seeks to replace her." The woman turned and headed into the orchard. "Come, walk with me. We have things to discuss."

Panthea hesitated for a moment. A creature out of legend, a tree-spirit, was asking her to go for a walk, issuing the invitation as casually as one of her sisters might. Calmly, composedly taking a stroll through the olive orchard on a warm summer's day.

A few paces ahead, the woman paused and turned back. A bite entered her voice. "Well, come on."

Panthea drew a deep breath, puffed it out between pursed lips, and offered a quick prayer to her family's patron goddess, Annanoe. Then, feeling simultaneously foolish and excited, she stepped off the path. An insignificant action on the face of things. Yet she felt as if she were abandoning the sane, orderly world inhabited by her family as she entered an unfamiliar place of shifting, unreliable shadows.

Shadows which lengthened and deepened the further she and her guide ventured into the olive grove.

"Tell me," said the stranger, pausing beneath a heavily laden tree, plucking off a plump black olive and popping it into her mouth, "why do you think your father seeks a new wife?"

She reached for another fruit and Panthea screwed up her face, imagining that intense, bitter taste on her tongue. Nobody ate olives straight from the tree; they needed to be cured and brined to make them palatable. For humans, anyway. Dryads—or whatever this creature was—obviously employed different criteria.

"I don't know. I'm not sure he does, either." Panthea twisted her hands together, squinting against a rare shaft of dappled sunlight in search of enlightenment. "He still loves Mother, I'm sure of it. But he says he needs more children and…and Mother agrees with him. You'd think ten would be enough for any couple, especially when none succumbed to childhood illnesses as so many others do."

The tree-woman growled. "Oathbreaker! Vile betrayer!"

Panthea jumped.

"Your father desires more children to delay the fulfilment of his oath to me. Your sister Berenice belongs to me, girl. As the final fruit of your mother's womb, she belongs to *me*. And to my goddess." She hissed, displaying a row of pointed, brown teeth—like olive pits. Her fingers hooked into claws. "Dimitri's goddess, too, supposedly."

She then outlined all that had happened on that very spot twenty years earlier, when it had been a dry and dusty patch of earth dotted with a few thirsty, struggling trees.

"Here's a message for your father," concluded Annanoe's helper. "Call off this wedding and bring me his youngest child as agreed—or face the consequences. And I promise you, he will not like them!"

Panthea blanched and backed away, her heart thundering in her chest. "Wh-what sort of consequ—" she began, forcing the words from a throat suddenly gone dry.

She spoke to empty air. Nothing stirred in the silent orchard. The dryad had vanished.

Stumbling, weeping, she fled back through the trees, through ever-shifting shadows which reached for her with claw-like limbs. Whispers wove through grasping branches and somewhere a crow cawed, its grating call harsh and bleak. None of the warblers, linnets, or thrushes who normally filled the grove with song made any sound, as if they, too, felt that pervasive sense of menace.

To her dismay, on reaching the path once more she discovered that although she'd seemed to spend less than an hour among the trees, the time was close to sunset. She entered the house with a faltering step and tears staining her cheeks.

"Thea, my little bird! Whatever's wrong! You've been gone all day; we were about to send out a search party for you." Her mother rushed to her and clasped her tightly, then shook her, relieved and furious by turns.

Panthea dropped onto one of the many colourful cushions spread around the living room, nestled between the tiled or marbled tables, potted plants, and vividly painted statues. "I...I need to speak to Papa." Her voice broke on a sob. "This is serious, Mama."

"What's serious? Where have you been?" Her father stumped through the door, his face thunderous. "Your mother was starting to worry."

"I'm sorry, Papa." How was she to deliver Mitera's ultimatum without upsetting him further? Panthea bit her lip, choked back her tears, and blurted out her tale in a jumble of words.

A shadow passed across Dimitri's face—a look of consternation. Or fear? Panthea had never seen her father display fear before. He quickly controlled his expression, scowling and folding his arms, feet planted firmly apart.

"No."

"But...but she said she'll make you pay dearly if you refuse her request, Papa."

"My wedding to Lymaris will go ahead as planned," shouted Dimitri, red-faced. "How can you expect me or your mother to agree to give up Berenice? Have you so little love for your sister that you would see her become a dryad, a creature concerned only with the upkeep of the orchards, with no human feelings at all?"

"N-no," replied Thea, conflicted. "But she said you'd agreed to this bargain. That by taking Lymaris as your second wife, you've broken your oath to her. I'm scared, Papa, Mama. I'm really scared."

"We all are, Thea-love," explained her mother earnestly, joining Panthea on the cushions. "We knew, all those years ago, that we could never, ever give any of you up. But we needed the goddess's favour. So, between us, we devised this plan. A woman's child-bearing years are finite, but a man can procreate well into old age. And the richer a man becomes, the more wives he's allowed. So, as each of us reaches the age where she ceases to bleed, your father will simply take another wife. The goddess's helper is old. We hoped that by the time your father joins his ancestors, she would have already gone to her gods."

A prickle of uneasiness crept across Panthea's shoulders. "Oh, Mama," she whispered, one hand to her mouth, "I don't think that will work. She seemed quite certain that she had a claim on Berenice."

A shadow passed across the open window. The shutters banged violently against the wall, and a ululating howl sounded from the direction of the orchard.

All three turned toward it, aghast, and in an upstairs room the baby started to cry. They heard Syrilda hush her, then begin crooning a lullaby. Against the wall the shadow grew, crept through the window frame, and crawled across the floor.

"How foolish do you suppose me to be?" asked the dryad Mitera, Annanoe's handmaid, transforming from shadow to substance before their horrified gazes. "My wording was perfectly clear. A year after your wife's courses cease to flow, I said. In other words, now!"

"But you didn't name her," faltered Dimitri. "You didn't specify Khloe; you just said my wife. Once I wed Lymaris it will be her youngest child you're entitled to, and Lymaris is young. You could have another two decades or more yet to wait."

Mitera sneered. "Foolish, foolish mortal. I said, and I quote, 'I'll put my energy toward reviving your grove *for the next twenty years.*' That time is now up, and I've come to collect my apprentice."

Khloe screamed. "No! No, I won't allow it, you can't take my baby!"

The dryad snarled. "Very well, Oathbreaker. If you can't bear to be parted from her, you and she and the rest of your accursed family can remain together *indefinitely*. I'll still need a helper, though, and as you've broken the terms of our contract, so can I. I won't wait until Berenice is old enough to be trained. I'll take Panthea instead, and she can begin her lessons immediately. Come, child, come and meet your goddess."

Darkness enveloped the villa. Eager, pulsating darkness, with a pale, gleaming figure at its core. More than twice life-size, with long, wheaten hair shrouding her nakedness and garlands of wildflowers looped around her long neck. Unlike Mitera, her expression conveyed regret rather than judgement. She shook her head sadly and brought her hands sharply together.

The resulting crack rent the heavens. Around them the earth groaned and tore, toppling the stately columns, rending the walls, dashing paintings to the ground, and strewing furnishings throughout the rubble. Syrilda rushed down the creaking, swaying staircase with baby Berenice in her arms, two of her brothers and another sister behind her. They'd barely reached ground level when the stairs collapsed, adding spears of broken timber to the chaos. The other brother still living under his parent's roof struggled through a splintered doorway, holding tight to his younger sister.

Mitera glanced around. "We have almost the entire family now, I see. Where are the others? The two eldest?"

Stumbling across to Syrilda, Khloe gathered her and the baby close, sobbing. The rest of the children huddled around Dimitri. All except Panthea, whom Mitera bound to her side with a striated brown hand.

The pale figure spoke. "They are married and have begun their own families, Mitera. We'll have to search a little further afield. But first, let me deal with these miscreants."

She extended a hand, scooping air through her fingers and drawing them close to her chest. As she did so Dimitri spasmed and an agonized scream tore from his throat. The ruins of his home crumbled to powder around him, and before the horrified eyes of his family he began to change form. Sandals and clothing shredded, decayed, and vanished as his feet sank into the earth and took root. His spread fingers and arms became branches, his body a trunk, his hair grey-green leaves. When the goddess was done, a forty-three-year-old olive tree stood before her, in its prime and ready to fruit.

One by one the rest of his family suffered a similar fate, even the two oldest siblings, whom Annanoe tracked down and hauled home. In place of Dimitri's once-sumptuous villa now stood a burgeoning olive grove. Young trees, all of them, the smallest just saplings. But they had room to grow. Small shrubs of lavender, rosemary, and artemisia took root beneath and around them, while rockroses and thyme sprawled underfoot. The little grove vibrated with the music of bees and cicadas.

"Don't cry," said Mitera, as a horrified Panthea watched her own skin turn grey-brown and furrowed. "Olive trees live for a very long time. Your family can remain together now for millennia, and you can visit whenever you please. But now, we'd better get moving. We have a lot of work to do, you and I."

After a while her tears did cease to fall, mainly because she no longer had tear ducts. From a distance Panthea now looked little different from the rest of her family, for a dryad took the form of the tree she was born from. Grey-brown limbs, grey-green hair, and fathomless dark eyes.

Her training under Mitera involved many journeys throughout her goddess's island and even onto the mainland. Through wheatfields, orchards, herb farms, and even humble vegetable patches attached to the common folk's cottages. That last brought a lump to her throat for a while. True, she'd always wanted to travel, but even more had she longed for a home and a vegetable patch of her own to tend.

A little after Panthea's sixteenth birthday Mitera's soul fled to the Elysian Fields, leaving behind a few lifeless sticks and a pile of withered leaves.

The goddess, wearing human form and draped in red-gold autumn leaves, paused beneath an olive tree and studied her new helper with interest. "You do not mourn her passing?"

Panthea lifted her shoulders slightly. They were no longer supple enough to achieve a proper shrug. "Why should I? After what she did to me and my family?"

"She merely followed my instructions," said Annanoe, turning her back on Panthea and continuing her inspection of the grove. "As you are now bound to do. I allow my helpers a great deal of autonomy; expect them to make decisions without bothering me needlessly." She twisted a strand of saffron-yellow hair around one finger, leaf-green eyes thoughtful. "I believe I'll miss Mitera. She was very good at her job—although perhaps she neglected her duties a little toward the end. I didn't notice. Possibly I should have."

Her shadow suddenly swelled and ballooned outwards, as if cast by a creature many times larger than the lovely woman who sauntered down the sunlit path. "It might be wise to keep a closer eye on you."

The words boomed through the grove, hollow and menacing. Then the shadows retracted, to once again resemble those cast by a human form. The goddess resumed speaking in a conversational tone. "Once you've mastered the intricacies of olive-growing, ensuring they have well-drained soil and adequate sunshine, we'll move on to the wheat fields on the other side of the island. They get more rainfall there, you see…"

Annanoe droned on, about the best conditions for planting, how to ensure the best harvests, how to recover from the disasters visited upon the island by the gods of sea, storm, and fire. Panthea nodded occasionally, barely listening. She'd heard it all before from Mitera, in exhaustive, mind-numbing detail. Gradually that numbness, that detachment, seeped into every pore, slowly leaching away her humanity.

Sometimes the sound of the wind sighing through the trees reminded her of voices, of the people she had known and the stories they had told. There had been a boy once, dark-haired, dark-eyed, brown-skinned, and prone to laughter. A warm-hearted, generous soul with whom she'd imagined sharing a future. Marriage, a home, children. Love. The things all girls long for. At first the loss of this simple dream cut deeply, but as time passed that desire—all desire—faded and died.

After a few decades as the handmaid of the harvest goddess, she forgot the touch of both joy and sorrow. By the end of her first century she could no longer recall the names of her friends, and after a millennium had passed even those of her siblings and parents had dimmed.

But for reasons beyond her understanding she would always be drawn back to the small, haphazardly planted olive grove within sight of the high mountain passes.

THE PRICE OF PROPHECY

INE GAUSEL

Outside the carriage window, the world moved past slowly.

The air was filled with the smell of summer as they drove past an endless stretch of trees covered in lilac-coloured leaves. The rhythmic clang of newly-shod hooves hitting the hard pavement sounded like a lullaby, whilst the uneven cobblestone made the carriage rock like a huge cradle, lulling the people inside to sleep.

After traveling for three days, Remalt was ready to arrive at the villa. Thoughts of resting his aching body and drowning in soft pillows consumed him. Knowing how comfortable he'd be in just a little while, he smiled to himself.

"That's the first you've smiled in several hours, my friend. Are you slowly going mad?" Faustus asked with a small laugh.

"Just thinking about going to bed and never getting back out," Remalt admitted without turning to look at his companion.

He did not have to look at Faustus to know that his long-time friend was grinning at him with attentive eyes. They had not talked for several hours, and while Remalt reveled in the silence, he knew the other man did not. Faustus loved to talk and could do so for hours if given the chance. The only reason they had even become friends was because Faustus had casually started a conversation one day. He always assumed people would like him, and it made him confident in his approach.

"I could have a good lie down myself! Three days of travel is tiring, but it's worth it to get away from the bustling activity of the city, don't you think? Just leaving your responsibility as a senator in the darkest corner of your mind for a few days. I know I need a break, and I'm sure you'll appreciate one too." Faustus put a hand on Remalt's shoulder.

Remalt turned his gaze towards his friend, and coworker, and was greeted by two piercing blue eyes and a smile which made his own lips turn upwards. Somehow, Faustus always managed to brighten his mood. "I'm glad you talked me into it."

Faustus's cerulean wings fluttered gently behind him at the answer. "I know, my friend. I know," he chuckled, gently patting Remalt's shoulder.

Remalt went back to gazing at the landscape outside until a gasp echoed in his ear seconds later. "Remalt, look! I love those flowers—irises. I've only ever seen them grow around here."

He had noticed them even before Faustus had pointed them out; it was hard to miss the blue petals amongst the green grass. "You're such a fairy," he teased.

Faustus's jaw dropped in mock outrage. "A fairy?" He chuckled. "A fairy would destroy the flower to make a potion. I'm just admiring its beauty."

"How wizardly of you, Faust."

"I wish I could go out and pluck some. They would look gorgeous in the dining room."

Remalt found no reason to indulge his friend. Flowers bloomed everywhere during the summer months, and he was certain Faustus would find plants just as beautiful right outside the country house.

"I hope you're ready to lose at some board games. Thought we could play when we get to the villa," Faustus went on.

"Yes. Sounds like fun," Remalt said absentmindedly. A few moments later, he wrinkled his brows at the sound of yelling. "Do you hear that?" He looked to Faustus for confirmation.

The other man nodded, his eyes wide and focused as the two men stilled and listened.

A sudden loud thump on the carriage roof made them jump. Remalt's wings instinctively perked up, preparing for flight, and Faustus let out a small shriek. The carriage grounded to a halt, and Remalt could feel his heart hammering beneath his ribs, though he was unsure whether it was out of fear or excitement.

"Bandits?" Faustus suggested with a whisper, grabbing hold

of Remalt's wrist. "I've never had to deal with bandits before. What do we do, Rem?"

"Stay here." Remalt got up from his seat, folding his wings back under his clothing. Faustus's ever-tightening grip on Remalt's wrist stopped him. His friend shook his head, silently begging Remalt to stay inside the transport with him.

"We're not safer in here, Faust," Remalt said. "At least I'll keep them distracted in case you need to run."

"I don't want you to get hurt, Rem."

"If *you* got hurt, I couldn't forgive myself. Let me take care of this."

"The Eternal Chaos be with you," Faustus said quietly at last. "*Please*, be careful." He squeezed Remalt's hand once more before loosening his grip.

Remalt took a deep breath, then headed outside. His first instinct was to look to the roof, but his attention was drawn to the scene in front of him: the carriage driver was leaning over someone. Remalt walked over. The ruby markings adorning the face of the man on the ground unmistakably identified him as a demon.

"What's going on?"

"He says someone shot him down. He was trying to fly away," the driver answered.

Remalt saw the arrow buried deep in the demon's side—he was lucky they hadn't hit him anywhere else. The injured man had no wings, but it was common knowledge that—unlike wizards—demons used magic to transform their arms into their instrument of flight. Tucking them in after being hit had probably caused his descent.

"Wizards," the demon whispered.

Remalt glanced at the injured man's face. Their gazes met, and for a moment he felt lost. Never had he seen such beautiful eyes, with irises as red as the blood that ran down the demon's body. Was this the man the prophecy had foretold? The man destined to love him? Those stunning eyes shone at him like a well-fed bonfire; this *had* to be him.

Composing himself, he leaned down to help the injured man stand. "We're not far from my friend's villa. We'll help you."

The demon's knees gave out as he stood, and for a moment, Remalt was the only one keeping him upright. "Thank you," he said as he let out a breath.

"What's your name?"

"Sitri."

"I'm Remalt."

Sitri looked confused for a moment, wrinkling his brows. "Senator Remalt, on the Council of Wizards?" he asked uncertainly.

"Yes," Remalt replied.

Sitri seemed slightly reluctant to follow, but was obviously too weak to resist as Remalt helped him up the step of the carriage and inside the transport.

"Hey," an unfamiliar voice called out. "That demon is mine."

Two men stepped out from the shadow of the trees, one of them carrying both a bow and a quiver of arrows—the attackers Sitri had mentioned. The one carrying the weapon was a wizard with a pierced lip, long dark hair, and deep brown eyes; standing with a puffed-out chest, he was clearly used to people finding him intimidating. The other one looked skinnier, but his bright white eyes were almost as intrusive as his companion's general presence—he was not a wizard, but a seer. Most likely a slave, brought along to tell the hunter where to shoot. In times like these, Remalt was glad titles mattered more than physique, though he wasn't in bad shape himself.

"Oh, you must be the man who shot him. I'm glad you've come to report yourself."

The dark-haired man scoffed. "Pardon?"

"Isn't that why you came over?"

The brute began to walk toward them, which made Remalt

take a few steps forward to meet him head on. Standing almost chest to chest, Remalt could see the hunter studying his face. The senator's own cheekbone piercings would likely reveal his wizard ancestry—and hopefully keep the man slightly more in check.

"If you don't step aside, I'll rip your wings off, *visart nol ve magik*," the hunter snarled.

Remalt stood with his back straight as the insult ricocheted off him. Was calling him a wizard without magic truly the best slur the brute could come up with? "Threatening a senator on the Council of Wizards is punishable by death. Would you like to repeat yourself, or will you and your slave be on your way?"

The man seemed to think it a joke at first—his mouth twitched in a smirk—but as Remalt lifted his hand to reveal the signet ring on his index finger, the other wizard understood the severity of the situation. Giving in, he took a couple of quick steps backwards, got on his knees, and bowed his head. "Forgive me, Domine. The demon is yours. Please, look at it as an apology."

"Tread carefully from now on. We don't want people to think wizards will harm them; that will just hurt our reputation. We are all children of the Eternal Chaos. If you want to shoot something, shoot the humans."

"Yes, Domine."

Remalt left the abashed men as he walked back to the carriage where Sitri still stood, slightly hunched over and clutching his side. Remalt helped the demon inside before getting in himself, sitting down beside Faustus, who looked fairly confused at this point.

"What happened? Who's this?"

"Sitri. He's a demon. Some big-mouthed wizard shot him with an arrow," Remalt spat, gesturing to the arrow digging into Sitri's flesh.

They all fell back in their seats as the carriage started to move again.

"You fell when you tried to fly away?" Remalt asked the demon. The pain was evident on the man's face as he nodded in confirmation.

"He's lucky they didn't hit his wings," Faustus mused, "and that demon wings are stronger than wizards'. My wings are so delicate, I don't know what I would do if someone shot an arrow through them."

"Yeah, I guess I'm lucky...." Sitri looked exhausted, as if he'd collapse at any moment.

Remalt got up, changing his seat to sit beside the injured demon. He pulled the man gently towards him, letting Sitri's head rest on his shoulder. Remalt had to close his eyes as the sweet scent of the demon made him dizzy with excitement. For a brief instant he wondered if he had caught Sitri's attention, too, when their eyes had met for the first time—if the demon also felt the fluttering of wings in the pit of his stomach.

"Don't worry," he murmured, "Faustus and I will patch you up. We have a potion that will help with the healing. You'll be better in no time."

∽

REMALT LIFTED his head as he heard bare feet running across the living room floor. A young slave girl stopped in front of him, staring at the ground as she spoke.

"He's woken up, Domine." Her voice was barely louder than a whisper.

"I should go check on him," Remalt said to Faustus, who was about to roll two dice onto the table.

"You're just saying that because you're losing this round. If you leave now, you won't know if I cheat," Faustus teased, grinning at Remalt with a row of pearly-white teeth.

"You always cheat. I know your dice are loaded, and yet I've still managed to win two rounds," Remalt stated with a satisfied smile as he got up from his seat.

Faustus acted offended, resting a hand over his heart to claim that he would never do any such thing. Before leaving the room completely, Remalt took one last glance at Faustus, who looked shocked as he picked up the dice from Remalt's side of the table. Faustus wasn't the only one playing with loaded dice.

When he arrived at the bedroom, Remalt knocked lightly on the wall before pushing aside the curtains to enter the room. The demon was sitting up in the bed, studying his own arms, but he looked up when he heard Remalt approach.

Now that the situation wasn't so dire, Remalt had time to study the demon properly. Those red eyes still stood out the most, but now he also noticed the long, curly brown hair. The man had a handsome face, with intricate markings enhancing his sculpted features. They smiled at each other as Remalt came closer and sat down on the edge of the bed.

"Let me see." Remalt held his hand out. Sitri did as he was told, and Remalt studied the bruised skin of the demon's arm in silence for a second. Sitri's bicep bulged, and it took all the wizard's strength of will not to place the palm of his hand against the tight muscle. Brushing his thumb over one of the bruises instead, he had to let go of the demon's arm altogether as Sitri abruptly pulled back.

Remalt straightened his back a little, composing himself. "How are you feeling?"

"My whole body is aching, but I feel better. But I worry that I won't be able to fly for a long time, looking at the state of my arms," he added quietly.

"Just take the time you need to heal. Forcing yourself to get better will only hurt you in the long run. You can stay here as long as you need." It was Faustus's villa, but Remalt knew his friend's generosity knew no bounds.

"I should be on my way as quickly as possible. My family must be really worried."

Remalt tried to hide his surprise at the fact that this man had a family. Not that it was unlikely; he just hadn't thought about it. Images of someone else holding Sitri in their arms flashed before Remalt's eyes, and a rush of emotions—sadness, anger, and jealousy—stalled his response momentarily.

"They must indeed be worried," he said. "Perhaps you can write them a letter? I'll send a slave out to deliver it."

"You would do that for me?"

"Of course. My duty as a senator is to take care of all the children of the Eternal Chaos."

The demon began to chuckle. As the chuckle turned into a wholehearted laugh, he had to clutch his wounded side.

Remalt's eyes swept over Sitri in confusion. "What?"

"Forgive me, Senator, that was really impolite of me, but I'm sure you're aware of what kind of reputation your kind—wizards—have?" Sitri calmed himself. "I don't want to imply anything about you personally, but all we hear about is how entitled and arrogant wizards are. It made your statement sound rather...bizarre. Apologies."

"Wizards are the strongest magic-wielders," Remalt explained. "Chaos blessed us with the power to wield magic outside ourselves. I know it's hard for you to understand, but all we want to do is protect you. Letting non-wizards rule alongside us in the council would be like letting a child be the head of the household—a disaster waiting to happen."

Sitri looked away. "Of course. I understand." He went back to studying his arms, caressing himself lightly.

"You don't agree?" Remalt asked with an amused smile. The demon shook his head. "That's fine. Most people don't," Remalt reassured him. He stood up. "I'll find some parchment, a pen, and some ink so you can write that letter."

A couple of minutes later Remalt returned to the bedroom,

carrying writing equipment. Sitri's face lit up as Remalt put everything down on his lap. The demon studied the materials, then looked a little disappointed. "Do you have a board or anything I can put the parchment on? It's not that easy to write on a soft surface."

Remalt slowly turned around but spotted nothing useful nearby. His eyes landed back on the demon, who sat with a hopeful expression. A moment of silence gave Remalt an idea.

"Here," he said as he sat down on the bed. "You can use my back."

"I... Are you sure?" Sitri stuttered.

Remalt turned his head to the side to get a glimpse of the man behind him. "Is the letter going to be very long?"

"I don't think so."

"Then why would it be a problem?"

Though Sitri was obviously reluctant, he eventually laid the parchment against Remalt's back. However, the demon never started writing.

"What's wrong?"

"Your hair...is a little bit in the way," Sitri admitted, before clearing his throat.

"Oh." Remalt grabbed the braids on top of his head, tearing the wig off to reveal his short, black hair. "I sometimes forget I'm wearing it. Is this better?"

"Yes, thank you, Senator," Sitri said as he pressed pen to parchment.

Remalt could feel the other man holding the parchment steady against his body, and the smooth movement of the pen against his back. Silence ensued once again, but Remalt searched his mind frantically for something to talk about. What would he have in common with a demon? No, that was the wrong way to go about it. What would he have in common with this specific demon?

"Sitri?"

"Hmm?"

"What were you doing when that wizard shot you?"

"Nothing that warranted an attack." Sitri stopped writing for a moment. "I know too many wizards who think they can get whatever they want." He pressed the pen against Remalt's back again, slightly harder this time, and sighed. "Senator?"

"Remalt, please." Faustus wanted to hear his name spoken by that soft voice.

"Remalt…do you think the Eternal Chaos actually prefers wizards? As a race, I mean."

Remalt had to think; no one had ever asked him this question before. "No more than a parent prefers their oldest child," he answered in the end.

"But a parent would interfere with injustice committed by an older brother or sister against the younger one. Chaos never interferes. It just watches passively as siblings slaughter each other." Sitri almost spat the last words.

"Maybe that is Chaos's version of justice. No matter the reason it stays passive, I doubt the reason is favoritism for wizards. I believe Chaos loves all its creations equally."

"Even the ones who commit heinous crimes?"

"Isn't that the purpose of unconditional love?"

Sitri scoffed as he removed the pen and parchment from Remalt's back. Remalt turned around to look at the demon, who now sat slouching as he read his own letter. His eyes moved swiftly over the words, then he rolled the parchment up and handed it to Remalt. "If Chaos loves us all unconditionally, yet still does not spring into action, I have no need for its love."

Remalt swallowed hard at the demon's statement. "I suppose not," he said after a moment of thinking. "Being loved only holds worth if it is noticed…felt." For a moment he wondered if he knew what he was talking about, if he himself had ever experienced what love felt like. Not in the mood to go into detail on this subject any more than they'd already done,

Remalt got up. "I'll go give this to someone who'll deliver it to your family."

"Thank you, Remalt, you've been very kind to me." Sitri gave a careful smile.

"Of course. It's my pleasure." Remalt returned the smile before turning to leave so the other man could rest.

As he lifted the curtains, the demon called out to him. "You won't read it, right?"

"Of course not, Sitri. I swear." He gave Sitri one last smile before heading straight for his own chambers, holding the scroll close to his chest, as if to protect it.

The slaves inside jumped slightly as Remalt ripped the curtains to the side and entered the room. "Leave," he commanded.

The slaves cleared out as quickly as they could, and he was left alone to confront his own morals. Why had the demon asked if he would read it? It just made him wonder even more.

He sat down on his bed, closing his eyes. Maybe he could remember the feeling of the pen against his back and decipher every stroke. "For Eternity's sake," he mumbled, realizing he'd given himself an impossible task. He searched his mind for just one valid reason to read the letter, but all he could find were several good reasons not to. But then there it was, the one realization that preserved his conscience: no one would know.

He gently opened the scroll.

My dearest Octavia,
I hope my absence has not worried you too much. I was badly wounded on my way back
home to you, but two of the senators from the Council of Wizards were kind enough to help me.
The senators have been gracious towards me, but I am uncertain of their intentions. Few
wizards are generous without expecting something in return.

With the help of their healing potions, I hope to be back at full health in a week's time. I already miss you and the children; I will be on my way back to you as soon as I am able.
I love you <u>unconditionally</u>.
Sitri

Remalt's eyes were glued to the word at the end. Jealousy made his chest tighten painfully. He remembered the prophecy the seer had told him when he was young—that he would meet a man with beautiful, piercing eyes, and that the iris would reveal they were meant for each other. All his life he'd waited for love, and now that he was so close to having it, he had already lost it.

He let out a deep breath as he crumpled the letter into a ball. Seers were able to look into the future, but it seemed like he would have to carve his own path.

※

THE MARKETPLACE SMELLED OF SEAFOOD, raw meat, blood, and sweat. Remalt lifted a perfumed cloth to his nose to keep from gagging. Had this not been a very personal matter, he would have sent one of his slaves, but he had to know that things were done correctly. He searched for the right shop as he passed several buildings.

As he did so, Remalt noticed a white-haired beggar at a corner. She was scarcely dressed, revealing more of her skin than he cared to see; however, that was not why she caught his eye. She was staring intensely at him with pale white irises, and her lips moved, but she made no sound at first.

"Re…" he heard her say. "Rem…alt?"

A shiver went down his spine, but his fear did not stall his approach. Her features revealed that she was a seer, and it would be even more terrifying to pass on an opportunity to know his own future. He stopped in front of her, sat down on his haunches, and took her hand in his. She gasped as he touched her.

"I am Remalt," he said quietly. "Please, tell me what you see."

Her eyes moved frantically around, searching. "A beast…" she mumbled. "Blood-red eyes…will consume you." She gasped again and tightened the grip on his hand. "True love reveals itself.…"

He thought about Sitri, certain that she spoke of how much the demon would lust for him. It made his heart beat hard in his chest. As she came back to herself, her grip on his hand loosened. He couldn't help but smile at her, even though she did not smile back.

"Thank you," he said, handing her a cowrie shell from his purse. This prophecy meant that his plan would work. Now all he had to do was execute it. He stood, then had to back up quickly as the seer tried to grab him. She looked desperate. "One cowrie was enough, wench, get off me!" How ungrateful; he had given her more than enough for the amount of information he'd received.

They studied each other for a moment, then she backed away. Remalt turned on his heel and kept walking, glad to be rid of such a horrendous woman.

When he finally found the shop, he was even more confident than before. This was the choice that would secure his own happiness. He stepped inside, taking in his surroundings. Two huge shelves lined either side of the room, filled with colorful spices from around the world. Remalt's gaze went to the man behind the counter, who was staring at him attentively. His slightly elongated ears and dainty features gave away his fairy nature. Behind him stood a tall shelf stocked with vials of vibrant liquids, revealing that this merchant traded in more than exotic spices.

"Can I help you?" the man asked, raising an eyebrow at Remalt.

"I'm looking for someone by the name of Magnus."

"That may be me, depending on what you want," the fairy said, chewing on his thumbnail.

"I need a potion." Remalt walked all the way up to the counter, staring back at the man. "I need someone who can make whatever I want. Are you skilled enough?"

The man scoffed, clearly offended. "As long as you have a big enough purse, I can make anything and everything you want." His eyes glanced over Remalt's purple toga. "What *do* you want?"

Remalt had thought about the details of the potion for several days; it was exciting to make it into reality. "I want something that will make the one who drinks it undesirable… ugly and distorted." He thought for a moment. "And…I want them to become a lustful creature, that they become dependent on…intimacy."

Magnus seemed slightly disconcerted, despite his professional politeness. He cleared his throat. "I see. How long do you want it to last?"

"Forever," Remalt stated definitively. He'd love Sitri no matter what, but he had to make sure nobody else would. "I want it done by tomorrow. That won't be a problem, will it?" He put his ringed hand on top of the counter.

Magnus swallowed hard at the sight of the signet ring. "Of course not, Senator. I'll have it done for you tomorrow at dawn. Does that sound good to you?"

"Excellent. How much do I owe you for this service?"

"It can be difficult to make something that lasts forever. To get the effect you want, it would also require rare—and very expensive—ingredients. I'll probably have to use my last unicorn horn, and let me tell you, you've never experienced fear until you've gazed into the sharp-toothed jaw of one of those beasts—at least that's what I've heard. And dragon scales—easier than the unicorn horn, but they're greedy bastards." He paused to think. "Would three hundred fifty cowries be...acceptable?"

"Absolutely," Remalt agreed. He couldn't put a price on his own happiness. Whatever the cost, he would gladly pay it. "I'll come back at dawn then."

"Good doing business with you, Senator. May the men of the council prosper," the merchant said, holding his hand out for Remalt to shake.

Remalt took his hand, sealing their deal. As he left the shop, the smell of animal cadavers and exhausted men entered his nostrils once again before he lifted his perfumed cloth to his face. Now, there was only one thing left to do.

∼

Sixty-one years earlier

The boy's eyes darted over the toned muscles of the marble statue. As he reached out to touch the rock-hard skin, his hand shook. Thrilling tingles surged through his body, as if he truly believed he was touching a real man. A small giggle left his lips as he stepped onto the pedestal that made the statue a head taller than him, evening out the height difference. His arms slid over the broad, snow-white shoulders that made his own complexion look darker than usual. He tilted his head, and for a second, he had expected the sculpture to do the same. Slowly, he leaned in, placing a small but lustful kiss on stone-cold lips.

"Remalt!" His father's voice rang out.

The boy froze. Untangling himself from his imaginary lover, Remalt turned to look at the angry man behind him. He swallowed loudly before speaking. "Father. I thought— You're home early."

"When you begged me to buy that statue, I thought maybe you'd grown to appreciate the arts—well, in another, more dignified way...."

Remalt thought frantically for an excuse. "I was...practicing. I'm nervous I might disappoint Caecilia."

"It looked more like you were practicing kissing her brother," his father retorted. "Why aren't you ready? I told you yesterday that we would visit Caecilia and her family."

"I lost track of time, I—"

"Obviously. Hurry, Remalt, we do not want to keep them waiting."

Remalt turned on his heels, heading for his bedchambers. His momentum dwindled the more he thought about that woman. He felt like a fool every time they had a conversation—as if he wore a grinning mask and danced like a monkey. She had caught him staring at her brother once, and after that she'd started to openly question his manliness. A boulder sank in the pit of his stomach, slowing his pace for a few steps before he halted.

"Father? Do I have to marry her? I don't feel like we're a good match, and I don't really feel comfortable when I'm with—"

"It is decided. Now hurry."

There was no reasoning with this man. Remalt's life was planned out—it had been for eighteen years now. Sometimes he daydreamed that his father would fall over and die right in front of him, freeing Remalt from arranged commitments. Other times he thought of running away with Caecilius—Caecilia's brother. Those were the thoughts that followed him everywhere, the thoughts that gave him strength to keep going.

By the time they'd reached the market, it had started to rain. Small drops of water landed on Remalt's cheeks, creating the illusion that he was crying. Maybe the Eternal Chaos wept for him? The thought that the universe was just as unhappy with his arranged marriage made him snort a laugh.

"I think we should buy a nice necklace for Caecilia," his father suggested. "Don't you agree? As an apology for being late."

"We'll be even more late if we stop to buy gifts."

"But at least we won't be late and without gifts," his father said, ending the conversation as he went to purchase the jewelry.

Remalt sighed and headed over to a nearby water fountain to wait. He watched as the water droplets landed in the fountain, creating tiny ripples, then frowned as he saw the reflection of a man. Their eyes met, first through the water, then when Remalt lifted his head to look at the stranger. The man was pale; both his eyes and his hair were as white as the marble Remalt had kissed earlier—he had to be a seer.

"Are you Remalt?" the white man asked.

"Yes...?"

"The Eternal Chaos has spoken to me about you."

Remalt's heart started beating hard and fast. Had the Eternal Chaos actually noticed him? The white man held his hand out, offering a view into the future. It scared him, the thought of hearing that he'd be miserably married to Caecilia. But in the end, he chose to lock hands with the man. It was better to know.

White eyes disappeared behind pale eyelids, and the man's grip tightened.

"I can see you, Remalt. You're happy." The man smiled. "Such piercing eyes.... He loves you."

"He?" Remalt blurted out. His knees suddenly felt weak, barely strong enough to keep him upright. "Not Caecilia? Caecilius, then?"

The pale face of the man twisted into a grimace before he answered. "No. None of them...." His grip loosened, and bright-white eyes gazed at him once more. "The irises, Remalt, they will reveal that you are meant for each other."

Remalt watched as the seer left. He smiled, and the raindrops landing on his cheeks turned to happy tears. He wouldn't have to kiss a stone-cold mouth forever; one day they'd turn into the soft lips of a man who loved him.

His father called for him, and he glanced at the man who had planned out his whole life, down to every last detail. Now Remalt knew differently; one day he would be happy, and he would do anything to find that happiness.

Caecilia entered Remalt's mind again, but his smile did not falter. His marriage could be arranged—but so could his status as a widower.

REMALT MET Faustus by the gate right outside the villa. His friend came running towards him, grabbing his shoulders with a worried expression. Remalt stood still as the delicate wizard looked frantically for the source of his wounds, lifting limbs and several layers of clothing. When he found nothing, he lifted his eyes to look at Remalt's bloodied face.

"Rem, what happened? Are you hurt?" He tenderly placed his hands on Remalt's cheeks.

"It's not my blood, Faustus. Don't worry."

"Then whose?" Faustus's eyebrows met in the middle, creating a concerned expression. "Rem…what have you done?"

Remalt lifted his hand to put it on his friend's cheek, caressing it gently with his thumb. "It was something I had to do, Faust, but they did not suffer."

When he tried to give Faustus a reassuring smile, his friend did not smile back, his eyes full of tears.

Remalt took a deep breath. "I need to clean myself. I have something for our guest, and I should look presentable."

"Rem, you're scaring me. You're not acting like yourself. This…" Faustus gestured to Remalt's bloody clothes. "This is not the man I— Why are you so obsessed with that demon?"

"Destiny showed the way, and I paved the road."

"That is blasphemy—the Eternal Chaos discredits Destiny. What has blinded you?" Faustus shed a tear at his last question, and Remalt caught it with his finger.

"True love," he whispered, and Faustus's gaze fell from his.

Remalt headed inside, ordering the first slaves he saw to ready some warm water and a cloth. It was brought to his room minutes later, and at his own request he was left to tend to himself alone. It took some time for him to wash the dried blood from his hands and face, but in the end he both looked and felt like himself again.

The slave who came to get the bloodied water would not meet his eyes. On her way to leave, he ordered her to wait. He could see how she tensed her shoulders, and how her knees shook.

"I need two cups of wine," he told her. "One of them just over half full."

"Yes, Domine," she answered, hurrying out as quickly as possible. When she came back with what he had ordered, she still did not lift her gaze. "To whom should I give the other one, Domine?" Her voice shook too.

He lifted both cups off the tray. "I'll take care of it. You can go back and tend to your master."

Left alone once more, he sat down on his bed and put the cups down on a small table beside it. He lifted his wig gently off his head, taking care not to make any sudden movements—

tied to and hidden between the braids hung a tiny ceramic jar. After untying it as carefully as he could manage, his hands shaking in trepidation, he opened the lid and put his nose to the jar, but there was no odor. He put the lid back on to give himself a moment to think.

What scared Remalt most was the thought that Sitri might not understand that he had done everything to bring happiness to both of them. If Sitri reacted the same way as the slave girl had, Remalt's heart would break. But then he reminded himself that the seer he'd met had predicted a happy future: true love would reveal itself. Remalt smiled, picturing Sitri and himself embracing.

Figuring that he had come too far to back out now, he poured the potion into the cup with the least amount of wine. Grabbing one cup with each hand, he headed toward Sitri's chambers.

"Senator," Sitri said as the wizard entered the room, "good evening."

"Good evening, Sitri. How are you feeling?" Remalt sat down

THE PRICE OF PROPHECY

at the edge of the bed, handing Sitri the poisoned cup with a smile.

"I'm feeling much better, thank you for asking." The demon accepted the cup, his expression slightly bemused. "Wine? Is it a special occasion?"

"I suppose," Remalt replied with a nervous chuckle. "I have some good news."

Sitri lit up. "Did you get a letter from my wife? A reply?" He held his hand out expectantly.

Remalt had to think for a second, but then he remembered the letter he was supposed to have sent several days ago. He moved to put his hand on top of Sitri's to comfort him, but the demon moved away as soon as they touched.

"I'm sorry, Sitri," he said, retracting his rejected hand. "I don't think she loved you the way you hoped she did."

"With all due respect, Senator, you do not know her. She always tells me that when Chaos made the two of us, it planted a part of each other in both of us, so that we would feel incomplete without the other. True love like that does not fade within a few days. Are you sure your slave gave the letter to the right woman?"

"Yes," Remalt barked. His vision went blurry and his body felt numb as he listened to the demon talk. Sitri looked surprised at the sudden, harsh tone, and Remalt managed to compose himself. "I'm sure." He sighed. "Drink, please. The wine is good."

"Apologies," Sitri mumbled, before putting his lips against the cup to take a few gulps of his drink. "You're right, it's good."

Remalt tried to peek at him through his peripheral vision, wondering how much the demon had drunk.

"So, Remalt," Sitri began, "I hope you know that I do appreciate everything you and Senator Faustus have done for me. I just want you to know that...you've sort of changed my opinion about wizards."

"Oh? In what way?" Remalt asked, taking a swig of his own drink to keep his nerves in check.

"I mean, obviously some of them can be cruel, but now that I've met you, I know that not all wizards are horrible. My impression of your kind was that you only cared about your own, but you've taken such good care of me. I just wanted to say thank you…so, thank you," Sitri concluded, giving him a gentle smile before taking another sip of wine.

Remalt smiled back, his heart warmed.

"Oh, I forgot—you said you had good news," the demon added, taking the last sip of his wine before searching for a place to put his cup.

Remalt took it away from him and put both of their cups down on the floor. Now all he had to do was wait for the potion to work. When he looked up, he met Sitri's gaze. The demon's magnificent red eyes gleamed with anticipation.

"I just wanted to tell you that I've arranged for you to come back to Rome with me in a couple of days," Remalt explained.

Sitri looked at him with utter confusion, the demon's eyes studying his face. "I don't understand."

Why had Sitri built a life with someone else? A useless attachment that hindered their happiness. Sitri wouldn't give up on his woman unless he understood what was truly at stake: *their* true love.

"There's…a prophecy," Remalt said. "A seer told me I'd find you, and that we were… That we would fall in love. Since I live in Rome, you should come with me so we can give it a chance."

The demon looked uncomfortable, rubbing his forehead with his palm. "I have a wife, Senator. I understand that you've…" He took a deep breath. "That you've been told we're supposed to be in love, but I've already found the person I want to spend my life with. I hope you can understand."

He had just managed to finish speaking before he started coughing violently, his whole body shaking. Remalt reached out to him again, wanting to help, but this time Sitri moved his whole body away, dragging himself further up the bed.

"Please, don't," he managed to push out between coughs.

"You need to relax," Remalt explained, wanting the transformation to happen as comfortably as possible.

The coughing stopped after a while, but Remalt's worry only grew when Sitri began to bleed from both his mouth and nose. Droplets dripped onto the demon's bare chest and the bedsheets.

"What's going on?" Sitri whispered as he touched his face, staining his hands with some of the blood. Big tears formed in his eyes, running down his cheeks as if they were racing each other to the bottom. "Senator, if you're doing this, please stop," he sobbed in between gulps for air.

"It's the potion. Just relax; it's not dangerous." Remalt gave him a gentle smile in the hope that it would be comforting.

"What potion?" Sitri looked to the empty cups. "What did you give me?" he demanded, his pupils dilating as their eyes met again.

Before Remalt could answer, Sitri squeezed his eyes shut and groaned. Remalt watched with fascination as the demon's body slowly started changing. His arms smoothly morphed into wings. His fingers became elongated and his skin stretched out to create membranes, so that they looked like bat wings. Sitri seemed to calm down for a moment, opening his eyes to look at himself.

"They're beautiful—your wings," Remalt said. He was used to seeing the more fragile dragonfly-like wings that wizards possessed; seeing the strong wings of a demon truly intrigued him. The demon lifted his head to look at Remalt, but his expression was not one of appreciation.

"It hurts. What did you do?" he managed to say.

"It will be over soon, I promise."

"Please, Rem—" The demon let out another groan as the

transformation continued. Everything started to happen at once now. His wings grew longer, creating a truly unnatural shape that made Remalt's stomach churn, and a lion-like tail appeared. Horns sprouted, bending all the way to the back of Sitri's head. His ears grew pointed, his nails turned into claws, and his heels elongated into a shape resembling the feet of a werewolf. Finally, his ruby markings disappeared and his skin greyed, making him look like he'd risen from a newly dug grave.

They sat in silence as Sitri caught his breath. When he seemed calmer, Remalt put his hand on the demon's cheek, caressing it gently. Small drops of sweat and tears were caught by his thumb. "You see? It's over now. You're fine."

Sitri growled at him, pushing his hand away. "Don't touch me." The demon wrapped his wings around himself protectively. "What did the potion do? Why do I look like…like a beast?"

"You don't look like a beast to me. I'll always be here for you, Sitri, that's what I want you to understand. We're meant to be together, and I need you to come to Rome with me."

"I'm not coming to Rome with you, Senator. I have a wife and children."

"They wouldn't want you like this," Remalt tried to convince him. "No one would desire you like this, except me." He edged closer, hopeful Sitri would not move away from him this time. The demon stayed still, but he turned his gaze to the floor. "Sitri, my dear, you have to understand. I did it for us. We are meant to be, it is true love—you'll learn to see that in time."

"I'm not in love with you," the demon stated harshly.

"Not yet, but in—"

"I will never be in love with you, Senator. I love my wife." Sitri got up from the bed in a swift movement, but Remalt could see that the wound from the arrow still caused him pain. "I will be heading home now."

"Sitri."

There was no reaction from the other man, who walked toward the doorway.

"Sitri, they're dead." This caused the demon to stop moving, but he didn't turn around. "I killed them. I knew they'd be a distraction, so I fixed it for you."

When nothing happened after his confession, Remalt got up and walked over to Sitri, who shifted away from him. Remalt turned quickly, grabbing Sitri's wing.

"Please, hear me out, I—" he began, but before he could finish Sitri pressed up against him, bringing their lips together in a soft but passionate kiss.

Remalt's whole body gave in, making him instinctively close his eyes and kiss the other man back. All he felt was peace and happiness. He put his arms around his beloved, letting himself be pulled back toward the bed without breaking the kiss. Sitri sat down on the edge and Remalt leaned forward, placing one hand on either side of the demon. They lay down without their lips ever breaking apart.

Remalt recoiled when he felt something hard shatter against his head. He groaned in pain, automatically reaching for the part of his head that had been hit. Sitri moved under him, but he was too dizzy to focus on what the other man was doing. His hand felt wet; he was bleeding.

As he moved his hand back down, he felt Sitri grab hold of his clothes and give a quick slash against his throat. Seconds passed before he started to panic. Hot, red fluid oozed down his neck and chest, but the only reason he knew it was happening was because of how it warmed his skin but made his insides freeze.

Sitri moved away, letting Remalt struggle for his life without the warmth of another person to soothe his descent into the eternal darkness of Chaos. Remalt found the silence almost more unbearable. He wanted to scream. Scream at the pain that weakened his body. Scream out the fear that overtook him as he realized that he would soon be gone. But he could do nothing but gurgle on his own blood.

He was dying at the hands of the person who had been prophesied to love him. It made no sense. Unless... Had he been wrong?

In one last desperate attempt to understand, he lifted his eyes to look at Sitri's red ones. They did not strike him as beautiful anymore now that they were staring at him with utter revulsion. But another's eyes flashed in his mind, blue ones that had looked at him with utter adoration for many years. It made him realize that he *had* known love; he'd just been blind to it.

Then he remembered, and all he could feel was regret. Enthusiastic words, spoken by the most delicate mouth, echoed in the distance. *I love those flowers—irises....*

WITCH-DRAGON

S. K. SAYARI

The Scourge neared.

Solveig smelled rot on the wind, tasted metallicity on her tongue, and heard beating drums in the distance. Death approached, and only human lifeblood could satiate it.

The Witch-Dragon of Barasthar was most likely close too. A being born of the Scourge—the blight that sought to turn everything to rot. The blight that only the Lightbringer could battle. Solveig's lips curled into a fierce smile at the thought of her mother who bore such Light in her soul, so powerful that no darkness could escape unscathed.

Solveig turned her attention south. The inky darkness of the Scourge pooled in the pallid sky, unhindered by the harsh winds of the Ahai desert as it glistened like oil. The white sands churned restlessly as if they knew it was near, and the sun battered down on Solveig's face as she stood on the crest of a dune. Beads of sweat trickled down her forehead and slithered down her nose. It was hot today, more than usual, though it didn't bother her too much.

"Ch...Chief!" shouted a squeaky voice.

Solveig turned, raising a hand to block the glare of the sun. A spindly boy, Aran, was running up the dune toward her. He panted heavily, his arms waving like cloth in the wind as he battled the incline.

"The...Witch-Dragon...is close!"

"I can feel it." Solveig wiped her face with her hand as Aran crested the dune. "How far away?"

"Eastward. About five days away on swift feet." said Aran, placing his hands on his hips.

Solveig nodded. Her muscles ached at the very thought of fighting the Witch-Dragon. "Tell my brother to come here."

Aran bounced on his toes and sped back toward the ragged tents littered below. Solveig turned her attention back to the darkness in the sky. She couldn't be sure, but it seemed as though the Scourge had either grown larger or closer—she couldn't tell which.

How long had Solveig and her people lived under a blanket of fear? The Scourge and its children had been 'alive' for longer than she could remember. Whenever she asked her mother, the Lightbringer simply brushed away her questions.

At the sound of muttered curses, Solveig looked over her shoulder. A man with thinning black hair, sunken cheeks, and a prominent, permanent scowl was ascending the incline. When he reached Solveig, his scowl deepened, and he clutched his dark robes tightly to his chest.

"Watching the evil won't make it any less powerful, Sol."

"I know that, Soren," snapped Solveig. "Did your silly little books tell you that, or did you by chance actually fight the Scourge as Mother and I are doing?"

"I'm a *scholar* and a *sorcerer*," hissed Soren. "My strength doesn't lie in savagery and prancing about with pointy metal sticks. It lies in information and deduction, as well as the art of magic."

Solveig snorted. Soren played with tomes of ancient magic that their father had gifted him. Though his magic was strong, it was still no match for immortality. Nothing but the Light was.

"If it weren't for my 'savagery,' you'd be dead, *Brother*. All of us would have perished at the will of the Witch-Dragon."

Soren grumbled, lowering his head. "You're right, Sol. I'm sorry."

It was unlike Soren to apologize. Solveig's heart twisted with guilt, and she bit her lip. "I'm sorry too."

"I suppose I'll go play my part, then. It's time for me to pay the Witch-Dragon a visit."

"So nonchalant about it. You know that it's immortal, right?"

Soren snorted. "Yes, I do. I won't get too close, don't worry. I'll just be scouting, but depending on how fast it travels, I might engage it. I should be back in around ten days' time. You get the others ready to run if the worst comes to pass."

Solveig nodded. The clan was about sixty people strong, but most were either elderly or children. "Take Dart and Bec with you."

"No. I'll go alone." With a pat on her shoulder, Soren descended the dune.

Solveig stayed on its peak, returning her gaze to the Scourge. One day, she would free the desert and her people.

One day, they would know no more fear.

∼

"WE'RE RUNNING OUT OF SUPPLIES," Solveig muttered to herself, mashing cactus in a crude mortar with a pestle. Her mouth watered as liquid oozed from the flesh of the plant. She swallowed around her parched throat, then smiled at a child, ushering him to come forward. "Here's today's ration, Elmir."

Despite how badly she wanted to devour the ration, her duty came first. She had always known that sacrifices would be necessary when the clan had named her chief after her father's death. Perhaps her mentality was why they had chosen her as opposed to Soren, who was three years her senior.

Soren.

The clan had begun moving northwest, away from the Scourge, three days ago. It had now been ten days since Solveig's brother had gone to fend off the Witch-Dragon, and her heart was full with needles of worry. She wondered if he was hiding or fighting, whether he was safe or hurt.

Elmir grinned toothily, snapping Solveig out of her thoughts. He gulped down the water as Solveig poured it into his mouth. When he was finished, she patted him on the head, and then he took off running.

"Is that everyone?" Solveig asked, scanning the others. Weary faces nodded back at her. "Good—then let's keep going. We will rest once again at nightfall."

A horn sounded, and Solveig's heart danced in her chest as she spun on her heel. Three camels appeared from the side of a dune, two loaded with sacks and satchels, the third bearing a woman who radiated Light itself.

The Lightbringer.

When the Lightbringer descended from her camel, Solveig threw her arms around her. She smelled of the cacti flowers that were woven into her auburn hair, and the smell made Solveig warm inside.

"I'm glad you were able to find us with your Light, Mother. I've missed you!"

"And I you, my child." The Lightbringer raised her hands to Solveig's cheeks, softly stroking them with her thumbs. "You've taken care of the people so well. You're a fine chieftain."

"One day I'll pass the role to Soren. I want to be a Lightbringer, like you."

Darkness flitted across her mother's eyes. "You will not become a Lightbringer."

"Why not?" huffed Solveig. "You help the people, too, by warding away the Scourge whenever it turns the sands dark. If I can help you in any way, I will."

The Lightbringer hesitated. A smile touched her lips, and she kissed Solveig's forehead. "My dear, sweet child. All life bears a signature—one that I am able to sense. But your brother's...is strange. I cannot sense him—, save for that he is in distress. Where is he?"

"Soren...Soren went to battle the Witch-Dragon." Solveig raised a hand to her chin, biting her lip. "He really thinks he can drive it away with his 'magic' and 'deduction.' I'm just worried about him. I wish he'd never gone."

Solveig's mother flinched and swayed, her head snapping east. Solveig looked in that direction—that was the way to

Soren. Her mother must have sensed the Witch-Dragon, she thought, prickles running up her spine. The Lightbringer lowered her hands, arms trembling at her sides.

"What is it, Mother? Did I say something wrong?"

"N-no.... I must go. Soren...my son. I need to..." The Lightbringer rubbed her right wrist, then smiled at Solveig. The gesture did not reach her eyes as it usually did. "I'll be back, my love."

Solveig stepped forward. "Do you want me to come with—"

"No!" shouted her mother, voice cracking, before she cleared her throat. "No, stay with the people. They need you."

With a slow nod, Solveig stepped aside, and her mother rushed back toward the camels. Throwing herself on one's back, she snapped the reins, ushering the camel into a gallop. Solveig shook her head, tempted to follow. With a sigh, she brought the remaining camels to the heart of the camp and removed the goods slung on to their backs. Food, clothing, and water.

She glanced southward. The darkness was close now, the stench of rot and mire threatening to overpower her senses. The clan would have to flee soon.

Solveig sighed yet again and clenched her fists. One day, she would herald the Light.

One day, she would become a Lightbringer.

∽

SOREN and their mother returned to the new camp the next morning. The Lightbringer's eyes were dull, her hair a mess, her clothing torn. Soren's cheeks were more depressed than usual, his posture rigid and his movement stiff.

Solveig ran toward the two, kicking up a flurry of sand in her wake. "What happened? Did you fight the Witch-Dragon?"

The two nodded, silent. Solveig swallowed. It was unlike Soren to be so dreary, and even more unlike their mother to look so tired. Something had happened, but Solveig didn't want to push them too hard for details. Details could wait.

"If either of you need to, rest up. We need to leave this part of the desert soon. I'm sure the Witch-Dragon is recouping, and when it heals, it will come for us."

"Hey, Sol," said Soren, kicking at the sand. "I, uh, need to speak with you."

"About what?" asked Solveig and their mother in unison.

Soren smiled, the lines deep around his mouth. He never smiled, and Solveig wondered if the battle with the Witch-Dragon had sent him mad. "Just to apologize for my rash actions."

Solveig tilted her head to the side. Rash actions? Did he mean how he had decided to face the Witch-Dragon alone?

"Finally, my son is learning respect." Their mother chuckled, then grimaced. "I am weary. I must rest.... Should either of you need me, I'll be in my tent."

Soren stood as still as a rock until their mother was gone from sight. Solveig tapped her fingers on her thighs, curiosity coursing through her body. "Well? What did you want to apologize for? We need to start—"

"Come with me." Soren grabbed her by the shoulder, his grip as cold as the desert night and as strong as the day's heat. "Quickly. Quickly!"

She protested as Soren led her past the tents, not stopping his course until nothing but sand was in sight. Solveig crossed her arms and clicked her tongue in irritation. Why in the world had he dragged her away from camp? "What is it?"

"I saw something," he whispered, his face ashen.

The expression sent spirals of fear through her mind. "What?"

He sucked in a deep breath. "I managed to wound the Witch-Dragon on its foreleg. A paltry wound that'll heal over time, considering it's immortal, but…"

"But?"

"Mother has a wound on her right wrist."

Solveig raised her hands in a questioning gesture, though something scratched at her mind. An inkling—but of what, she didn't know. "And?"

"It's the same shape as the wound I caused on the Witch-Dragon's foreleg...its right one, at that."

Solveig's fear turned to red-hot anger. "Just what are you implying? She's our mother! She raised us!" she snarled, fire coursing through her veins. "The Lightbringer is the only one who can combat the Scourge and the Witch-Dragon. Her Light is *everything* to us!"

"I'm not implying—" began Soren, his eyes guarded, his lips trembling. "I'm simply telling you what I saw. The rest is up to you...Chief."

Solveig opened her mouth to retort, but Soren was already marching back to camp. She shuddered, her breaths ragged, and then she fell to her knees.

∼

Nothing made sense.

Solveig avoided eye-contact with her mother, fiddling with the hilt of her dagger. It had been but hours since Soren had told her what he'd seen, and already doubts wormed through her mind like maggots, corrupting every image of the Lightbringer she had in her head.

What could it mean, that the Witch-Dragon and her mother had the same wound? Coincidence, perhaps. It had to be coincidence. Solveig couldn't think—or perhaps *wouldn't* think—of anything more, nor anything less.

She jumped, letting out a yelp, when someone gripped her shoulder.

The Lightbringer smiled at Solveig, tilting her head to the

side. "It is time for us to travel far away, my sweet daughter. The Witch-Dragon approaches; we could only stave it off for a short amount of time. We must tuck our tails and flee."

Solveig ground her teeth together. A dull throb pierced her forehead, and every breath she took reeked of cacti flowers. "No."

The Lightbringer blinked. "What?"

"I said no. I will battle the Witch-Dragon."

Her mother jerked as if she'd been slapped, spreading her arms. "You cannot!"

"Why not?" challenged Solveig, narrowing her eyes.

"Because you are not a Lightbringer." Her mother smiled and raised her hands to Solveig's face, but Solveig turned her head away.

The gesture had once soothed her soul. Now, it raised the hairs on the back of her neck. She cast her gaze toward the Lightbringer's right wrist—but it was covered in cloth.

Solveig sucked in a deep breath, raising her chin. "Then you shall come with me."

Her mother's smile faltered, darkness flashing across her eyes, but only for a moment. "Very well, Lady Chieftain. I shall accompany you to battle the Witch-Dragon of Barasthar."

"Good. Bring Soren too."

The Lightbringer nodded, deliberate and slow, before she stepped back, allowing Solveig to pass. The chieftain shouted orders, and the clan scrambled to the ready, gathering their supplies and beginning the march west. Solveig's fingers trembled at her sides, her flesh crawling. She would find out the truth.

Or die trying.

THE LIGHTBRINGER WAS QUIET. Eerily so. She lowered her head, her illuminated robes rustling in the gentle breeze that brought with it the stench of death. Solveig stood to her right, and Soren to her left. Solveig couldn't help that her gaze kept slipping to the Lightbringer's right wrist, even though it was still covered. Her mouth was dry with fear, or anticipation, or perhaps both.

Light had barely begun to tip over the horizon, but it was enough for her to see the tar-like sphere in the sky, now hovering above their abandoned camp. It dripped, the mire sizzling as it hit the sand.

The Scourge contorted and expanded into a black maw, churning and twisting. It pulsed as if alive, and three creatures oozed out of its core, falling to the desert sand. The creatures would have resembled humans were it not for their rot-riddled forms, their skin peeling as bones jutted out at odd angles. Where they stepped, the sand turned black and steamed, as if it were smouldering.

Solveig pushed down her urge to retch at the acrid stench of burning sand. "We have to deal with these abominations first. Come, Soren!"

Drawing her dagger, she bared her teeth at the Scourgelings. They uttered guttural laughs in return, striding toward her. Beside her, Soren raised a hand, purple mist oozing from his skin. The Scourgelings burst apart as the mist made contact—but more kept falling from the pulsing sphere.

Solveig slashed and whirled, the Scourgelings barely faltering at her strikes. She gritted her teeth, leaping at another one of the dark creatures, but it lashed out with inhuman speed. Solveig stumbled, her breath catching in her chest.

"Behind me!" shouted her mother, pushing Solveig to the side.

Light pooled in her mother's outthrust palm, spilling out toward the Scourgelings. They screamed and withered, turning to dust, and the Scourge shrank in size.

Solveig's heart rampaged in her chest, the maggots of doubt receding. Instead, a scathing guilt grew within the pit of her stomach. Her mother was Light. There was no way she would do anything to harm her people. And now Solveig had put her and Soren in danger, all because—

A thudding stole her attention. As rhythmic as drumming, the thudding grew closer.

A behemoth stalked over the dune, freezing her limbs with its gaze—piercing jet-black eyes, deep-set and reptilian, bored into her soul. Dark, rotting skin peeled away to reveal wasting muscle and black bones, as pitch-black as its long horns, deadly claws, and sharp teeth. The only things that weren't black were the ribbons—scarlet satin tied around its horns, fluttering madly in the frenzied breeze. A Witch-Dragon. *The* Witch-Dragon.

"Mother," Solveig whispered, the dagger slipping from her grasp to thunk into the sand. "Mother, do something!"

The Lightbringer opened her mouth, her lips trembling. "We must run!"

Solveig nodded, backing away, but purple mist whirled on the wind, streaming toward the Witch-Dragon's face. It howled, clawing at its eyes. The Lightbringer screamed.

Her face was marred.

Solveig's vision went hazy, her breaths becoming ragged and heavy. Why? Why had her mother's face been hurt too? Solveig wanted to scream, to cry, to rip her hair out one strand at a time. Nothing made sense!

"They are tied together! Light and Dark are one!" shouted Soren, running toward her.

Their mother shook her head, wringing her hands. "My daughter, don't listen to your brother! I'm your *mother*! Help me —save me! You must run from the Witch-Dragon—you mustn't—"

"You lied to us this whole time. You betrayed me," hissed Solveig.

"I had to! The only way for me to wield the Light is to betroth the Darkness…. Do you really think I'd—"

"I don't know what to think!" screamed Solveig. The woman in front of her was no longer safe and kind and gentle.

Soren grabbed at Solveig's shoulder, squeezing tightly. "I'll take care of this. Don't worry, Sol." He waved at their mother. "Mother…I'm sorry. This is for our people. This is for Sol."

The Lightbringer gasped as purple smoke touched her hand, singing it, and the Witch-Dragon snarled as well, its foreleg burnt.

"You wretched traitor!" screamed their mother. "How dare you turn on me!"

"If I kill you, our people will be free." Solveig snatched her dagger from the sand, advancing on her mother. "If I kill you, we'll be free!"

Soren raised his hand back at the Witch-Dragon, battling the creature with his magic. Solveig spun on her heel, whipping her dagger at her mother's face. The Lightbringer screamed as steel sliced flesh.

"*You* are the traitor! I am your mother! I am the Lightbringer! I—"

Solveig pounced, colliding with the Lightbringer. They rolled in the sand, her mother's grip like a snakebite on Solveig's throat. Solveig convulsed, her vision darkening as the Lightbringer's grip tightened. Using the last of her strength, she slashed at her mother's throat. Remembering the way her mother had always picked her up when she fell, sung her to sleep, and patched her wounds, Solveig's heart shattered the moment the blade connected.

Crimson spurted from the Lightbringer's throat, and she choked, her hand slipping from Solveig's neck. Solveig took a deep breath, her fingers shaking.

The Witch-Dragon collapsed, its own throat dripping black blood, its breaths rattling. The Scourge twisted and writhed, growing smaller until it imploded. Soren fell to his knees, lowering his head.

Solveig sobbed, stumbling to Soren, helping him to his feet. He was panting, his body quivering. "We did it, Soren. We..."

The Witch-Dragon shuddered, rising once more, black flames licking its lips. The Witch-Dragon...how was it still moving? Solveig looked frantically to her mother's still body, then back to the beast. Were they wrong about the Light and Dark being connected?

Or was the Witch-Dragon stronger than the Lightbringer?

It growled, low and guttural, and ice pierced Solveig's heart. She grabbed Soren's robes, dragging him away, but he was slow, exhausted.

"Run, you fool!" Soren hissed. He lurched forward and Solveig ran after him, looking frantically over her shoulder. She couldn't take her eyes off the Witch-Dragon as they scrambled up a dune, her mouth dry. With its dying breath, it breathed black flames that tumbled and sizzled as they ripped across the sand.

The flames were unearthly, too fast. Solveig sobbed, faltering. They wouldn't make it.

She reached out, and Soren took her hand.

CURSED IN BLOOD

JAY ROSE

Selena let go of the knife, propelling it from her hand and into the piece of wood a few paces away. She ignored the groans of men around her and picked up the second knife. All she needed was one more strike and victory was hers. The knife sat against her palm as though it belonged there. With a simple flick of her wrist, she threw the blade at its intended target and smiled when it hit the red circle.

A perfect score.

"Pay up." Selena held out her hand to the man who'd challenged her.

His face was grim as he counted out money from his wallet. None of the other patrons in the pub dared speak as he finished.

Around her, smoke twisted and curled in the gloom. The patrons that weren't watching the massacre were caught in their own conversations. A jukebox at the far end of the room played a fast and hard tempo, the rhythm on the verge of hypnotic.

"I knew you were going to regret that challenge. Now she's going to gloat." Paul, the bartender, shook his head as he wiped a glass.

"It's what I do." Selena shrugged, pulling herself from the music, and snatched her winnings out of the man's outstretched hand. She gave a sigh of relief as she stuffed the bills in the pocket of her jeans. This would get her a few more nights at the motel. It wasn't as luxurious as her former home, but staying there had brought too many memories, too much pain. The smell of blood and decay didn't quite help matters either, and everywhere she went she was reminded of the one who had turned her into this beast. Her master.

Her recent opponent pursed his lips and started to open his mouth before his friend grabbed his shoulder.

"Are you willing to lose more money, Frank? Let it go."

"Listen to your boy." Selena winked, waved to Paul, and left the man to gawk at her recent target.

Outside, the moon peeked between the clouds, full and bright—which meant she had more work to do before retiring to the tiny room she called a home. She threw on her leather jacket, fending off the cold. This side of town was quiet tonight, save for the thump of music from the few pubs that littered the street. One of the lampposts flickered on, and she stuck her hands into her pockets.

Selena sucked in a deep breath, allowing the monster that lived inside her to awaken. It writhed within its cage, wanting nothing more than to break free of the reins and take control. Learning how to deal with the demon that shared her soul had taken a long time. While the monster craved blood and the need to kill, Selena despised the desires it hungered for. The worry of what would happen, of what it would do if she let go of the restraints, was a constant battle. Imagining a never-ending storm of blood and death, she worked every day to keep a firm grip on it, to never lose control over the monster.

Today, though, with the full moon at her beck and call, she could afford to bring it forward while still holding tight to her leash. For werewolves, the moon's magic was a curse—but for her it was a blessing, increasing her control.

Closing her eyes, she released her hold ever so slightly and tucked herself into the alley behind the pub. When she opened her eyes, a rush of power coursed through her veins and a darkness enveloped her. The monster within was ready to take down whoever stood in their way. But there was only one kind of life she would allow it to take.

Those most deserving of death.

"All right, let's find us a criminal, shall we?"

Selena sprinted toward the darker side of town, where all the bad humans liked to parade. She kept to the shadows, heightened senses giving her an edge as she found her way to the place she'd gone almost every full moon since the killing of her master. The man responsible for her bloodlust.

It had been months since she escaped that boarding school—since she ended his life with her own bare hands.

As she slipped through the streets, she slowly neared the town's center. From ahead came the sound of chanting, and she stilled. Tonight was Worship-the-gods-who-damned-us Day—or to them, Blessed Saint's Day.

On light feet, Selena kept to her cover, not wanting to be seen as she spied on the spectacle. A dozen or so women stood around an altar of the goddess Freya. Each of them bowed while holding a dim candle. One by one, they placed the burning light next to the altar and returned to their prayers.

"Almighty Freya, we call to you. Bless it be that you give us strength and the means to bring life back into this—"

"Lunatics. All of them," Selena huffed as she climbed up the side of a building.

She hopped her way from rooftop to rooftop, closing the distance to the darker side of town until she could see over the crowd of thugs—the men and women who prowled the streets like rabid dogs. Looting and stealing, bootleggers and murderers. All the bad Selena loved to gnaw on. She sat there a while, looking for the right one.

A soft breeze brought their scent to her, and the need to jump down and take a man's life was almost too much. She pulled back the reins of the monster, who lashed against the restraints.

"Not yet," she hissed.

"Talking to yourself?"

The voice behind her sent Selena to her feet with her dagger drawn. To sneak up on her when her senses were stronger than a normal human's was nearly impossible; damn her to hell for allowing herself to be distracted by the alluring scent of the men below.

The one who stood before her looked no different than the thugs she wanted to sink her teeth into. His unkempt hair sat shaggy against dark skin while his blue eyes looked her up and down. Her lips curled into a snarl, and the monster within her wanted to tear him to pieces for interrupting their hunt for dinner.

"What do you want?"

"Are you Selena Russo?"

No one had called her by her surname for so long; she almost didn't recognize it. "Who's asking?"

"Just someone hoping to have a moment of your time. My name is Xander."

Selena breathed deeply. Nothing about this man smelled supernatural. Then again, neither did she—and she wasn't exactly human. Sure, she had a human heart—and pretty much every other organ—but the monster inside would never be anything more.

"You should go."

"I know what you are."

Xander took a step closer, and she fought the monster, who wanted to sink its sharp teeth into his neck. The pulse of his veins begged to be sucked dry like a drug. It took her a second to realize what his words meant.

"Do you now?"

"An Infuriya."

Unaware that humans had ever heard of her kind, Selena stilled. Vampires, werewolves, and witches, sure, but she was something else—something far more dangerous.

Taking a step closer, she sucked in a sharp breath, but again, he smelled like nothing other than aftershave.

"Then you know what I can do."

"I also know you have a certain set of skills and that you're closer to a human than any other supernatural predator. I need your help."

Selena laughed. "You're asking *me* for help? Someone that could kill you in a single heartbeat?"

"I'll pay well." He held out a sack and opened it, displaying a large wad of bills.

Her eyes widened. Was her need for money so bad that she was actually considering helping him? The beast inside wanted to simply take the money and run, but the look of desperation on the man's face was almost too much. Selena could have cursed herself for what she was about to do.

"What kind of help are you looking for?" she asked wearily, keeping an eye on the sack.

"I need help finding someone."

"I'm sure law enforcement is better equipped for such tasks."

"Finding my sister is not exactly their top priority in a town full of thugs and things that go bump in the night. Plus, I don't want them. I want you. Please—I can offer more than money if it means you'll do the job." Distress layered the man's words, his plea pathetic but real, and Selena needed the money.

"What are you offering?"

"A place to stay. I know you've been living in the motel on Fifth and Park, which has more roaches and rats than the gutters. Come, see what I can offer, and if you still refuse, I will take that as your word and leave you be."

Selena narrowed her eyes. "You've been watching me?"

"I—"

"Forget it. Take me to your home."

Even if he was leading her into a trap or a ruse, all she needed to do was let the monster loose and move on. She supposed finding a new town to live in wouldn't be so bad. Getting away from the manor at the top of Floyd Hill would probably be for the best anyway. Visions of killing her master still flooded her dreams, but maybe being away from this place would ease her mind a little.

Xander led her through the dark streets, and the monster within grew wild with hunger. Once she was sure the man's words were true, she'd find food. If not, well, then they had already found their dinner for the night, hadn't they?

The house they stopped in front of sat between two taller structures. It appeared abandoned, with the front gate hanging from broken hinges while the lawn sprouted to the tops of her knees. Most of the yellow siding was faded or missing, leaving the wood exposed. The only window, a small oculus with a crack from one edge to another, remained covered by a curtain on the inside. Nothing screamed quaint or inviting.

"This is where you live?" she asked.

"The outside is rough, I know. But the inside is updated and not as pathetic. It's my job to take care of these things, but that's hard to do when all you can think about is finding your sister." Xander shrugged and pushed open the gate, which desperately needed some sort of grease.

Inside, much to Xander's word, had been updated but still begged for a good clean. Selena slid a finger against the round table at the entrance and grimaced at the amount of dust she collected.

They walked through the front room and into a kitchenette. Nothing here showed a speck of grime. Xander was right; this was way better than the crummy room she was staying in.

"All right. I'll help you, but I need to know every detail—places she could have gone, people who had a grudge against her...anything that could lead me in the right direction. I'll also need something of hers, something that carries her scent."

"Her name is Alexi." He withdrew a picture from the pocket of his jeans and handed it to Selena. "She never went anywhere except the park a few blocks down. I told her she needed to stop going there alone, given that she's deaf. No one dislikes Lex—she's a beautiful ray of sunlight—but one night when I returned home, she was just…gone."

Selena looked at the picture in her hand, a child no older than ten with bright gold pigtails and a face she found herself smiling at. She bit her lip, forcing the beast to stand down, its thoughts overpowering her mind as she witnessed its need to taste such a delectable treat. Xander fidgeted with the collar of his shirt, his nerves only making her hunger worse.

"Give me something so I can recognize her scent. I'll head out to the park and see what I can find. How long has it been?" Selena slid the picture of Alexi into her pocket and looked to Xander, whose gaze wouldn't meet her own.

"It's been a year today."

"A year!" Selena shook her head. Finding anyone after that long…he had to know the odds by now. She felt sorry for him—and the need to comfort him. An emotion she'd thought lost to her.

How peculiar.

"I've been searching and done everything I can to no avail. If I had any other option.… Just help me find her."

She owed this human nothing. Walking away from this would be as easy as throwing another knife at the red target. Yet, it was as if something compelled her to help him—a stranger she'd only just met. She couldn't put a finger on why and huffed a sigh. "Okay, fine. Though I'm not sure I can find someone who's been missing for a year with no leads."

"Well, there was one lead. The police found her favorite hat in the trunk of some thug's car. He claimed he found it and was going to give it to his daughter. The police never found any sign the man was lying, but…"

"Go on."

"It was one of the Marzden brothers."

Selena groaned. The Marzden family were a whole clan of vampires, nestled into the rich side of town in luxurious houses, and part of the mob. They were as close to her kin as any of the supernatural families, and she despised them. More than likely they had done the job, but they also had all of law enforcement in their pocket.

"I know where one hangs out, and he and I have an understanding. Let's go. But I have one request before we do—I'm going to need some of your blood."

Xander nodded, a little too quickly. Had he been expecting this? It made her skeptical of his intentions, and she hesitated—but only for a moment. The beast's hunger outweighed any worry. She let the monster show, just enough to take what she needed. His blood tasted sweet, a little more so than normal, but still, nothing seemed out of the ordinary. She pulled away, wiping her lips on her sleeve, before looking back at Xander, who seemed unperturbed, like he did this all the time. No look of horror, no shiver or sway in his body.

"Are you sure you're human?" Selena narrowed her eyes.

"As human as I look." He shrugged.

"Tell me the truth." Selena gazed into his eyes, pulling on what magic she possessed. It wasn't much, but it aided her when needed, and she was wary of this man's intentions.

"I have not lied to you."

She could feel his truth as if it were her own, yet the monster inside was unconvinced. Being at odds with herself didn't sit well, but what else could she do? His truth outweighed her monster's worry.

Suspicious still, Selena continued to keep her guard up as they drove away in Xander's car. They headed across town to a strip club owned by the Marzdens that also served as one of their illegal casinos. A place Selena frequented often when needing extra cash, though the last time she'd been told to never return. Lucky for her, she never listened to orders.

Selena couldn't help gazing at Xander. Before they'd left, he'd changed into a nice button-up top and pants that matched his dark skin tone. She found herself staring and pried her eyes away. Odd that she'd find herself attracted to a human. Another question to the riddle that was Xander.

After an awkward and silent car ride, while Xander continued to rub the sore on his wrist, they pulled up to Fangs and found themselves being eyed by the bouncer. Selena recognized him and smiled. Purely human, but a blood bank to the vampires inside.

"Selena! It's been a while. You know you're not allowed in here."

"Hey, Cliff. I know, but Bruno isn't here. I can tell by the level of stench that hasn't wafted my way. I just want to show my new friend here a good time." Selena grabbed Cliff's hand, placing a few bills in it before closing his fingers and winking.

"No fighting this time, *please*."

"I can't promise to be on my best behavior, but I can give you this." Selena looked into Cliff's eyes, letting her monster peek out from behind the human guise. "You never saw me; you have no idea how I got into the club or who I was with."

Cliff swayed on his heels. By the time he caught his balance, Selena and Xander were already walking into the club. She hated using her gifts on good humans, but she liked Cliff, and the less he knew the safer he was.

"What now?" asked Xander.

"Stay close and let me do most of the talking. You being a human is going to put us at a big disadvantage. We need to find who we are looking for and get out before someone important notices. Got it?"

"Loud and clear."

As they pushed their way through the crowd of people,

Selena sensed Xander's gaze shifting between the dancers on the stages that surrounded them. Most were human, and judging by the collars around their necks, they were nothing more than pets to the vampires. It had taken Selena a long time to stop asking if they needed her help. They never listened anyway. She pulled on Xander's arm, doing her best to keep him from being enthralled like the rest of the room, and made her way toward the back of the club. Standing there with arms crossed was someone else she knew all too well.

"Are we going to have another problem, Max, or are you going to let me pass?"

The guard looked at Xander and then back to Selena. The black eye he had was finally going away, though she wouldn't mind giving him another if needed. "Keep your puppet and your hands to yourself. I give you one hour; after that you have to leave."

Good enough to find her man, ask for answers, and get out before Bruno showed up.

They entered the casino, a much classier sight than the dancing buffoons they'd left behind. Here, people were dressed in cocktail dresses and suits more expensive than anything Selena would ever be able to afford. She only had a few moments to check out her surroundings before the man she'd come for entered her line of sight.

"Come with me." Selena linked her arm with Xander's, and her heart sped up as she felt the muscle beneath his shirt.

They approached the bar where Alonzo sat. His bald head and bulky shoulders were too easy to spot in the crowd of young beauty. She slid into the seat next to him, motioning for Xander to take the other, and huffed.

"Do you really think that thing is going to keep people from noticing your shiny head?" She pointed toward the fedora that sat on the bar.

"Selena. I thought you weren't allowed back." Alonzo's deep

voice vibrated within her. She might have worked with him in the past, but the vampire was scary. Vibrant green eyes drifted down her torso and back up until they stopped on her lips. He licked his own, causing Selena to shudder.

"You didn't come here to play, or you wouldn't have brought that," he grumbled, nodding toward Xander.

"I'm here on business, and I wouldn't play with you even if you paid me."

Alonzo snorted. "And here I thought you were all about pleasure."

"I'm looking for a girl. Name's Alexi." Selena ignored his seductive tone, pulling out the picture and handing it to him.

His brows furrowed as he studied the girl's face. "Who wants to know?"

Ha! So he *did* know something. Satisfied, Selena snatched the picture back. "I do. You know where she is?"

Alonzo shook his head. "I remember her though. Cute girl. She and Hailey played together at the park. Haven't seen her in a long time."

"Hailey?"

"She's a Marzden's kid. A human girl turned vamp. Parents thought it was a good idea to let her be with people who knew how to take care of her."

Ignoring the fact that a vampire child was running around somewhere, she pulled her questions back to finding Alexi. "Police said one of the brothers had the girl's hat in the trunk of his car. You think they turned her?"

"Turned?" Xander shot out of his chair, sending it skidding back. "What are you saying?"

"Not now," Selena hissed and turned back to Alonzo.

"You better watch yourself, Lena. They hear you're investigating them—"

Selena threw her hands up. "I'm just looking for a girl, Al. I don't care about the brothers."

"Is that so?"

Shit.

Selena turned in her chair and came face-to-face with the one person she'd been trying to avoid. This vampire was straight class and could fool any human into thinking him normal. He was anything but. If Selena had to guess, he was kissed by the goddess Hera herself with how he walked about. A dark-grey suit curved along his muscular build, contrasting perfectly against his dark skin. His emerald eyes were deep and inviting, but that wasn't what caught her attention the most. The military-cut hair he sported was almost enough to make her wonder what it might feel like between her fingers. Though, sadly, she'd only ever felt his face on her knuckles. Which was how she preferred most of her men.

"Bruno."

"And here I thought we'd banned you. Good to know we need to take Cliff off bouncer duties. Who do we have here?" Bruno eyed Xander, sliding his tongue against his bottom lip, showing off his fangs.

"Not your dinner," Selena said. "I'm here on business, and we were just about to leave." She stood from her chair, but Bruno blocked her way. His smile sent her legs into jello. Damn her for letting him get to her again—this was why she tried to stay away from this place. How'd she let Xander talk her into this? She looked over at him, but his eyes were transfixed by Bruno.

"But the fun was just getting started. Tell me, *Selena*, what kind of business could you possibly have in my casino?" Bruno's sly tone against her name sent chills down her back.

"We're looking for my sister, Alexi." Xander took a step in front of Selena to stand between her and Bruno. A bold move for someone unaware of who he was confronting. Or maybe he did. Maybe Xander knew exactly what this man was. Had he planned this? But then why would he need her? Panic laced her thoughts; something didn't feel right.

"The deaf girl—the one my daughter speaks so fondly of? Surely you don't think we have her here?"

"I'd like to know what happened. What did you do to my sister?"

Selena watched the two men and their stare-down, worried about what might happen if she let this continue. After all, she needed Xander's money, and his death would put a damper on such transactions.

"Oookay, I think it's time we leave." Selena grabbed ahold of Xander's arm, but he didn't budge. His strength overpowered her own, which was something else she wasn't used to. There was no way Xander wasn't more than he claimed to be. His strengths, secrets, whatever he was keeping from her—it was time he fessed up.

"Oh, please stay, I was just about to have dinner. It would be an honor to have you join us." Bruno smirked.

"Did you turn her? Is she a bloodsucker like you? Fucking *tell* me!" Xander spoke through gritted teeth, his hands balling into fists at his side.

Bruno no longer held on to his righteous demeanor, narrowing his eyes until his forehead wrinkled. Selena could smell his anger rise, and with speed much like her own, Bruno had Xander pinned against the wall with his arm across the human's throat. His teeth bared as he hissed.

Sweet mother of Odin, this is about to get ugly, Selena thought, rubbing her face at needing to get physical inside Bruno's establishment yet again.

"You dare accuse *me* of such things? Do you know who I am, human boy? I could slit your throat with a single fang and drink you dry. Disposing of your body would be easy, and you have no one that would miss you. Not even your sister. Your very *dead* sister." Bruno cackled, a laugh so chilling Selena couldn't move.

The monster within her took that little weakness and burst into action. Before Selena could stop herself, she threw Bruno across the room and was on top of him. The monster surged forward, unleashing a barrage of thrashing swipes. Bruno cried out, calling for his men, who approached as fast as Selena retreated. Blood dripped from her mouth and her hands; she'd have time to worry about what she'd done later.

Selena tugged Xander's shirt, dragging him out of the casino and the club until the fresh air brought her back to her senses. This was really bad. Her control had faltered back there, as if someone had flipped a switch and before she knew it, she was attacking Bruno. What was wrong with her?

Xander ripped himself from her grip. "I had him right where I wanted him!"

"Shut up and get in your car before we both die."

Xander jumped into the driver's seat just as some of Bruno's men came hurtling out of the club. Selena slammed the door and held on as Xander swerved out of their parking spot.

A smile played at the corner of Xander's lips, only for a moment before vanishing. It sent both Selena and the thing she shared a soul with into a rage, but she bit it back.

Neither of them dared say a word until they were safely back inside Xander's home. His anger boiled within him, her own matching his and then some.

"Did you know?" she snapped.

"What?" He whirled around to face her, his lips pursed.

"Did you *fucking* know she was dead? You asked him questions as if you were sure he had her. You told me—"

"I wasn't sure. I—I had a feeling, just something inside, that she was gone." Xander dropped to his knees, cupping his face in his hands.

Seeing his silent sobs, she swore. This was exactly why she hated dealing with humans. Though, was he human? He'd told her he was telling the truth. So why did all of this *feel* wrong? She needed answers.

"Do you have anything to drink? Something stronger than water?"

If there was one thing Selena knew, it was how to make the pain go away, even for a short time. And alcohol would help her nerves.

"Cupboard above the fridge."

Selena found a bottle of whiskey among the many vodkas and disregarded glasses. As she turned to walk back into the living room, her eyes fell on an open door—a light green glow illuminating the dark space beyond. Curiosity sent her snooping. Selena stepped through the door, turning the corner, and covered her mouth to stop a gasp. Along the wall, glowing green paint blended into the wood. The paint, though dry, looked as if it would smear the second she touched it. It curved and arched with such a graceful hand that she barely noticed what it depicted. Two snakes, circling one another to form an 'S' shape, each biting the tail of the other.

"What is this?" She stepped toward it, her hand outstretched, though the beast inside thrashed against her in protest.

"Did you find the cupboard all right, Selena?" Xander called from the living room.

Selena jumped back, closing her eyes tightly before opening them again. When she opened them, the paint was gone, leaving behind nothing but dark wood.

She was clearly losing her mind.

As Selena returned to the living room, she found Xander setting the fireplace ablaze. The glow of the flames licked his cheeks, glistening against the blue of his eyes. She could have stood there and watched him for a long time, mesmerized by the muscles through his thin shirt. Shouldn't she have been furious, not admiring his beauty?

Clearing her throat, she held out the open bottle to Xander, who snatched it and threw his head back. He took two big swigs before handing it off.

"I'm trying really hard to understand you and what's going on. I need you to tell me everything," she said, deciding to keep her little venture to herself.

"I haven't lied to you. Maybe skirted the truth a little, but I *do* need to find my sister. I can tell that you don't trust me and are wondering whether to take my money and walk away. I wouldn't blame you, but I swear, I mean you no harm."

"If that's true, if what you want is to simply find your sister, then I'm willing to still help you so that you can put her to rest, but I can't say this all adds up. For starters, you're not like any human I've ever known, and that tells me, whether you know it or not, that you possess magic." The way he acted and the strength he carried was sure to be paranormal. The more time she spent in his presence, the more she knew it to be true. After all, there were many kinds of creatures, even humanlike ones, that didn't even know what they were.

"There have been magic practitioners in my family. A long time ago, but I assure you I'm no threat to you."

That would explain the vanishing painting she'd found in the room.

"That might be true, but you're freakishly strong, your blood tastes sweet, and something about you just feels…off." She hadn't meant to say that last part; it was as if her filter was gone.

"I don't know what you want me to say, Selena. Alexi is all that matters right now. If you don't want to help me—"

"No, it's not that. My head has been spinning since we met. You make me feel different, I guess."

Xander huffed. "That's one I've never been told before. But I assure you, I'm only paying for your special skills, nothing more."

Selena could feel herself believing him as his words swept through her. The desire to believe him was strong, and even if he was a threat, Selena was much more of a predator. The monster inside agreed and wanted to rip into Xander's flesh rather than listen to his words. Its hostility was something she'd lived with since becoming an Infuriya, but trying to hold it back just then was difficult.

Will you chill out? What's wrong with you? she told the beast.

Needing a distraction, something to calm herself and the monster before they did something they couldn't undo, she sucked in a deep breath, already regretting what she was about to say.

"I haven't always been like this, you know." Selena slid down the wall, sitting close to him as the heat of the fire warmed her. She was cold by nature—the Infuriya didn't need heat—but she still enjoyed the warmth nonetheless. "I used to be human, a long time ago."

"What happened?" he asked, taking the bottle from her hand.

"It's a long story, but my mother used to say it was the work of Hel. Cursed by my conception. A rape baby." Selena swallowed. It had been too long since she'd told this story.

"Hel—really?"

"What, you don't believe in the big guy downstairs? What really happened was my mother got sick of my crying and sent me away to the boarding school on Floyd Hill. Come to find out the owner of that school was a master Infuriya. He took children in and raised them to be his army."

"The crazy man of Floyd Hill was an Infuriya? I'll be damned."

"After he turned us, he starved us and forced us to attack one another. He was trying to find his perfect soldier. To this day, I still don't know what he meant by that. There was only me and one other left by the end. He tricked us, said that we'd passed all his tests and were cured. He called our parents to come get us, but really he hadn't given us the final test." Selena closed her eyes, recalling the events that had forever changed her. The moment she'd known nothing would ever be the same. "When my mother got there, I had been starved of human blood for weeks. The monster inside me was so hungry that I couldn't control it. When he let her into my room and closed the door...there was nothing to stop me. My control was lost to the monster, and before I knew it, I'd killed her."

Selena's hands shook as she let the alcohol slide down her throat. It burned, and she welcomed every bit of it. Flashes of her mother's face, the terror and betrayal at what Selena had done, rushed into her mind. But most of all, she sensed the truth —could feel her mother's truth. She *was* the monster her mother had made her out to be; a monster who'd killed the one who had given her life.

"That's tragic as hell." Xander slurred his words, leaning his head back against the wall.

What's even more tragic was that Selena had enjoyed it. The monster had never felt so alive, and when it was all done—when her mother's dead body lay still—she'd smiled. Because it was her own mother who had subjected her to this life.

But she would never tell Xander that.

"Yeah, well, my life is a tragedy and I'm just living its nightmare." Selena passed the bottle back to Xander.

"I'm sorry I haven't been upfront with you." Xander sat up, moving closer to Selena until she could feel his breath on her face. "I didn't know if you'd still help me. My sister is my world. I needed...I had to be sure it was the Marzdens. But I also had to be sure you were who they say."

Selena raised a brow. "What do you mean?"

"I want you to bring her back."

"Back? You mean like, from the dead?"

Xander nodded. "I know what happens when the blood of an Infuriya is mixed with that of someone who is gone."

Selena couldn't believe her ears. It was wrong to do such a

thing. Bringing her back would only create an abomination, and Selena would have no part in it.

"I can't do that. If I bring your sister back...Xander, she won't be your sister anymore. When a life is taken, that soul is gone forever. There is nothing that can bring her back, not even my blood."

"Damnit, Selena, I have to try. She's all I have. *Please.*"

A feeling urged Selena to stroke Xander's cheek. She raised her hand, and as soon as she brushed his skin, the desire to do much more rushed over her. She blinked, trying to focus, but even the monster within wanted more. Though she was sure their wants were very different.

"Doing this is wrong, Xander. I won't do it. Your sister is gone, and you don't have to deal with this by yourself. I'm here."

Xander brought his gaze to Selena, hot and intense and inviting. She wasn't sure if it was the alcohol or the way he looked at her, but she wanted him. Needed him. Never in her life had she felt such need. Sure, she enjoyed the occasional partner, a fun night of heat and arousal, but this felt different somehow.

"Promise me, Xander. Promise me you will never ask me to do this again. Promise to forget about this and let your sister rest. Do this, and I will help you through whatever you need."

Xander leaned in closer, his lips inches from her own, until they connected. Fire blazed between them as the soft kiss turned into passion and passion turned into lust. His hands were in her hair, pulling her harder against him. Her own hands searched for the bottom of his shirt and ripped it from him. She rubbed her hands over the hard muscle of his chest and groaned beneath his kiss.

She pulled back, only for a moment, wondering what the hell she was doing. Having someone to care for, having anything besides the beast for comfort, was a liability. She could never afford to let herself have emotions other than hatred and pain. It was the one thing her master had made sure of, that the thought of love was impractical—a weakness. To jump into bed with someone she'd just met was a mistake. Then again, hadn't she had plenty of one night stands before? How was this one any different?

"If you don't want this, I under—"

Selena was on him, closing her mouth on his to keep him from speaking anymore. She'd have time to regret her choices in the morning. As he laid her down in front of the fireplace, ready to take her on a trip to Valhalla, he whispered into her ear.

"I promise."

~

SELENA WOKE to rays of light casting through the slit in the curtains. She left her eyes closed for a while, basking in the euphoria of last night's pleasure. Even her monster slept peacefully, though that would only last for a while. Before long it would require her to feed again, since last night had only just been enough to get her by. Tonight, she'd have to find someone to feed from. Until then, however, she would enjoy the day with someone who made her heart feel again. It seemed silly, to feel this way about someone she'd just met, and maybe it was just the aftereffects of sex—which was a human thing she never could get tired of—but she didn't think so. With anyone else, she'd have refused to even stay the night. Selena huffed; what had she gotten herself into?

She opened her eyes and rolled over to find a single white rose on top of the pillow Xander had been sleeping on. Her lips curled into a smile as she brought the flower to her nose. Something weird fluttered in her stomach, and she pressed her empty hand to it. She'd never felt this way before, as an Infuriya or a human. The odd feeling vanished the second

Selena noticed the small puncture mark on the inside of her arm. She dropped the rose, anger replacing the wash of emotion she'd been having. Something—no, someone—had drawn her blood.

"Xander?" Selena cried out. She scurried to her feet and rushed through the house, searching every room. Her gaze fell on a piece of paper that sat on the kitchen counter.

Selena,
I hope one day you can forgive me.
—X.

She crumpled up the paper and threw it into the fireplace. How *dare* he take her blood and use her like this. Inside her, the monster thrashed and begged to be let out. It wanted blood, and not just anyone's. It wanted *his*. She couldn't allow it, not when they'd been doing so good at keeping it in since leaving the boarding school. She needed to track him down and stop him before he did something stupid, but she barely knew him. Where would he go? How did he even know where his sister's body—

"Son of a..." Selena ran out of the house and, using the strength of the Infuriya, raced toward Fangs. This time of day the entire place would be closed, but Bruno would still be there with whoever he'd bedded that night. If there was one thing for certain, it was Bruno's habits.

Fangs came into view. Several people stood along the sidewalk, all with terror-stricken faces. Selena slowed and approached the crowd. Cliff gave her a nod.

"Hells, am I glad to see you. Your friend is in there with Bruno."

"How did you—"

"Remember? Yeah, remind me to thank you later for that. Bruno has a witch on retainer who cleared my mind. Apparently he wanted to know more about your friend—who I didn't know was a warlock."

"A warlock? No, I would know if he were. Even I can tell the presence of a full-fledged warlock."

Would she? After everything, she didn't know if she could trust her instincts. Xander had said his family were practitioners, but even the taste of his blood had brought no sign of such potent magic.

And then it hit her, like a wave clearing the clouds from her mind. She thought about his smooth words on the rooftop—the way she'd fallen for him harder than any man before. The snakes on the wall, the way he smiled after nearly starting a brawl in Fangs. How he'd been able to seduce her and steal blood without even the monster knowing. Most of all, that he'd been able to hide it all from her. He was more than she could have imagined, and that scared her to her core.

She pinned her red curls up and out of her face before pushing past the crowd. While entering the club, rather than pulling out the dagger, she let the monster free. It accepted her offer with pleasure and launched itself through the cage. Selena looked to her left, where a mirror hung on the wall. Her once bright blue eyes were now as red as the fire that had warmed her just hours ago. She made her way into the main room.

Furniture lay in shambles across the floor, with broken glass and spilled drinks strewn about. How long ago had this happened? It couldn't have been *that* long if everyone was still outside. Yet, no one was in this room, and the quiet worried her. The monster didn't care as flashes of killing Xander entered her vision.

"Yes, I know. We need to find him first."

The door to the casino was wide open, hanging from a hinge, and Selena did her best to ignore Max's body, which lay in a heap. Well, at least that meant one less vampire in the world.

Inside the casino the war had been even worse. Shattered slot machines lay tumbled on their sides, card tables were toppled over, and chips rolled in every direction. Many of Bruno's men were dead or just knocked out. It took all of Selena's strength to keep the monster from ending their lives.

They weren't here for the vampires; they were here for the warlock. She tugged on her will and pulled the monster back to their task of finding Xander.

Alonzo stirred a few feet away, and she ran to him, cupping his face in her hands. "Easy, Al. What the hell happened?"

Red eyes blazed as they opened, focusing on Selena. His teeth bared as he swatted her hands from him. "You did this."

"You have to believe me—I had no idea he was a warlock."

Alonzo smiled. "It's nice to see that you let the monster out to play."

Selena sucked in a breath and turned away. "Where are they?"

"It was a compliment. Your buddy took Bruno and they left. I think they went searching for his sister's body. Which means they're headed to the Marzdens' cemetery."

The cemetery. So Bruno did know what happened to Alexi, and he'd been the one to do it.

Selena wasted no more time and started back toward the front of the club. The monster may have been out, but they were both in agreement: they had a warlock to hunt down.

"Lena, wait! There's one more thing you need to know. I think that crazy warlock is trying to bring—"

"—her back from the dead. I know. And he's trying to use my blood to do it."

Alonzo's face paled. "Your blood? He can't do that."

"Apparently he can."

The monster thrashed harder, its need burning against her skin. It wouldn't be much longer until it took control and anyone in her path would feel its wrath.

She needed to sink her teeth into someone.

Back in the club, one of the vampires' minions stood cleaning up the mess of glass. She knew this was wrong, but no matter how firmly she told herself that, the desire ached in her throat. Before she could stop the beast, it sank its teeth into the man. The taste of his blood like a juicy steak hot off the grill, Selena wrapped her hands around his head and let the beast's hunger be quenched.

Stop, she commanded. *Enough, no killing. Not him, not when we have a warlock to maim.*

To her surprise, the monster listened and let go of the man, who dropped to his knees, finally able to let out a scream as he crawled away.

She hated that—the way humans feared her. Hated that she had to harm even a single one of them. Yet here she was, on the hunt for one.

Betrayed. Lied. Broken promises. The beast repeated the words over and over, only fueling its anger as they took off toward the cemetery. Only a few blocks and she'd be face-to-face with her enemy.

The Marzdens' cemetery was the oldest in the entire town, owned and operated by the brothers and their family for centuries. Only those in the family—or close to it—were allowed to rest here. Selena walked up to the iron gate, where an 'M' nearly half the size of the gate was carved into the iron. It was already open, so she slipped through. Row upon row of once-white tombstones surrounded her, and chills ran down her back as she pushed on further through the dead. Cemeteries were something she tried to stay away from—though death wasn't something the monster would allow. She'd tried a long time ago to take her life and had been most unsuccessful.

Without warning, the deafening silence was pierced by the deathly shriek of a blackened crow. It perched itself atop a blank tombstone, watching her with curious eyes. Ignoring it, she traveled on.

She walked a bit further before a familiar voice echoed against the stones.

"Awaken, my dear sister. Come back to me with the blood of the damned. Arise as one."

Selena was too late.

In the shadow of a large obelisk, Xander stood with the already decaying body of his sister laid on a raised cement slab. There was no way this girl had been dead for an entire year. Days, maybe weeks, but definitely not longer than that. So what had happened to her in all that time? Her withered frame was barely noticeable underneath the clothes she wore, all dirt-covered and stained with dried blood.

Next to the slab lay Bruno, his head red with his own blood. She couldn't sense whether or not he was still alive and held on to hope that he was still with her. She might not like Bruno most of the time, but if anyone was going to end him, she'd rather it be her.

"Xander." Selena stepped out of the shadows and into the light of day. She held out her hands and took small steps closer.

"You can't stop this, Selena. She is about to wake, and when she does, she and I are leaving."

"Leaving where?"

"Not your concern."

"I still can't let you do that."

Selena begged the monster inside to hold on, to wait for the right moment to strike. She needed to know just how strong Xander was before they took him down.

He laughed, a deafening screech that pierced her ears. "You can't stop me. Once my sister has risen, she will slaughter both of you and we can finally be free without worry. I can finally have the power to best those who oppose me, with her at my side."

"Is that what you think, you fool? You *fucking* lied to me. Betrayed me and used your magic so that I would sleep with you, all so you could gain power? And your sister—you've done nothing but curse her, damn her to the life of a mindless monster. Don't you get it? An Infuriya without a soul is just that, mindless and damned. A creature of destruction and death. She will kill and kill until there is nothing left. She doesn't know who she is, and nothing you do will change that. I know because I have seen this before, Xander. End her suffering once and for all, or I will, and I will not do so mercifully."

A flash of light zipped through the air, striking Selena where she stood. It sent her flying back into the obelisk. Bits of stone shattered around her. In a heartbeat, the monster inside charged. They had almost made it to Xander when a small child crashed into them, moving like a woken zombie. Alexi screamed, lifting her face toward the rising sun. When she looked back at Selena, a smile crept onto her boney face.

Selena knew that this child's death was inevitable the second she looked into the girl's cold, dead eyes. There was nothing there but emptiness and the monster's anger. She noticed, then, the vampiric glint in the girl's eyes and the sharp canines protruding from her mouth. She had been turned.

There would be time for answers later, she thought, knowing what needed to be done now. Selena knew how to take care of one of her own, having done it more than once back when her master still controlled her. She kicked toward the girl, the blow landing straight into her chest. Quickly rolling to her feet, Selena waited for a blow from Xander that never came. Her ears pulled her attention to Bruno, who was now back on his feet, fully conscious, fending off Xander's attacks. Each jab calculated and precise, it left Selena glued to the show. Until something grabbed the back of her shirt and tossed her to the ground. Her head slammed against the ground, sending stars into her vision, and then Alexi was on top of her.

All Bruno had to do was keep Xander occupied. Selena swallowed and hoped like hell the monster would allow her to regain control after this was all said and done. She took one final breath, and the monster sprang to life. Selena tore the girl off her. Fast as a lightning strike, the beast sank its teeth into the side of Alexi's neck.

Alexi screamed and moved to strike Selena, but missed—a trained fighter this one was not. She managed to scurry away, and as predicted, she ran. Infuriya were fast, faster than vampires and werewolves combined, but an untrained newling was nothing compared to Selena and her beast. They caught up and pulled Alexi down by her hair. With one quick, solid motion, the monster within Selena grabbed the Infuriya child by the throat, severing the head from its body. Alexi didn't even have time to cry out in pain. Though Selena wanted to. Having to do such a thing to a child would leave her scarred, and above all else, angry at the one responsible.

Behind her, Xander did the crying for them both. He launched Bruno off him with one of his spells and looked at Selena, his anger more prevalent than ever before. She'd killed his sister for good, and now he was prepared to ensure she paid the price.

"I should have just taken your blood the moment I saw you. Taken it, and you wouldn't have even known. But I had to be sure, I had to know that you were what they said. Filthy, bloodsucking bitch."

"And you're a ray of sunshine." Selena curled her hands into fists, preparing herself to end a second life today.

"You're not even fully human, a disgrace and—"

"And you betrayed me, lied to me, and made me believe that I actually felt something for you." Selena laughed. "It's good to know it was all just a trick, an illusion caused by your spells. This time, though, I won't let your tricks fool me."

Selena leapt forward, crashing down on top of Xander, but

agile as she was, he still managed to shove her off and throw her into a nearby tombstone.

Disoriented and seeing stars, it took her a second to sit up. "Why did you even recruit me? What was the point of this whole ruse?" Selena coughed as she got up, pain coursing down her back.

"Because he's a fucking *god*." Bruno was bent over, a hand placed against a gash in his side. Dried blood covered the side of his face.

"What?" Selena furrowed her brow.

"Ha! Point to the bloodsucker."

Selena covered her eyes as a bright, green flash emanated from Xander. As the light died, what it revealed left her in awe. Dark wavy locks cascaded down his back while his face paled from once-dark skin. Black and green robes covered him, save for a hand that held a wooden staff. Pieces of twine curled up its curves like barbed wire, and the top of it wrapped around his hand as though it were a part of him. Glowing yellow eyes turned to Selena, who couldn't move. The monster tried to free them, but even its strength was nothing compared to a god.

"Wh-who are you?"

"The trickster, of course."

Trickster? A god of deceit and illusions. There was only one who fit that bill.

"Loki?" Selena swayed, and as the beast within howled, the truth came crashing back at once. The rich smell of the otherworldly, the way his eyes had twinkled on their first encounter. The intertwining snakes—the damn symbol of the god himself. Her attacking Bruno at his club like a savage beast. The strong feelings of need and lust that had her throwing herself at him. The constant doubting of what he said, of what he was. Not even the taste of his blood had given any indication that this god was more than just a simple human.

Selena fell to her knees, panting and cursing as Loki showed her just what the beast had been trying to tell her. Through each bit of anger, it hadn't been confusion or a hungry desire for blood. The monster had simply been trying to open her eyes to this illusion.

"You played me."

Loki waved his staff, sending Selena back against a tree.

"It sure was fun, wasn't it?" Loki laughed.

"Fun? What the hell was the purpose of all of this? Is Alexi even your sister?"

"Tsk, tsk. Don't you try figuring me out, Selena. Many have died trying. But, thanks for playing my game anyway." Loki winked before vanishing.

Selena fell to the ground coughing and sputtering as she cursed the sky. Damn her, damn *him*.

A game? Selena growled, a sound that would make any werewolf proud. Getting to her feet, she looked at the carnage around her. The girl's body in two, blood splattered on broken tombstones. So many answers, and yet she still had no idea what he'd wanted from her. What was the point?

Bruno closed the distance between them. "He told me he has a job for you. I didn't know what he meant by that until we got here."

"What do you mean?"

"He said he has plans for you and wanted to know what power your beast possessed. Apparently, this was just him gearing up for something."

"And this girl?" She pointed toward Alexi.

Bruno shrugged and turned to leave, but stopped. When his eyes met hers, they were lit with rage. "Don't think I haven't forgotten what you did to me, Selena. Compulsion or not, I don't ever want to see you in my club again." He looked away and left Selena to deal with the aftermath of a god's game.

All of it, every bit of the last few days, had been a test for her.

Selena tried to understand but was left with more questions than answers.

"I swear to Odin himself, Loki. If I ever see your face again, I will end you." Selena's hands shook with anger while the monster inside slid back into its cage.

Whatever the trickster had done, whatever he was planning, he'd certainly made one thing clear:

She would never trust another soul again.

DEATH'S REQUIEM

INE GAUSEL

He felt her presence long before he heard footsteps approaching. It would be so good to see her again—it had been a while since she'd last visited.

"Good evening." Her elegant voice rang out through the damp air of the dungeons.

He opened his eyes. The flaming torches outside his cell lit her up, making it look like she was the one burning.

"Good evening, Princess. Didn't know you could walk on the ceiling."

"I'm afraid I cannot," she chuckled. She rolled her eyes before holding a tray of food out toward him. "Are you hungry? I brought your favorite."

Floating in midair, Beyond rolled around to look at her. "Bread? That's very kind of you." He put his feet back on the ground and walked over to her, grabbing ahold of the golden bars between them. The tip of his fingers tingled, then the feeling spread through his arms and started to sting.

Seeing her face up close again made him smile. He'd missed those dark, almost black eyes, her naturally blood-red lips. Those beautiful lips smiled back at him, and he could not resist reaching out between the bars to caress her cheek. She leaned into his touch.

"I missed you, Avita."

Princess Avita had visited him for years, ever since she was just a curious child. Their friendship was something he treasured—he would almost go so far as to say that he loved her, something he hadn't even thought himself capable of before meeting her. He appreciated her small gestures: how she came to him with food and drink, told him about her day, and the games they played when there was nothing left for them to talk about.

"I missed you too, B. I'm so sorry that I have not been able to come visit you before now; I've been preoccupied." She put her hand atop the one he held to her cheek.

"I don't expect you to come and visit me," he tried to assure her before retracting his hand.

She remembered the tray and held it out to him, letting him choose between a slice of bread, some meat still stuck to a bone, a cup of wine, and a cup of water.

To be polite, he picked up the wine, drinking it all in one quick gulp. "You should give the water to someone else. It is—"

"—the source of life, which makes it special. Holy," she recited, reassuring him that she remembered his former lectures. "Just thought I'd give you the option, but after all these years, I should have known."

Beyond put the cup back onto the tray. "Will you stay with me for a little while, my dear Avita?"

"It would be my pleasure," she said, sitting down on the hard floor. Her dark-green dress fell elegantly around her, making the neat bump on her belly slightly more obvious. At first, nothing had made him happier than knowing she was about to bring more life into the world, but his happiness had faded quickly.

"Is your husband treating you well?" Beyond asked, kneeling down. The cell bars blocked his view a little, but he still met Avita's eyes. The dim torchlight reflected in her dark-brown irises.

"Yes, Lun takes very good care of me. He brought me four slices of cake yesterday. I'm no longer certain how much of this is cake and how much is baby." Her laughter was so lively it filled him with joy.

"When is the baby due?"

"In two months. I hope it's a boy. I want to name him after you and his father." She looked down at her ever-growing stomach. "Don't you think Beylun would be a good name for a boy?"

"It would be a beautiful name for your son, Avita. I'm honored."

A moment of silence brought her attention back to the untouched food. "Take some," she offered again.

He shook his head. "Please, give this to the same person you give your water. Give it to someone who needs it."

Sometimes he wondered why she would ever bring sustenance to him rather than the healthy portion of the realm's population; she seemed to have food to spare, and the people needed it. He didn't.

"I promise," Avita said. She paused, thoughtful. "Maybe I could give it to my father? He's come down with the sickness. He's been bedridden for a week now."

Beyond lifted his brows. "No. Someone who needs it. Your father does not."

"He's the king. The people need him to recover," she countered. "And I want him to meet his grandchild." Her eyes fell to her stomach. She stroked over it with a gentle hand, as if already soothing the child.

"He won't recover. Give it to someone not affected by the sickness."

A small tear traveled down her cheek. She didn't understand anything—poor child. Beyond sighed quietly before reaching his hand out to her again. She took it in her own, and he caressed her knuckles gently with his thumb.

"He knew what to do about the people who are sick. I feel helpless, B," she said. "The harvest has been so bad the last few years. People don't have time to work because their afflicted family members crave their attention. And the people give much of their food to the ill—so much that they fall ill themselves because they're starving. I don't know what to do...."

The royal family had no idea how much they tortured the men and women living in their kingdom—the world, even. They had sentenced every being on the planet to live in an endless limbo. The sick would not be cured, and the ones who were fit would never stop caring for them. In the end, there would be no one left to keep everything running. The world would fall barren because people would no longer find the time to live. They were forgetting how.

"Avita. My dear. I wish I could help you, but I'm trapped here. If you'd let me out, I—"

"Are you serious? Why do you always bring this up in my moments of weakness?" She let out a deep, exasperated breath. "The doctors have tried for decades. What kind of magic can you possibly have that they haven't already tried?"

"I *can* cure the sickness. The reason why the sickness came to the kingdom—the world—in the first place is because your great-grandfather locked me up in this cell. Let me out, and I'll cure the king."

A small glimmer of hope shone in her eyes, but it lasted a mere second before it again turned to skepticism and anger. "You have to let go of this delusion, B," she said, her voice breaking. She stood up and grabbed the tray with unusual temper. "I have to go back and tend to my father."

Without taking another look at him, she strode away from the dungeons, and he was once again left alone.

Beyond put his forehead against the bars. He could feel the gold sting and burn, making his entire body itch. He knew it could not hurt him, and he could ignore the discomfort when spending time with the princess; however, in his solitude, it was all he could focus on. It weakened him, drew the energy out of him like a leech. Had it only been the bars, maybe he could have gotten out himself, but the previous king had thought of everything—covered the walls, floor, and ceiling in the same metal.

Drained of his strength, he floated back up into the air, the only part of the cell void of the king's cherished gold.

He remembered a time when he was not bound to a physical body. When his vision extended all over the world. But even though he was banished from the world outside his cage and most of his powers were gone, he could still hear the anguished cries from the souls affected by what they'd decided to call 'the sickness.' No amount of gold could break his connection to them. They were calling for him. *Please, take me away. Make it stop.* Dead souls trapped in a living body—what torment.

∼

"So, you are the man she's been visiting." An unfamiliar voice spoke—a man.

Beyond floated on his back, arms stretched out as if he were swimming in a gentle stream. "The princess? Yes. I'm her friend. You must be her husband—Lun, is it?"

When the prince did not answer, Beyond rolled around to see if he was still there. He was. Touching the golden bars, Lun looked mesmerized.

"A waste of precious metal. What did you do to earn such a prison?"

"I did my job, nothing more. And gold is the only metal able to contain me," Beyond explained, studying the young man. Lun's footsteps echoed as he restlessly walked alongside the cell, sliding his fingers across the bars.

"An unorthodox prison for someone so obviously affected by the sickness. I'm certain a normal cell would hold you just fine."

"Have you not heard the poem, Your Highness?" Beyond asked.

The prince looked back at him, and for another silent moment, they stared at each other. "What poem?" he finally asked.

Beyond grinned, then let his voice echo throughout the dungeons:

"It is true what they say;

> That whatever your role,
> Only one thing matters
> When Death wants your soul.
>
> Bread might sate your hunger,
> And water your thirst—
> But if own ye not gold
> Your blood will drip first.
>
> He cares not for titles
> Nor about wealth;
> Gold slows him but briefly.
> Take care of your health."

"I find no meaning in this poem," the prince admitted after a second of trying to comprehend the words. "It must be from before my time."

"From a time where I was free. Last I heard it was a hundred and fifty years ago. And you are right, it holds no meaning. At least, not as long as I'm trapped here."

A frown appeared on Lun's face. "A hundred and fifty?" he repeated, though mostly to himself. "The sickness came to our land—"

"To the world," Beyond corrected.

"—a hundred and fifty years ago."

Beyond cocked his head curiously to the side. Was this his chance? He planted his feet on the golden floor, walking over to the finely-clothed prince. Lun backed away with two small steps. For the first time, he looked scared.

"The sickness came when the king locked me up here," Beyond said, hoping the other man would take a hint.

"People are sick because of you?"

It was not exactly what Beyond had wanted to convey, but

he could work around it. "In a way. If I were free, everyone would be *cured*." He laid the bait, hoping the prince would bite.

"How is that possible?" In Lun's voice was a spark of hope that hadn't been there before. Now all Beyond had to do was blow more life into it.

"Have you ever heard of Death?"

The prince thought, then nodded. "From your poem. I do not know what—or who—it is."

Beyond pitied the man in front of him, and for a brief moment he imagined that it was the prince who was stuck in a cage. How could any creature appreciate life when to them it seemed endless? Only the ones affected by the sickness now knew the agony.

Beyond knew he had betrayed them by being captured. Many had been trapped for over a hundred years, too exhausted to move their bodies, never satisfied by any amount of food or drink. People who knew they needed something, but could never figure out what it was.

"Death," he said, "is peace."

He spoke his own truth, but by the never-ending anguished cries he heard day and night, he was certain it was everyone else's truth as well. Fear of endless torture or empty space could frighten any soul; but now the only torture they would experience was in not dying, and that vast dark and empty place would never feel anything but peaceful once they were there.

"The people who have the sickness want peace, and I am the one who brings it. The king's grandfather feared it, so he locked me inside this cell. The current king was fearful, too, so he also refused me freedom. I heard he's come down with the sickness."

"Avita feels helpless," Lun said, his expression revealing his empathy for her.

"I told her I could cure it, but she didn't believe me. All she has to do is let me out."

"Why would His Majesty be frightened of peace?" Lun asked,

as if he'd just then understood what Beyond had said to him. He took a step toward the cell again, regaining his courage.

"It's a different kind of peace, Your Highness. It envelops your whole body, it numbs you." It was difficult to explain such a thing to someone who hadn't experienced it. "Before they imprisoned me, everyone feared it. Now you've all forgotten it—the fear, and the accompanying appreciation of life." Beyond looked straight into Lun's eyes, peered into his soul. "It is your birthright to experience peace, but only I can give it to you, the king, the people, and the world. Would you deny every living being such a thing?"

Lun shook his head. "Everyone deserves peace," he agreed. "But how can I know you're being truthful?"

Beyond thought for a moment, then reached his hand out between the bars. "Place your hand in mine. You'll feel it."

The prince looked skeptical, but he quickly seemed to decide that an old, sickly man could not harm him too severely from inside a cage. As their hands met, Lun's breath was knocked out of him; few people had ever touched Beyond and lived to tell the tale. Avita knew the feeling, but she had grown numb to it over the years.

Lun closed his eyes as he slowly but steadily regained his ability to breathe. When it seemed like the prince was about to lose his footing and fall, Beyond let go of his hand.

"No, wait!" Lun cried out, grabbing Beyond's wrist. Seconds later, he found his senses, releasing his hold with a confused frown. "I've never experienced anything like that. It was so…divine."

"Peace is the cure, Lun. Help me bring it to your people. To the king."

"I will," Lun promised.

They had an understanding now, and as Lun turned his back to the golden cell, Beyond knew that he was going to do whatever he needed to free him. Lun loved Avita, and Beyond had just shown him the way to save her father. The prince would never pass on such an opportunity to help his princess.

Left alone once again, Beyond felt a sinking feeling in his chest at the realization that soon he would truly have his freedom back. Was he experiencing fear? Grief? It had to be similar; he was certain. He was used to people's hatred, but knowing that Avita's revulsion would soon be directed at him stung worse than gold. The king would be his target, and even though it would be an act of kindness, his beloved would condemn him for it.

His brows wrinkled as he felt something wet trail down his cheek, toward his ear. Avita had made him shed tears, made him feel things he was not supposed to.

Equally a blessing and a curse.

∼

THE TURN OF A KEY, a cell unlocked. Shadows on the ceiling revealed the door opening. He didn't know how long he'd been alone, if it had been days or weeks, but Lun was back and had brought freedom with him.

"Please, cure the people of our kingdom."

"The world," Death corrected. "I will cure the world."

He was on his feet in an instant. For a moment all he wanted to do was look, just to make sure the gold hadn't made him delusional. A small step at first, then another, and another. In the end, he stood firmly planted on the stone floor outside his cell. Waves of energy surged through his veins and almost knocked him off his feet. His body tingled with rejuvenation. His soot-black hair grew, cascading down his shoulders. His skin tightened, making him young and beautiful once more. Now his eyes could see again, past the things directly in front of him; as his presence grew, he could observe the world and every living being roaming it.

Dividing his consciousness to help the afflicted as quickly as possible, he lent a guiding hand to thousands of people at once. They were ready to pass, letting him lead them to the other side without any hesitation. Their peace became his as they were finally able to rest. Mere moments later, only the king's voice was left plaguing his mind. Avita was there with him, and Death wanted to talk to her before blessing her father with peace well-deserved.

"I'll see you again, Lun. Hopefully when you're old and tired. Thank you."

Lun's slightly confused expression was the last thing Beyond saw before disappearing from the dungeons.

One second later, he stood outside the king's chambers. Two guards watched the entrance to the room, but people couldn't see or hear him unless he wanted them to. Three knocks for Avita and her father to hear.

Knock. Knock. Knock.

He headed inside through insubstantial doors, solid matter that no longer held any meaning to him. Avita sat beside her father's bed, looking up toward him as he entered the room. Her lips turned down in a frown of uncertainty.

"Beyond?"

He didn't have to answer for her to come to her own conclusion.

"You don't look like…. How did you get out?" Her hand gently let go of her father's before she stood up and walked toward him. "He's gotten worse, I couldn't visit you…."

"I've never expected you to come and visit me, Avita," Death reassured her. Looking at her, he knew that he had broken an ancient promise—to love all beings equally. He was no longer in balance. She had removed the ground from under him, and he had fallen. He had started to envy the mortals, and it was all because of her. Yet, he knew that the feeling was not mutual. It made everything easier, to know that no mortal could ever love him while their souls still clung to life. "I've come to cure your father."

"You didn't lie to me? You actually know how to make him well?" For a moment, she was the sun, shining like a million lights fueled by hope.

"It will hurt, Avita."

"How long will he know pain?"

He put her face between his soft hands, caressing her cheeks with his thumbs. "It will hurt you, not him. He will be at peace, I promise."

He leaned in and kissed her forehead before stepping away, walking towards the sick king. He was met by tired, brown eyes. The king's dry lips opened, as if he wanted to speak, but no words were uttered. Death put a gentle hand on the old man's chest. One small touch was all it took.

"Who are you?" the king asked. He looked young and strong again. There was pride in the way he carried himself.

"I am Death, the son of our Great Mother, and your servant and guide. You have suffered in my absence. Please forgive me." Death bowed before the dead, the way he always did.

"Why are you here?"

"To lead you to the land of eternal peace." Death gestured to the space beside himself. To him it was empty, but he knew the king would see something beautiful. It would be his own paradise, something that would lure him in.

The king's soul came closer. Death held his hand out in a welcoming manner, ready to lead the way at the king's command. Then the king stopped, looking around the room as if he'd suddenly become aware of his surroundings.

"Avita. My daughter," he said, recognizing the face of the seemingly frozen woman in front of him. *"She's been with me every day since I fell ill. She's a wonderful woman, I'm proud of her,"* he remembered. *"Will she come with me?"*

DEATH'S REQUIEM

"Eventually, but right now only I can walk this path alongside you. Come. While we walk, you can tell me your favorite memory."

The king finally took Death's hand. "The birth of my daughter. She is my greatest accomplishment. Never have I loved someone so thoroughly."

As they walked together towards paradise, the king began to smile. From his perspective, he was treading into the most wonderful place he could ever imagine, but all Death saw was a soul slowly turning into a million tiny particles that shone bright like stars.

"Neither have I," Death mumbled before noticing that he was back in the land of the living.

Avita stood beside him, looking at him with worried eyes filled with unshed tears, like a layer of ice upon water.

"When will he wake up?"

"Avita, your father is dead. He will never wake up."

Her wandering eyes revealed her incomprehension. She turned to the king, putting her hand on his arm, shaking it gently to seek his attention. With a soft voice, she once again begged for a response. When nothing happened, she turned back to look at Death. The tears that had collected in her eyes had now crawled down her cheeks.

"What did you do? You promised a cure," she cried.

"Death is the cure. I told you it would hurt, but it's a bittersweet pain that can only be felt after having loved and lost."

She turned to her father once again, shaking him more and more aggressively when he didn't respond. "Father, please," she called out. Tears rained down from her eyes as she punched the dead man's chest.

Suddenly, the doors to the bedchambers opened, and a man in a guard's uniform came bursting in, filled with adrenaline. "Your Highness, hundreds of people from all over the city are standing outside. They say that their sick family members aren't responding—they're not breathing or moving their eyes, it's like they're not here anymore. No one knows what's going on."

"The same thing happened to my father," she said, her voice quivering. She looked towards Death, her eyes red with rage. "This is your doing. You have sent my kingdom into ruin. What kind of magic is this? Undo it!"

"Death cannot be reversed. Your kingdom will prosper now that your people no longer are left caring for the living dead. I promise."

"Guards!" she called out, and the two sentries came rushing to her aid. "Escort this man back to his cell." Avita's command made Death pause. "Put him in golden chains and place guards there day and night. I never want to see him again."

"My dear Avita," he said quietly as the guards came towards him, "sorrow clouds your mind. Death is a natural part of life; it happens to everyone. I'm so sorry that your great-grandfather stole your ability to experience and prepare yourself for the grief it causes. However, locking me back up will only hurt your people."

The guards grabbed his arms and started pulling him towards the doors. As he let them guide him down the path that led to his own personal death, he closed his eyes, placing a part of his consciousness in the king's chambers. Avita stared at him with big eyes as she turned around and met his gaze.

"How did you...?"

"We are friends, are we not?"

"Not anymore. Leave."

"Your father was not scared, he welcomed me. Keeping him alive caused him only pain and suffering, I brought him relief. Only the living shun me." He held his hand out towards her, hoping to feel the warmth of her touch. She took a step back instead, denying him his only wish. "If not for my sake, let me go free for the sake of your people. You are condemning them to a crueler fate than I."

"In the same breath as I command your freedom, will I not

sentence my child to both witness my own demise and for him to experience it himself? What horrible mother would I be?"

"Not only would you be a great mother, but you would also be a great queen."

"You spit lies," she barked, putting her arms around her growing belly as if trying to protect the life within.

"I'm almost back in the cell. Avita, promise you'll free me."

"No. I'll make sure you'll never leave that cell again, you monster."

Emotion welled up in him, but he was uncertain whether it was sadness or anger—maybe it was both? His cheeks felt wet as tears streamed from his eyes for the second time in all of history. As they hit the floorboards, the wood rotted. He was not supposed to have feelings like this, and the world would fall to ruin if he could not compose himself.

Their eyes met, and hers too were filled with salty tears. Looking into her dark eyes, he realized that he had one thing left to teach her.

"Avita...I love you. You're the only one I would ever break my promise for."

Only a few steps from the cell, his body melted from the guards' grip, turning to smoke. He'd given her the chance to make the right choice, but it seemed he would have to make the decision for her after all.

"If you're not ready to experience death, you're not ready to give life either. I will help you, so that next time...you'll be ready."

Her instincts did not tell her quickly enough that she should've moved away. Death reached her, placing his hand on her swollen belly.

FEED THE SEA

AISLING WILDER

*Shouldst thou encounter one with Song, swiftly rid thyself of him,
like unto the cur casteth out the flea.
Likewise, if Song is found within thine own house,
or the house of one who serves thee, so shalt thou cut it out.
For even the slightest melody is an abomination,
and thou shalt not suffer a single note to sound.*

~ The Book of Light, Illuminations 12:14

Burhan Terana, Fifth Hand's Fist, strode purposefully through the Great Hall of Hand's Keep. So purposefully, in fact, that Cadan—his second—struggled to keep pace as he approached.

"My lord! My lord?"

Burhan turned, annoyance bending his brow. "What is it?"

Cadan caught his breath, gasping out his pronouncement. "Her ladyship, my lord."

The larger man frowned, his steel-grey eyes growing dark, his lips a tight line beneath his grey-streaked goatee. "What about her? I do not have time for this. There are whispers along the Arm."

The smaller man nodded. "Yes, my lord. I know. Dark-Dread is creeping west from the Shadow Moors."

"If you know, then you also know that men and supplies must be sent immediately." Burhan turned to walk away again.

Cadan nodded. "Yes, my lord. Only…"

"Only what?" Burhan stopped, but did not turn.

"Only she wishes to confess, my lord."

Burhan did turn then, fixing that steely stare upon his second. "You are certain?"

Cadan flinched, but to his credit, did not drop his gaze. "Yes, my lord. She told the Luminaries. She has said she will confess. But only to you, my lord."

Silence filled the Great Hall then, the only sound the creaking of leather as the larger man clenched and unclenched his gloved fist. She wanted to confess. Just when he had begun to think she would carry her secret to her death.

Why?

Without another word he turned on his heel, heading back the way he'd come, with Cadan hurrying after. Deeper into the Keep and down to the dungeons.

Servants and guards bowed and made way as he passed. They said not a word—they wouldn't dare—but they stared their thoughts. It gnawed at him, the way they whispered behind his back. He saw the sideways glances, encountered the sudden silences when he walked into a room. He was not a fool. He would have them all killed if he could. But the Keep was poor enough in people. And he was Hand's Fist, charged with defending The Western Reach. He needed his men, and their loyalty. So he whipped some, flayed others, and executed the worst of them—making certain fear would ever check the rest. They might whisper, but they would obey.

"Wait here." He barked the command at his second, who nodded with obvious relief as they reached the next door.

It had been months, now, since he had commanded his wife's imprisonment. Six months near to the day since the girl had been born, and not even his. His would have been a son. The Luminaries had proclaimed it after conception. After two babes had been born and died, they'd told him he'd have a son who would thrive. No, this girl was not his. Could not be his.

Yet his wife had insisted. Even after he'd had her arrested, even after the Luminaries had questioned her, and her screams had echoed throughout the Keep. Even after that. Even after he'd had the babe cast in after her. She'd still insisted the child was his and his alone.

Until now.

He nodded to the last guard as the man opened the heavy iron door and handed him keys and a torch, then he made his way down the spiral stone steps into the lowest and darkest dungeon.

A foot of water sloshed about his boots as he ducked beneath the damp archway and made his way to his wife's cell. The tide was low, then, and ebbing. At high tide the water was up to his chest. Higher even, under some moons. The lowest dungeons were rough-hewn, carved out from a sea cave, the farthest walls still open to the ocean. It made for a brutal imprisonment. Those jailed were always wet, their flesh wrinkled and festering, and they were always cold.

The Hand was a peninsula reaching into the sea from the northwestern-most part of Westbreach, and the water surrounding it was never warm. The waves roared and raged at the cliffs beyond the Keep; you could hear the constant thunderous echo everywhere. Especially here. Eventually, all those cast into this dungeon would feed the sea. One day, so would she.

He stepped closer, stopping just outside the cell, lifting the torch and peering through the barred hatch. The firelight flickered and bounced dully off the iron door, forcing him to squint to see.

The enclosure beyond was dark, and it took a moment for his sight to adjust. He heard them before he saw them: a little wail above the slosh and slap of water. The babe. Then his wife's voice, soft and soothing. The sound pulled a pang from his heart. But he pushed it down, swallowing hard.

"Eliina." Six months since her name had left his lips.

He heard movement beyond, more coos from the infant—then his wife stepped into the circle of amber torchlight.

"Burhan."

His name on her lips. The pain stabbed again, a dagger to his heart. He had loved her once. Such a beauty she'd been. Bringing up the keys, he fumbled through them a moment, then found the right one, unlocked the iron door, and stepped within. A rush of water flooded in with him, adding to the murky, filth-ridden pool already there. It stank. He lifted his sleeve to his nose and held the torch higher.

A beauty she had been—but no longer. Her flesh, ghost-white, stretched over her bones like goatskin over a new drum. No give in it. She was covered in fetid, rotting boils and oozing sores. Her eyes, once glittering and fierce green, were mould-dull with hunger and pain, and her hair, that glorious amber that had first caught his eye long ago—her hair hung in tangled and listless strands. Her gown was wet grey rags, and her hands, clutched tight round the babe in her arms, were twisted—fingers bent from repeated breaks, joints swollen and arthritic from the constant damp.

The babe kicked and fussed, and she bounced it up and down. It was dry, at least—she'd somehow kept it so. It was also well fed and blanketed in new wool. Some foolish guard, probably. Showing mercy. He'd find them out. Have them whipped.

His gaze trailed back to his wife's face as she stepped closer. He drew himself up and met her gaze. "I have come to hear your confession."

She smiled, and for a moment he saw a glimpse of the young woman who had once held his heart. He shoved the pain away once more and found anger, familiar and cold, to take its place. No matter that he'd loved her once. Soon she would die, and he would wed another. Another who would give him sons.

"Well? Speak. I will not wait."

"Oh, I know. You never were patient, Husband."

He frowned. "I neither need nor accept your criticism. I have no time for such things. Give me your confession."

She stepped even closer, until she was only an arm's length from him.

"I wish to confess." She shifted the babe in her arms, looked down, then back up at him. "I wish to confess that I still love you, as I have always loved you...and that this child is a testament to that love."

He smiled, tightly, righteous anger hot in his breast. "That child is a girl and cannot be mine. Mine would have been a son. The Luminaries proclaimed—"

Eliina scoffed, then coughed for a few long moments, her broken body wracked with spasms. He watched, wincing a little, and waited until she could speak again—which she did, spitting the words out between each gasping breath. "The Luminaries... were wrong...as they often are. The girl is yours, Burhan. And... I can prove it."

He frowned and took a breath to protest—but she continued, her voice growing stronger as she spoke.

"This is my confession. I know the truth. The truth of your line, of your blood, oh Great Hand's Fist. Lord Beyond the Arm. Protector of The Western Reach. Bearer of Light." She backed away a step and held up the babe so that he could see the child's face. "Carrier of Song."

He paled. "Lies. You lie before the Light!"

She laughed, a scraping sort of sound, and the babe in her arms whimpered. She turned away, soothing the child until it was quiet once more, and when she turned back to him a strange light glinted behind her eyes.

"The Light. Oh yes, the Light. I've sworn many things to the Light, over the years. As have you, Husband. To the Light you swore to keep hearth and home and family. To protect the Hand and the lands beyond. And for my part, I swore to bear you children. And all for the Light. All things to the Light."

She recited the familiar blessing in a tone that bent more and more toward madness as she carried on.

"So many oaths, Husband. I never broke a single one. But you did, didn't you?" She turned away again, rocking and shushing the babe in between her words. "I have often wondered about your family. You told me your brothers were killed in battle, and your mother—you told me she went mad and murdered your father. You told me these things, and you wept against my shoulder as you spoke. Remember? I felt sorry for you, and loved you more because you were sad, and alone. It explained and excused your cruelty. Made it easier for me to forgive you. I thought I could heal you. Change you."

She moved closer to him in a rush then, causing the water to slosh and splash against his knees in her wake. "But 'twas all a lie."

Startled by her sudden movement, he stepped back, and nearly stumbled. "I did not lie! They are all dead!"

"Oh, yes. They are dead. But not by battle, nor your mother's madness. They died by your hand."

Anger burned in him again, and he raised a leather-clad fist. "Liar! Witch! Who told you these things?"

She smiled. "It is strange, what one overhears when one is in a dungeon, Husband. When one is tossed away. Forgotten. One finds others, also forgotten."

He gaped at her, staring, shaking his head while he searched his memory, trying to recall whom else he'd thrown in the lowest dungeon—whom she could have spoken to—as she went on.

"Your brothers. You murdered and then mutilated them. Made it seem as though they were taken by the Dark and its wretched children, but it was you. And while your father still mourned their loss, you murdered him and blamed it on your mother. Your poor, wretched mother. She went mad, you said. Killed herself after that, you said."

And he remembered. His mother. Here. He'd put her here. In the dungeons. But that had been years ago, years and years. No. It could not be. He backed away again, and this time he did stumble, falling against a low shelf carved into the wall: a mockery of a bed, slime-slick with algae and covered twice a day with water. He stood up abruptly again—and shoved Eliina away with a cry.

"No! You could not have spoken to her. She's dead. Long dead!"

Eliina grinned, slowly, the smile splitting lips that cracked and bled. "Oh, yes. She is dead. But it is passing strange, what Songs the sea may learn, and sing back on the tide. One only need listen. Listen, Husband." So saying, she held up the babe, now wide awake and staring at him from its bundling.

He looked down—he could not help it; it was as if an unseen hand pushed at his head, bending his neck. He gasped, then, as he truly saw the girl for the first time. She had the look of her mother. Slight and pale—with a shock of red curls sticking out from under the wool, and bright, glittering green eyes. Eyes that sought and caught his own. Caught, and held. She smiled with a tiny mouth that reminded him of his own, and then she made a sound—soft and sweet, little more than a murmur. No words that he could discern, but somehow the sound surrounded him. Like water, or wind. It was everywhere at once, and suddenly he was no longer ankle-deep in cold saltwater in the lowest dungeon, but instead stood in a field, bathed in warm, golden light. A gentle breeze brushed his cheek and stirred his cloak, and the scent of flowers, heady and summer-sweet, filled the air.

He looked around, dazed, uncertain. Where? He felt heavy. Drowsy. He looked down at his feet and saw that his boots were sinking, slowly, into the earth. Or was the earth rising up to envelop him? He could not tell. Dumbly, he reached to free himself, but his arms flailed, useless as loose cloth. Then he heard a new sound and looked up to see his mother. Young and beautiful as she had been when he was a small child. Blossoms rained down around her, white petals resting in her dark hair like a crown.

"My son." She nodded at him, reaching out a hand to brush his cheek.

"Mother?"

"Yes, Burhan."

"No. You—you're dead."

She smiled. "Yes. Long dead."

"Then how—?"

"The blood of the line is strong. It carries the Song. And the Song remembers."

"The Song...."

"Yes, my son. I sang it to you, as a child."

She took a breath, like autumn wind through trees, and let it out, filled with sound. Sound that joined the gentler warbles of the babe, turning and weaving around him, filling his heart with an ache that he had not felt in years. The joy of a childhood of innocence, the pain of that same childhood lost. And he remembered.

His father. Fourth Hand's Fist, beating his mother. Himself cowering in fear under his bed, watching. What had she done? He'd been afraid, a nightmare. She'd hummed to him, some simple and sweet and wordless thing. Not a Song in truth. Yet still forbidden.

His brothers, older, taking their father's lead, taking turns beating him until he cried, and beating him more for crying. His mother finding him, soothing. Soft—a whispered Song this time. That one kept secret, but not forever. More beatings, none of which he could stop. Too weak. His father saying it was her fault; the fault of her blood in him.

He loved his father. Wanted to make him proud. So, one day, he'd agreed, and he hadn't seen his mother much after that. He trained, took after his brothers. Learned to take the beatings and then to give them. Took his heart and made it hard. There was no place for softness in Hand's Keep.

His brothers, always better, always had his father's praise.

They had needed to die. A simple task. He hadn't known, really, until he'd done it. Hadn't even known it was singing. So easy to take a breath, send it out with sound, and see the power shimmer. Aim that out in turn to stab, to flay, to rip skin from flesh and flesh from bone.

His father then, mourning the death of the two he'd loved more than he'd ever loved Burhan. But he was true. Hard. He showed him. So easy again: take a breath. Find the right tone. Let it out. Sever his father's head from his neck with a single note. Watch the blood flow.

And his mother had seen. He wished she hadn't seen, hadn't known; she couldn't know. But she had, and had tried to sing to stop him. And so another breath, another note—one that had torn her tongue from her mouth.

No. Not him. That wasn't him. The Song had done that. Had done all of it. It was evil—made him do evil, vile things. And it came from her, she had sung it first. Given it to him, like a disease.

So he had sent her here, to be taken by the sea. To be forgotten. Like the Song in her—in him. He cast it out and invited the Luminaries in, to pray over him, and raised them up as he ruled Hand's Keep. They would silence the Song. Quench even the shortest note. Any hint of a melody and the bearers would be tortured. Killed. And he would remain pure. Strong. No Song in him. Never had been. And he would have many sons and they would also be strong, silent, pure. No Song in them either.

But then Eliina...and the babe. No. No!

Distant thunder roared past the somniferous sound all around, and he clenched his fists, focusing on that. Familiar and fierce. Yes. Pounding, like his heart. The sea. The dungeons. Eliina. The babe. He gasped awake—he could not see, the torch was gone—but he reached out, grasped the bundle of wool in his fist, and ripped the babe out of Eliina's grasp. Raising his hand over his head, he flung it hard across the cell.

"Abomination!"

The Song was silenced as the babe gave a single wail—and Eliina screamed, turning toward the child as it hit the wall and fell lifeless into the water; water which was now rushing swiftly out of the door, across the floor and toward the sea.

With a roar, Burhan leapt upon his wife, crushing her down into the darkness, to the floor of the cell, beneath the water. She thrashed and flailed in his grasp, but he did not let go. He would not. Could not.

It was over in moments.

He stood then, breathing hard and soaking wet, blinking in utter blackness, and listening. But he heard nothing. No Song. Nothing but the roar of the sea without and the water within, rushing, wave upon wave, reaching—taking first the babe, and then his wife, out across the floor and further away.

To feed the sea.

HEART OF SHADOWS

A. M. DILSAVER

*T*heo stared out the big bay window to the fog-shrouded forest beyond. Not an actual forest—real plants could not grow here—but something close enough to mimic the trees of Earth, a shadowy configuration meant to disguise the bland nothingness of the space beyond. If he could not conjure the sun, then he would surround himself with shadow instead.

An eerie howl broke the silence of the ever-night, long and high, followed closely by two more. Vorgs, probably, out hunting. Sounds erupted all around him as the veils opened under the Solstice moon, allowing passage between worlds, inviting all sorts of creatures into his solitary confinement in the Other-Realm.

Theo kept a close watch, though not for danger. The menacing presence surrounding his manor was enough to keep most creatures at bay. If not, the iron gate surrounding it made a decent enough deterrent. No one—or *thing*—had crossed the gate in thirty years.

Theo couldn't help but wonder why. Isandra had sent heroes after him for decades. Tall, strapping lads sent to slay the wicked jinn and bring back his heart. Every year, without fail, they came. Every year, without fail, they died.

And then they had stopped coming altogether.

This year would be different. He could feel it in his bones, in the shadows that wrapped around his torso and slithered around his arms and legs. He itched for excitement, even if it ended in a grizzly death.

Especially if it ended in a grizzly death.

"Help!"

His eyes snapped to the right, where a flicker of red danced through the shadow trees. Foolish humans, always choosing such vibrant colors. No wonder they were killed so easily. The figure screamed, high-pitched enough to make Theo wince, even from inside his manor. In the pervading silence of the Other-Realm, he had forgotten how piercing a human voice could be.

As the flicker of red moved closer, Theo recognized the flare of a long skirt. A sacrificed maiden, perhaps, though he had thought humans had moved past those archaic rituals by now. A distant howl let Theo know the vorgs had noticed the intruder as well. She would not be the first female to die in the Other-Realm, but he had never enjoyed seeing a woman in agony.

She fell against his gate, then yelped in pain, as if the iron bars had burned her skin. When she pushed her hood back to scan the forest behind her, a long braid fell out. Long, and completely white. Only one species he knew had hair like that.

Fae.

Theo stopped breathing. It couldn't be. The Fae were all dead. He had watched them die. So why did one appear to be banging against his gate?

A vorg howled again, calling out to its companions, and Theo found himself moving, running down crimson-carpeted hallways, shadows trailing him like soot. By the time he reached the front gate three vorgs loomed in the distance, great hulking masses charging toward them, shadow trees swirling out of existence with every pounding footfall.

The woman screamed frantically, banging against the bars with the heel of her hand, and he knew he should not let her in. Knew he should have stayed inside his manor while the realms collided and let her perish like the rest.

Instead, he opened the gate with a brush of shadow against lock. The woman tumbled through, letting the gate slam closed behind her. The first vorg crashed into it, rattling the iron bars as the woman in red huddled against Theo, burying her face in his collarbone. Theo had time to catch a whiff of something sharp and biting before she shoved against him, dancing just out of his grasp. The worn, black handle of a dagger jutted out of his carefully pressed vest.

Theo stared at the woman in shock. She cocked one hand on her hip, watching him with an arrogant smirk, eyes twinkling in triumph. Then her gaze dropped down to the knife in his chest, the tendrils of shadow twining around it. The smugness faded when she realized he did not collapse in pain, that blood did not stain the very expensive shirt she had just ruined.

A second dagger appeared in her hand, lithe fingers spinning the blade as a frown of determination creased her forehead.

Intriguing, the thought that she would merely try again, but Theo did not need to fight. He caught her wrist easily, leaning forward to whisper a single shadow-laced word into her ear, and she collapsed into unconsciousness.

∼

Theo sat in front of the fireplace, idly watching the shadows twist and twirl through his fingers, the warm amber flames doing little to chase away the confusion.

His fingers brushed across the spot where she'd stabbed him, shadows converging to swirl around the skin as if to assure him the wound no longer existed. He should have known it was a trap, should have sensed something off. Isandra had never sent a woman before. And her hair…

Theo sighed, recalling the harsh scent that had burned his nostrils as he'd carried her to a dungeon cell. Some kind of compound, a mixture of chemicals, used to change the color of her hair. What petty emotion had clouded his judgement enough to let that cheap trick work? Hope? Hope had no place here, and he did not deserve the fleeting warmth it provided.

Twisting his hand around, Theo drew the shadows into a sphere that hovered just above his palm. "Show me Isandra."

She appeared in the orb almost immediately, her pale skin

contrasted by the dark shadows framing her face. A wide smile cut across her face, lips still full and sensuous even after centuries on Earth.

"Theo! How *lovely* to see you alive."

He did not rise to the bait. "A woman? Really? Why would you send a woman to a place like this?"

Isandra's eyes hardened, crystal-blue shards that threatened to cut him. "I didn't send a woman."

"Interesting. Because one is here, and she seems to want me dead."

The blood drained from Isandra's face with uncharacteristic fear. "Mira..."

Theo cocked his head, gauging how much of her reaction was sincere. At least he had a name. "Mira. A friend of yours?"

Heat rushed into her face, staining her cheeks with roses. The anger, at least, was real. "If you harm a single hair on her head—"

"Silence." He cut off her petty threat with a snarl. "I will not be spoken to like I am the villain."

"Please."

And that was where she went too far, gave up the ruse too soon. Isandra had never said please.

"I think of her as a daughter," the ageless woman pleaded, and if Theo hadn't already been convinced it was a lie, he would have been impressed at the quiver in her voice. "Give her back, Theo. This isn't Mira's fault."

Something in his chest hardened at the sound of his name on her lips. "I did not take her," he said coldly, then he crumpled his fingers into a fist. The orb dissipated, shadows sweeping out to curl around his hand.

Now he just had to decide what to do with her.

THEO WOKE with a weight on his hips and a blade in his ribs.

The cool metal sliced through skin, immediately met by a rush of shadows. Mira sat on top of him with a cruel smirk, white hair flaring out around her head in a halo of death. The skirt of her dress spilled around him like a pool of blood, tiny gemstones from her bodice glittering malevolently in the weak light.

"Good evening, my dear," Theo said, voice still gravelly from sleep. "I take it you were displeased with your lodgings?"

"You left me in the dungeon," she snarled. "For two days." Anger seethed from her, an almost tangible entity that forced the blade deeper until it clicked against a rib.

Theo blinked—not at the blade but at her words. Had he really let two days pass? Time moved like a shadow in this forgotten realm, sometimes a jerk, other times a languid spiral, never something he could quite grasp.

"Yes, well...you seem to want me dead." He raised an eyebrow and glanced down at the dagger's hilt. Ribbons of shadow twined around the frayed leather, healing Theo's wound even as the blade forced it to remain open.

Mira frowned, smacking his chest with her free hand. "I stabbed you before...didn't I?" Her fingers slid over bare skin, desperately searching for a wound that no longer existed.

He gently took her hand and pushed it back. "They will not let me die." No matter how many times he tried—and he had tried often. The inability to feel pain allowed for some creative methods.

Confusion flitted across Mira's face. "They?"

He glanced down to the dagger, and she followed his gaze, finally noticing the shadows, almost imperceptible in the dark. They whispered around her fingers now, pushing, forcing the blade out of his body.

She released the weapon with a gasp and stumbled off the

bed, shuffling across the room until her back thudded against the door.

"What—how—you're a monster!"

"And you're free to leave," Theo said casually, propping himself up against the headboard. "Although you probably won't get far. The veils won't open again for a year."

"You're lying." A breathless whisper, a desperate hope.

"I never lie."

Mira gulped, her face so pale it almost glowed. "It doesn't matter. I came here for your heart. I'm not leaving without it."

Theo smirked. "Interesting. And how do you plan to do that?" He shifted his torso, revealing the smooth, unblemished skin where not one but two daggers had now failed to injure him.

Mira's breath came too quickly—he could hear it across the room—but her chin tilted defiantly. "I'll figure it out."

"And if I kill you first?"

Her eyes hardened around a flash of fear. "Then the world will always remember you for what you are—a beast. A monster. A murderer."

Theo's smirk faded, shadows slithering across his chest and twining around his neck as if they could sense his changing emotions. "The world has already forgotten me. If I had a heart, I would gladly give it to you."

"But you won't?"

"I can't."

"You're a *jinn*." She spat the word like it tasted bad on her tongue. "You can do whatever you wish. Whatever *anyone* wishes."

A heavy feeling settled in Theo's chest as he thought of the last time he had been summoned, of Isandra's wicked smile as she demanded her wishes, of the mirror he'd shattered to make sure no one ever summoned him again.

"Mother told me what you did," Mira snarled. "How you destroyed an entire race of people for—"

Theo crossed the room in an instant, shadow-laced fingers pressing against her jaw, aborting the heinous words. "You do not speak of the Fae," he hissed into her ear as shadowy tendrils curved a pattern against her pale throat. The words stung his tongue, a bitter reminder of the past he could not blot out, no matter what realm he lived in, no matter how many years had passed.

The acidity of Mira's hair made him want to gag. How could he have ever mistaken this harsh falseness for the feathery, swan-white hair of the Fae? He let her go with a sneer of disgust and leaned over a low fireplace built into the wall, the dying embers providing the room's only source of light. A swirl of his finger sent bright orange flames bursting into life.

"I did not want to kill them," he said quietly.

"But you did."

"Yes."

He sensed her movement but did not turn, did not fight the knife that found its way into his back, a perfect throw with deadly aim. Theo closed his eyes, waiting for a flash of white. For the swell of blood on skin. For the warmth of pain, or the coldness of inevitability. Every blade inserted, every rope twisted, every bone broken brought with it a surge of hope, a breath of hesitation, but they always ended the same way.

With life instead of death.

Twisting his arm, Theo yanked the knife out and hurled it across the room. The blade buried itself in the headboard of his bed.

"When are you going to learn that doesn't work?" he growled, stomping back toward her.

Mira's eyes widened as he grabbed her arm, but she did not move, stiffening her spine as he searched for more weapons. The red dress had grown dirty from her stay in the dungeon, and Theo felt a flicker of guilt at having left her there so long. She had hacked away the train, shortening the skirt to something she could move in more easily, but he knew the alluring fabric hid more than one kind of danger. He pulled out two more daggers and a garrote, slinging them across the room.

The shadows that wrapped around his body writhed and stretched, reaching for her bare shoulders, her torn dress, her false-white hair. Mira's breaths came out in short bursts, eyes wide and fearful. Good. At least she had the sense to be afraid.

"You're a monster," she whispered as he released her, finished with his search, though he had no faith he'd found them all.

"I did what I was bound to do," he snapped. She had not come for the truth, but he would shove it down her throat anyway. "Isandra is the real beast."

Mira backed away to stand near the door, as if preparing to flee. "Mother told me what you did. How you stole her magic, left her stranded in a realm that no longer believed in magic."

"I stopped a wicked sorceress from taking over the world," he snarled. "She's a brute who doesn't know when to stop. If you're not careful, she'll destroy you too." He glanced down her body at the dress that had concealed so many weapons, poisoned honey luring in the fly. "If she hasn't already."

Anger surged across Mira's face like the shadows cast by the fire, but a seed of doubt sparked in her eyes as well. She smothered it with a frustrated shake of her head. "I don't believe you."

"I told you, I never lie." And though he hadn't intended to convince her of his innocence—knew he couldn't even if he tried—he found himself wanting to anyway. Wanting to warn her, at least, before she made the same mistakes he had.

"You know it's true," he said, his voice as quiet as the smoke that danced in the air between them. "Somewhere deep inside, you know what she's capable of."

"And what are you capable of?" Mira asked with fire in her eyes and a stubborn set to her chin.

A familiar feeling wormed its way into Theo's chest—a flame that had burned out long ago. He pushed the thoughts away, letting familiar apathy replace the anger that had fueled him moments before, leaving a cold emptiness in its place. "I guess we'll see."

He fell onto the bed, not bothering to cover himself with the sheet. The fire had heated the room too quickly, combining with the passion of her fury and melting the shell of ice he'd protected himself in for so long.

"What am I supposed to do now?" Mira demanded, sounding less like a scared prisoner and more like an irritated house guest. The thought amused Theo.

"Make yourself at home," he said, with only a trace of sarcasm. "You are free to sleep where you like. The dungeon obviously won't hold you anyway." He raised his head off the pillow, turning to glance at her over his shoulder. "How did you get out, by the way?"

"Well, it's not exactly state-of-the-art, is it?" Theo could hear the sneer in her words. "I used the garrote to saw through some of the bars."

He collapsed back on the bed, unable to keep a grin from creeping across his pillow. "Of course you did," he murmured.

"So that's it? You're just going to leave me to wander around for a year? Tell me my mother is a monster and then go back to sleep like everything is fine?"

Theo wanted to tell her that the things he knew about Isandra would turn her stomach. That he lay on his bed not to sleep, but to hide the pain that lived in his eyes. That nothing would ever be fine again.

Instead, he said, "You may join me for dinner tomorrow evening."

"And if I don't?"

He shrugged, letting the apathy suck him back down, a comfortable cloud to numb the pain. "Starve, for all I care."

Mira hmphed, and Theo tried to calculate the odds that Isandra really hadn't sent her, that the next year living with a fiery assassin wouldn't somehow end in his death. Tried to determine whether fear or hope sliced through his chest like her daggers could not.

But it was too late for calculations, and Theo had relived enough nightmares for one night. He closed his eyes, though sleep danced far out of reach, as elusive as one of his shadows.

"Trust me," he said. "There are worse ways to die."

∼

Mira moved through the manor like a wraith. Or one of his—she shuddered—shadows. A chill passed down her spine as she remembered the way they had curled around her hand, twined through her hair, a cool menace brushing against her skin. Inhuman and terrifying.

Not that she had expected him to be human. Mother had told her jinn could be tricky. Could take on the form of a human and twist it to suit their needs.

She could have told Mira about the knives, though. Mother *knew* daggers were her favorite weapon, and yet she had failed to mention the jinn could not be killed by one. She wondered if he were telling the truth, that a heart did not beat beneath his surprisingly human chest. Was it an item, then? A keepsake hidden somewhere in this shadowy manor?

Apparently, she had a year to find out. Another tiny detail Mother had neglected to inform her.

A canvas on the wall distracted her: a portrait of the jinn and the likeness he wore. The same lean body; wavy black hair that curled around his ears and fell over his forehead; a sharp, angled jaw; eyelashes even longer than her own.

The eyes, though…the eyes were different. In the painting a flat, lifeless grey, but in person they had been hungry, almost alive, as if actual shadows swirled around his pupils. The expression didn't fit either, too arrogant in the painting, too sure of himself, and no shadows twined around his arms or wrapped around his neck. The jinn she'd seen in the bedroom had seemed weighted, heavy, exuding a sadness that belied his eternal youth and power.

"How do I kill you?" she murmured to the portrait, and she could have sworn the eyes flickered in response.

∾

MIRA STARED at the feast spread before her, the long dining table hidden beneath dozens of food-laden trays. He hadn't been kidding when he'd said he would have dinner. This looked much more appetizing than the snacks she'd found in her raid of the kitchen last night.

She stiffened as the jinn entered, the steak knife she'd tucked into her—*his*—pants suddenly feeling like rubber as she noted the way those infernal shadows twisted and curled over his lean form, seeping out of his dark blue suit like smoke.

"Hello," he greeted her, taking a seat at the opposite end of the table. "Glad you decided to join me."

"Did I have a choice?"

He didn't answer, his eyes dropping to the shirt she'd stolen from his room that morning. A plain white one, ridiculously soft, and rolled up at the sleeves to accommodate her shorter arms.

"What am I to call you?" she asked. "If I am to be here for a while."

"Theo. Please."

She cocked an eyebrow. "Theo? Really?"

"My true name is Theodorizain. I assumed Theo would be more palatable for your…human tongue."

She flinched at the reminder that he was not human, that something otherworldly lived in his veins. Then she shrugged. "Call me Mira."

Theo smirked. "Does this mean you no longer wish to kill me, Mira?"

"I haven't decided yet," she responded, eyeing a platter of roasted duck.

"Shall we eat while you figure it out?"

Drool practically dripped down Mira's chin, but she hesitated.

"It's not poisoned," he assured her, as if reading her fears. He cut a bite off a chunk of steaming venison, scraping his teeth across the fork as he exaggerated the bite.

The gesture did little to ease Mira's fears, but she grabbed the plate closest to her anyway. If he wanted her dead, he'd had plenty of opportunity before now. She still wasn't sure why he hadn't killed her last night—in retribution for stabbing him, if nothing else.

She shuddered, disguising the tremor by picking up her fork. There was something inherently terrifying about trying to kill something that wouldn't die.

"Tell me about my mother," she said around a mouthful of duck. The juice burst in her mouth in an explosion of flavor and she nearly swooned, temporarily forgetting the nightmare she'd landed in.

"Enchantress. Sorceress. Slayer of babies and destroyer of an entire nation."

Mira paused in her chewing to glare at him. "Some might say the same about you."

To her surprise, he looked chagrined. "I have paid for my sins," he said quietly. "Many times over."

A haunted look passed through his eyes, and Mira hoped she

never had to face the thing that could scar an immortal being. Well, almost immortal. There was still that business about his heart. "My mother doesn't think so."

"I do wish you would stop calling her that."

"My parents were killed when I was a baby. Isandra raised me. What else should I call her?"

"Murderer, perhaps? If your parents were killed, she is sure to have done it." He idly stabbed a piece of meat with a fork, rose-colored liquid oozing onto the plate.

"Why would she do that?"

"Isandra kills without shame or regret. Ending the lives of two humans in order to obtain a baby would mean nothing to her."

Mira forced herself to swallow, the perfectly cooked meat suddenly tasting like ash on her tongue. As much as she wanted to brush his words off as slanderous, the lies of a beast, she had seen Mother's darkness for herself, the callous way she could talk of ending someone's life. The many ways she had taught Mira to do the same.

"And, what?" she demanded, thumping her fork against delicate china. "She *asked* you to destroy her family, her entire race? Earth doesn't even believe in the Fae anymore. They've been debased as fantasy, a story to tell children!"

"Yes." Theo's eyes turned impossibly dark, laced with the same shadows tattooed across his neck. "It was her second wish."

Mira shook her head, not wanting to believe. Theo did—that much she could see in a glance. Though he sat calmly in his chair on the other side of the table, silky black tendrils slipped over his fork, and his eyes glittered with an otherworldly malice.

"Why?" she breathed, her voice barely audible in the aching silence of the dining room.

Theo placed his fork on the plate and leaned back in his

chair, a soft breath escaping in a sigh. "She wanted to be the only one."

"The only what?"

"The only one with gifts. Being Fae was not enough for her. She used her first wish to demand magic. But pure magic is... unreliable, at best. Malevolent, at worst. I only gave her a shadow, but it...changed her. Evil loves a good host. It fed on her ambitions, her desires. Corrupted her."

Mira thought of Isandra's study in their mansion on Earth. Floor-to-ceiling shelves of ancient books and tomes. Scrolls with ink no longer legible. Dozens of jars and vials whose contents Mira did not want to think about. Her adopted mother had been obsessed with magic, trying every possible combination of spells and potions to get it back. Mira had entered the room once by accident. Isandra had made sure she would never do it again.

"She became convinced the Fae were a threat," Theo continued. "For her second wish, she ordered them destroyed. I tried to talk her out of it, tried to resist, but—"

He broke off, jaw clenched so tightly a tic appeared in his temples. Mira's heart jolted in response to his pain, and she tried to convince herself he was lying. How many times had she seen her mother fake tears, manipulating people with her emotions?

"And her third wish?"

At this Theo almost smiled, though his black eyes still reflected bitter regret. "That is where she made her mistake," he said, voice hissing in triumph. "She wished to be as powerful as a jinn. But she did not say which one. I split my own power in half, then secluded myself here before it could reach her."

Mira shook her head in confusion. "Before what could reach her?"

He held his hand up, showing off the black tendrils that whispered over his skin. "Magic."

Mira watched the shadows in fascination rather than fear, seeing them in a new light. The other half of his magic. Sentient power looking for its host.

Looking for Isandra.

"And the wish overrode her previous magic," Theo said almost proudly. "Even her natural Fae powers."

"Leaving her with nothing," Mira finished, the pieces snapping into place with a bone-jarring thud.

"As long as I stay here, in the Other-Realm, she cannot access magic there on Earth."

"Why does she not just come here herself?" Mira asked, thinking of all the training, all the plans, all she had endured to come in her mother's place. "If you're in the same realm, couldn't she get it that way?"

"Yes, but at a price. This is the Other-Realm. The space between. The place from which jinn are summoned. On Earth, the magic is merely a part of her wish. Here, she would become a true jinn, linked to a mirror, bound to the wishes of others. She will not come here, even for magic."

Mira nodded, long and slow. "That's why she wants your heart. She thinks if she can destroy you, she will become a full jinn."

He nodded.

"Is she right?"

Their eyes locked across the table, and Mira forced herself not to blink.

"If I am destroyed, the curse will be broken," Theo said quietly.

"And the only way to kill a jinn is to destroy its heart?"

He shrugged, mouth quirking up a little at the edges. "So they say. But it will not help Isandra. As I told you before, I have no heart. And if I knew how to kill myself, I would have already done it."

Mira nodded idly, scraping her fork across her plate,

drawing designs in the rich gravy that seeped off her uneaten duck. "I think," she said slowly, "that I believe you."

The air hung heavy with unspoken promises, untethered hope. Mira wasn't sure which was hers and which was his.

"So what will you do?" Theo asked. Though he looked calm, she noticed the shadows had stopped moving, hovering above his skin in quiet anticipation.

Mira pushed her chair back, the stillness broken as he rose with her.

"That," she announced, "is something I will need to think about."

~

To Theo's best guess, unreliable as that was, a week passed before Mira made her decision. He was sitting in his study, nothing moving but the fire in the hearth and the shadows against his skin, when she finally approached him.

"Theo."

He turned at her voice, pretending he didn't know she was there, that he hadn't sensed her presence long before she'd reached his study. "Mira."

She entered the room slowly, with a mixture of caution and respect. He tried to ignore the way his borrowed shirt flattered her slender frame, the collar hanging loosely over one shoulder, the black pants somehow a perfect fit. She must have ripped up a pair of his own, found something sharp to sew them back together with. She seemed never to lack a sharp object.

"I've decided what to do."

She stopped in front of him, the fire turning her pale skin amber, and he tried to ignore the buzz in his ears, the way the shadows quickened around him. "It does not involve death, I hope."

She took a breath, her eyes never leaving his, the shadows from the fireplace flickering dangerously across her face.

"It does," she said, her voice brushing against his skin like a caress. "You're going to help me kill my mother."

∽

Mira held her breath, the heat from the fire making her arms prickle with sweat.

"Interesting," Theo said, his grey eyes reflecting nothing. "And how do you propose we do that?"

"I take it she cannot be killed with a knife to the chest?" Mira asked the question lightly, but all her hopes hung on his answer. If he could tell her how to kill Isandra, maybe she could do the same to him instead.

"The same restrictions apply to her as they do to me," Theo answered vaguely.

Mira crossed her arms, irritated. "Which means she can only die if her heart is destroyed, but she doesn't have a heart either?"

A soft grin played on Theo's lips. "Something like that."

"Well, she wants to kill you to get both halves of your magic. Does that mean if I kill her, you'll get both?"

He shook his head, eyes tight. "We are bound irrevocably now. If one of us dies, so does the other."

The words hung in the air, then crashed around Mira like broken glass, destroying days, months, years of planning. "Does Mother know about this?" she whispered.

"Would she have sent you to kill me if she did?"

Mira opened her mouth to deny it, then shook her head, trying to unscramble the pieces of what he'd said. The idea was so absurd she wanted to laugh. Three times—she had stabbed him three times. What if one of them had worked? Would Isandra have died as well?

And would that have been such a bad thing?

Mira dismissed the thought for now, tucking it in that dark place of her soul she tried not to think about, full of dangerous whispers and promises not yet broken.

"Can't you just undo it?" she asked.

"Once a jinn grants a wish, it cannot be undone."

Sorrow laced his words, and Mira thought of the Fae, an entire race of people destroyed, a wish he could not undo. As much as she tried to ignore the idea that Isandra had been the one to order it, Mira couldn't deny that Theo's confession at dinner last week had left a bad taste in her mouth. Still, she had a job to do.

"Is there a way?" she asked. "To separate the magic again? To kill one but not the other?"

Theo shrugged, the movement as casual as if she'd asked what he wanted for supper. "You're welcome to look. The library here is quite extensive."

"Now?"

He shrugged, waving an arm in invitation, and something sparked in Mira's chest as she followed him down the hallway. Excitement? A silly emotion for an assassin to have, and yet when he opened the doors to reveal dozens of bookshelves, her chest swelled in delight. Lights appeared instantly, sconces bursting to life, a large fireplace spontaneously erupting in a glow of ember and flames. The shelves seemed to go on forever, row after row of gleaming mahogany, each one framed with ornate columns reaching for an impossibly high ceiling. Elegant spiral staircases bore entry to a second and even third story, where open mezzanines revealed even more bookcases.

"Do you like it?" he asked.

"It's incredible," she breathed. She had already resigned herself to a bleak stay in a manor full of dark rooms and shadowy hallways, but this...this made a year in the Other-Realm almost worth it.

"I'm glad," he said, and for a moment she forgot to hate him, forgot the reason she had come to this realm in the first place. Then she saw the shadows inking over his skin, remembered the two nights she'd spent in the dungeon, and snapped herself back to reality.

"Well," she said, shoving her excitement into the black box with everything else. "I guess we should get started."

◊

THEO WATCHED HER.

For months Mira scoured his boundless library, poring through dozens of books a day. She drank the words, feasting on knowledge, her papercuts lined with ink.

Some days she curled up in a chair with a stack of dusty tomes beside her. Other days she scribbled frantically on the smooth wooden tables, papers collecting in messy heaps around her. Still other times she read right from the shelves, lost in a book for hours while she hung precariously on a tall ladder, or sat on the floor with her back to a shelf, oblivious to the harsh imprints it left on her skin.

He watched her hide weapons all over the manor like a squirrel burying nuts, not trusting that he wouldn't take her daggers away again. Occasionally she still stabbed him with some of them, but usually only when she was bored. Then she would watch in morbid fascination as the shadows oozed out of his skin to heal the wounds every time.

He watched her cautiously try on the numerous dresses he conjured for her—green velvet, amber taffeta, shimmering azure silk—easing into them like a caterpillar trying on its wings for the first time. Eventually she stopped waiting for him to offer and met him in his bedroom first thing every morning, demanding his newest creation. Then she would watch wide-eyed as his shadows slithered over skirts and bodices, leaving delicate lace and twinkling jewels in their wake.

He watched her trace ancient pictures of Fae with a trembling finger while tears dripped down her face and collected in the scoop of her collarbone. Then she would stare into a mirror with the same look of desperate hatred that always seemed to linger under the surface of her skin.

He watched her dust the shelves when she thought he wasn't looking, or casually straighten a three-hundred-year-old vase, humming a quiet little ditty from Earth while a dainty foot tapped the carpet.

He watched her hair lengthen, exposing roots of a rich auburn color, so different than the harshness of her false white. She twirled it through her fingers sometimes when she was deep in thought, leaving the ends gently curled.

He watched her hunt for answers, and he watched her run away from them, and he couldn't say for certain which one scared him more.

~

MIRA SLAMMED THE BOOK CLOSED. Nothing. Months of research, a million books, and not a single clue how to break the wish.

"Are you okay?"

She jumped as Theo appeared right beside her, silent as always. She'd never been able to figure out if he appeared at will, or if he was merely part shadow himself.

"Yes," she answered, the word clipped. "Just frustrated."

Frustrated that she couldn't find anything. Frustrated that her time was almost up. Frustrated that she was no longer sure whom she wanted to kill, and whom she wanted to save. The choice was easy—kill the beast. But which one of them was the monster? Theo, or Isandra?

The longer she looked into Theo's shadow-kissed eyes, the more she saw human emotions: pain, regret, concern, guilt... love. And the longer she resided in this haunted manor, the more something loosened inside her, allowing her to breathe freely for the first time in her life. Theo controlled the darkness, kept it away from her, rather than constantly shoving his own agenda in her face like Isandra had done, forcing her to become someone else. Here, she was only Mira, and that was enough.

"Come with me." Theo extended a hand and Mira took it with a smile, used to the cool feel of the shadows brushing against her skin and the comforting warmth of his palm underneath.

"Where are we going?"

"I want to show you something."

He led her to the middle of a random hallway and opened a wide glass door—a door she was positive had not been there a moment before. She stepped through the entrance, overcome with the same sense of awe at seeing his library for the first time, except that instead of books, now she found herself surrounded by paintings. Hundreds of them, filling up every inch of the room. Oil paintings rendered on sturdy canvas; delicate watercolors encased behind glass; half-finished pieces draped over easels. He had even painted the ceilings.

"Did you do all this?" She turned and found Theo watching her from the doorway with a soft smile.

"Yes."

"This must have taken ages," she breathed, spinning in a circle to take it all in.

He shrugged, a light smirk playing at his lips. "Couple of centuries."

"What is it all?" She ran a hand lightly over a scene of a rose garden and half-expected to prick her finger on one of the thorns.

"These are my memories," he said quietly.

Mira examined the paintings with a fresh perspective—the dark-haired woman selling colorful woven rugs; a sunset sinking over the ocean; a child eating a pastry, icing dripping down his chin; the tips of the pyramids gleaming in a moonlit desert. Peaceful moments frozen in time. Moments of joy and wonder and beauty that Mira hadn't realized the human world could contain. Something twisted in her heart, an emotion Isandra had not taught her.

"You lost all this?" She turned and found Theo standing with his hands behind his back, somehow looking both younger and older at the same time.

"A just recompense for the horrors I have caused."

"So these people..." She stopped in front of a scene of a little girl with wide brown eyes and a soft smile. Her hair hung in tangled curls down to her lap, where dirt-stained fingers curled around a half-wilted rose. "They all summoned you...didn't they."

Theo stepped forward to stand behind her. "That's Grace."

Fondness softened his words, and Mira felt a pang of jealousy at the affection in his words. He had loved these people, had helped them simply because they'd called him. She had grown up believing jinn were wicked, malicious spirits who existed to torture humans, to twist their words, to defile their wishes. But they were not that way at all.

At least, not this one.

Mira turned away so he could not read the emotion in her eyes. A flash of red drew her gaze to a corner, where a single red rose floated in a glass dome on a small table. She approached it with wonder, eyeing the dark ribbons of shadow that twined around the stem.

"What is this?" she breathed in fascination.

"A gift," he answered with a reminiscent smile. "I keep it alive as a reminder."

Mira took his hand and trailed her finger across his palm, watching the shadows respond to her touch. Watching *Theo* respond to her touch. The pain of hope collided with reluctant fear before settling into a sort of morbid finality.

"If there was a way to set things right," she asked softly, "would you?"

"I would do anything to take back what I have done."

"Even if it kills you?"

His eyes glittered with a fierceness she had never seen. "Especially if it kills me."

∼

Mira picked at her dinner—the last meal she would eat in this shadowy realm—and wondered why she did not want to leave. Tomorrow she could go back, return to Earth, to the sun, to her mother.

"Theo, I need to tell you something."

"It can wait." He pushed back from the table, crossing the room to fiddle with some half-ancient machine in the corner.

She watched the strong slant of his shoulders, the curls that gathered at the nape of his neck, and wished she could run her hands through the dark locks. Wished she could hold him close and tell him what he had grown to mean to her. Wished her first dagger had worked and ended it all a year ago, so she wouldn't have to make this choice now.

"I think I found a way," she said. "To kill Isandra, I mean."

Theo turned and the haunting melody of a song she didn't know floated across the room, as sad and peaceful as his eyes. He approached her slowly, his eyes smoky and soft, like the fur of a wolf—but she knew he was no beast.

"I'm going to try it," Mira said, wondering why her pulse raced so quickly, why her hand longed to reach out and touch his. "But I think it will—"

"Dance with me."

"What?" Somehow his simple request invoked more fear than any threat he could have made.

"Dance with me." His voice was laced with midnight velvet,

full of promise. He reached out a hand, a symbol of trust, an offer of peace.

"Okay."

When her hand clasped his, the shadows rushed forward, twining around them. Mira took comfort in his arm, strong and firm around her as he led her to the center of the floor. She pressed herself closer, using his body as a guide, letting her feet get lost in the dance. Her yellow skirt spun around her in an aura of sunshine as music filled the room, pushing against years of pain, breaking down the walls she had forged so carefully.

Theo smiled, and Mira felt something melt inside. Tomorrow she could put back up the walls. Tomorrow, she could be what her mother had made her.

Tonight, she would dance.

∽

MIRA SHIVERED in the surreal stillness of the Shadow Forest, where nothing moved except wisps of grey fog slinking between her feet. The stunning yellow dress she had worn last night was gone, replaced with black leggings and a dark grey sweater.

Theo appeared at her side, a faithful shadow, an ever-attentive host. "Here," he said.

She looked down at the weapon in his palms, a dagger unlike anything she'd ever seen on Earth. Instead of a single, flat blade, two thin blades wrapped around each other in a dangerous spiral that ended in a wicked point. The handle was formed from bone, dark as ash, and tailored to fit her hand perfectly.

"A goodbye gift," he said, folding her fingers over it. "Perhaps we will meet again. In another life."

She drew in a sharp breath, unfamiliar emotion catching in her throat.

"Are you ready?" he asked gently, gesturing to the air that

shimmered before them. The veil between the Other-Realm and Earth. All that separated them from Isandra.

"Yes." A breath. A whisper. A lie.

Then she stepped through the veil to the other side.

∼

THEO WATCHED the air ripple around Mira, spreading as her body disrupted its natural flow. He had stayed up all night, listening to the vorgs and other creatures disturb the hushed darkness as the veils opened at midnight. He had waited as long as he dared, giving the sun ample time to rise, and he caught a glimpse of it now. Of white snow glistening in a pine forest with real trees. He imagined running his hands over the rough bark, imagined the pine needles brushing against his skin.

His face hardened as Mira stepped out of the way, revealing another figure. Isandra.

"Theo!" she chirped with delight as she spotted him. Her mouth split open like a crack in quartz as she gave him a wicked smirk, coming to stand just in front of the veil. The air still shifted and swirled, blurring her image slightly.

"Isandra," he growled, keeping his feet firmly planted on the shadow ground.

"Well, child," Isandra said, turning to Mira. "Did you get what I asked for?" She extended a hand, her nails painted the color of blood, long and sharp.

Mira looked back at Theo, pain etched across her face. "I'm sorry," she said, pulling a rose out of her pocket. Not a rose—*his* rose. "This is the only way to kill her."

Theo's eyes widened as he realized what she was about to do. "Mira, NO!"

But it was too late. She threw the rose on the snow, grinding it under the heel of her boot.

MIRA SUCKED IN DEEP BREATHS, the cold burning her throat, tears stinging her eyes. She did not want to look, didn't want to watch Theo fall, or dissipate into shadows, or scream in agony as she crushed his heart beneath her shoe. But it was the only way. He would have wanted her to do it. Would have wanted her to kill him if it meant killing Isandra too.

Except that neither one of them was dead.

Mira opened her eyes, her tears blurring the crumpled flower at her feet. The shadow that had twined around the stem, keeping the rose alive in the Other-Realm, slithered across the snow toward Isandra's feet. Mira's stomach lurched as she remembered what the shadows represented—jinn magic. Isandra's magic.

And Mira had brought it right to her.

Isandra's eyes lit up with centuries of greed and impatience as the shadow jumped to her hand, circling her fingers before crawling up her arm. The inky tendril brushed against her neck like a lover's caress, and Isandra opened her mouth, sucking it inside. Mira watched in horror as her mother smiled, eyes glittering with malice.

"I'm sorry," she said sweetly, her voice laced with a warning. "Did you say it was the only way to kill *me?*"

Mira froze, fear clutching her chest, chilling her bones. "No, I mean—it's his heart. That's—it has to be his heart. There's nothing else."

"Oh, but I think there *is*," Isandra crooned, stepping closer to Mira. "What you both don't realize is that I finally figured it out —how to steal a jinn's heart. It's you."

A SHIVER RACED across Theo's skin, shadows buzzing around him in frantic desperation as they tried to leap across the veil, to join the sliver of magic that now lived in Isandra's blood.

Isandra turned to face him, her ice-blue eyes taunting. "Isn't that right, Theo?"

He shook his head, intentionally avoiding Mira's face. If he looked at her, he would feel things, and he couldn't afford to feel things right now.

"Jinn don't have hearts," he said gruffly, praying she believed him. Praying they both believed him. "I've told you that."

"So if I kill Mira right now, nothing will happen?"

Mira's hand flashed, Theo's dagger in her palm, but Isandra was quicker, pinning Mira's dagger arm and twisting the other behind her until she winced.

Don't look.

"Well, your daughter would be dead," he answered with as much apathy as he could muster. "But I don't see how that would affect me."

"Won't it? Are you saying if I crush her right now, you won't perish as well?" Isandra's arm tightened around Mira's chest, making her slender body squirm in pain.

Don't look.

"Oh, I will perish," he answered calmly, a twinge of triumph flaring in his chest. "But so will you."

Isandra narrowed her eyes. "What are you talking about?"

"We share a soul now, remember? If you kill me, you die too."

One of Isandra's eyes twitched, a flicker of doubt. "You're lying."

He smiled. "I never lie."

Isandra's face twisted in anger as she lashed out, shoving Mira forward, toward the veil. Mira stumbled, gasping, falling, and he instinctively lunged forward to catch her.

He didn't realize he'd crossed the veil until the sun warmed his face, cold snow soaking into his pants. He looked up at Isandra, horror sinking into his bones as the shadows that had hovered around him for centuries rushed toward Isandra instead, finally completing the wish.

"Yesss," she hissed, closing her eyes as half of his magic flowed into her, filling her veins with power that now equaled his.

"Theo..." Mira twisted in his arms, struggling to look up at him. "I forgot...I'm so sorry."

He stroked her hair, admiring the way the auburn roots burned like fire in the sunlight. "It's okay, my love. You were right to try."

Tears dripped down Mira's face. Tears of confusion, and frustration, and regret. "Your heart...the rose...I don't understand."

"The rose is nothing more than a flower, a reminder of a happier time." He wrapped his arms around her, throat tight, and pressed a kiss to the top of her head. "I gave my heart to you a long time ago."

She buried her face in his chest, sobbing silently as grief replaced years of bitterness and apathy, an almost welcome pain.

"How sweet," Isandra taunted. "True love, together at last. And now you both must lose it."

Mira looked up at Theo and smiled, sad and triumphant, a small smile meant only for him. "Maybe we'll meet again," she whispered, her breath warm on his cheek. "In another life."

Theo raised his hand, wet with snow, and gently cupped her face. "In another life, then."

Mira leaned forward, pressing her lips to his, and Theo closed his eyes, letting the pain and bliss and rage and joy all blend into one chaotic breath. Isandra laughed behind them, but they ignored it, and when Mira broke the kiss to press her forehead against his cheek, Theo tasted the salt of her tears.

"I hope you are quite finished," Isandra declared, striding toward them with evil delight, her long black skirt trailing behind her like ash.

Mira leaned back, her lips brushing Theo's jawline. "Whatever it takes?"

He nodded and felt the world crack with the gesture, a tiny movement that would end it all. "Whatever it takes."

Her fingers slid into his, the beat of her heart pulsing against his palm, and then she drove his dagger into her chest.

Isandra's hand shot out in alarm, sinewy shadows streaking toward them, but too late. The shadows faded, Isandra's body dropping to the ground as she faded with them.

Theo's breath stilled in his chest, the sun warming his face for the first time in centuries. He gently stroked Mira's cheek with transparent fingers and a peace he had been searching for his whole life.

She smiled faintly at his ghostlike touch then closed her eyes for the last time, while beside her, pushing through pine needles laden with snow, a ribbon of shadow twined around a single red rose.

THE END

WYRMS OF AVASAL

S. K. SAYARI

Zana snarled and lunged at her enemy, her longsword glinting crimson in the blazing heat of the midday sun. Steel ripped into yielding flesh, and her bulky foe stumbled back before collapsing, his wounds gushing scarlet.

Zana took a moment to glance around. Her father, King of Arinta, fought a few feet away, roaring at the Titans who besieged his castle. The smell of blood and steel, mixed with the stench of sweat, permeated the grassy battlefield.

Zana...

She squinted, shaking her head. The multitude of whispering voices had appeared the day her mother had died, five months ago. They never uttered their purpose, only saying her name. As she leapt at another foe, the voices called to her again, lighting a flame within her soul that itched to break through her mortal body.

Zana...

King Tarin shouted, and Zana's head whipped to the side to see him stumble backward as a Titan brought down his blade. Zana sucked in a breath and leaped toward him. She had already lost her mother—she would not lose another parent.

"Father!"

King Tarin roared and swung his axe at the foe, and Zana hissed, lashing out at the Titan's legs. Together, they slew the giant, offering each other a grin of triumph. King Tarin's brow was slick with sweat, but otherwise he bore no signs of fatigue.

"We're winning the battle, Father. The Titans are almost defeated!"

"Do not rest," said King Tarin, hefting his axe. "There are far greater enemies of Arinta than the Titans."

As if his words were ones of summoning, the wind carried shrill screams to Zana's ears. She whirled around, looking west —to the mountains separating Arinta and Kalakan. Specks on the horizon grew larger, gleaming brown and russet red. Rocs, hailing from Angalnar.

Zana shuddered and bit the inside of her cheek in worry. Rocs were the Titans' allies, both races bearing bloodlust and craving man-flesh.

Zana!

The voices boomed throughout the battlefield, yet the expressions of those around her stated that only she could hear them. In her heart, Zana knew who the voices belonged to.

The Wyrms of Avasal.

"Zana, the enemy grows stronger! You must command the Wyrms to rise from the Gate!" boomed the king as he struck down another Titan.

"But..." The thought of her mother sent twinges of pain through her heart. The queen had been the Wyrmskeeper once —now it was up to Zana to follow in her footsteps, however difficult.

"You must take up her duty, for the sake of the kingdom! Go!"

Her mother's duty had been noble—commanding the Wyrms to protect Arinta. But the thought of forcing them—or any being, for that matter—to obey her will made Zana want to retch. On one hand, she wanted to save Arinta, but on the other, she wanted to be kind.

She shook her head, chasing away her doubts. Arinta was in trouble.

Zana leaped away, toward the soaring grey walls of the castle she and her comrades defended. She whirled past trembling soldiers with wide eyes and fearful grimaces, over the wooden bridge, past steadfast stone walls that hosted white banners with the Arintan sunflower. Flying up stone stairs that were rarely stepped on, her legs and lungs burned, sweat dripping down her temple. She took a moment to catch her breath when she reached a pair of looming black doors, serpentine creatures depicted on the glinting iron. Zana raised a hand to stroke the intricate embellishment, the cool metal a reprieve from the heat of summer and battle.

Wyrm's Gate, it read. Within lay the Dragonspool.

She pushed open the doors, stepping into an enormous chamber that opened to the cloudless blue sky, a massive circular pool of inky water in the center. The water was still and did not tremble as Zana stepped her way to the edge. She sniffed, unable to make out the subtle scent that lingered in the chamber. Curious if the scent was coming from the water, she knelt, lowering her face so her nose almost touched the liquid. It smelled of brimstone and smouldering wood.

"Zana," whispered voices emanating from the pool. "You have finally come, Littler One."

Zana shivered, raising her head. So the voices truly did belong to the Wyrms. Why had they been calling to her? How could they have spoken within her mind? Why could no one else hear them as she did?

"Y-yes, I have come. I have come to ask you to help us. Our people face the might of the Titans of Kalakan and the Rocs of Angalnar."

"Ask us?" the Wyrms said, their voices slithering across Zana's skin.

The pool entertained a small wave that lazily spread from its midpoint to the outer edges. The water slopped as the wave bounced off the stone and returned to the center, then fell still once more.

"Yes. I will not force you to help should you not wish to. I am not unkind."

"Little One spoke the same way. But Little One feared the true monster of this castle more than she longed to be kind to us."

"The true monster?" Zana tilted her head to the side. The 'little one' must be her mother. But who was the monster?

The sound of chains jingled throughout the chamber, though no metal was to be seen. "We are prisoners in your castle, Littler One. We hail from Avasal, the Everland."

"Twenty-seven years ago, when the sun was high in the sky and the heat of summer was at its strongest, we were attacked by the monster. The monster broke a pact between it and the Wyrms—a pact of peace and prosperity," rumbled another voice.

"It enlisted the help of a druid, who bound us to this watery grave for eternity," roared the first voice.

"The monster…" Zana shook her head, chills running up her spine. The monster sounded like a person, a human. Yet who could the Wyrms be speaking of?

"The monster is your father!"

The voices reverberated against the stone walls, and Zana shuddered, before hot tendrils of anger snaked through her muscles. The Wyrms were mistaken. Her father couldn't have been the one to imprison them! Yet seeds of doubt grew in Zana's stomach. Her father was known to ruthlessly crush their enemies and imprison those who defied him. But it was all for the sake of Arinta…wasn't it?

"My father may be ruthless, but—"

"That man is not all he seems."

Zana bit her lip. "True, he has been cruel to our enemies. But that is the price to pay for Arinta's prosperity and safety!"

"We miss Avasal, the Everland, our home," whispered a third voice, lilting and icy. "The land where no man has ventured, unsullied by his lust for power, his incessant greed. The land that your so-called father wishes to conquer."

"S-so…called?" A sharp pain pierced Zana's heart, which squeezed, beating to a primordial rhythm.

"You know the truth. You are one of the Blood. Your mother sought to free us, and the monster rid himself of her. Just as he will you."

Zana's fingers were trembling. "Are you saying...my father killed my mother?"

The pool was silent.

Zana looked at her feet. It couldn't be true. Her father had loved her mother. Yet she couldn't detect any sort of malevolence in the Wyrms' voices, any sort of deceit. What was the truth?

"I cannot believe your words about my mother in haste," she whispered, her voice breaking. "But...I believe in your confinement. I hear the truth ring clearly in your voices. I swear I will help free you, however I can...if you help save Arinta."

"Tanwyn of the seas, Gurgaran of the skies, and I, Naryth of the earth, bear witness to your words. Seal your oath with blood, Littler One!"

Zana nodded and unsheathed her hunting dagger. She sucked in a deep breath before raising the sharp steel to her palm, slicing a shallow cut. Blood, scarlet-bright, oozed from the wound. Three tear-shaped droplets fell into the inky liquid of the pool as her palm stung. The water rippled violently and burst. Zana cowered and shielded her face, scrambling back to the entrance of the chamber as dark beads rained down.

When the eruption of water subsided, she lowered her arm and sheathed her dagger—and met the gaze of three creatures emerging from the pool; they took her breath away.

A slick, obsidian tongue flickered from a gnarled, serpentine head, ochre-brown in complexion. Eyes of deep, burnished copper, ringed with flecks of charcoal, challenged Zana with their primordial blaze. A long neck with formidable spines disappeared into the water, where the horned heads of two more drakes emerged, one golden, one cerulean. The Wyrms snickered without a movement of their lips and sizeable, pearly teeth, and Zana jerked, her jaw dropping.

"*Zana of the Blood!*" they said in unison, a guttural cacophony.

"We shall fight off the Titans of Kalakan and the Rocs of Angalnar, and then you shall free us!"

Zana's breath left her as Naryth, with a guttural roar, leapt from the pool and shot up into the sky, leaving a violent disturbance of air in his wake. Gurgaran followed in a golden flurry, while Tanwyn took a moment to snatch Zana into her claws before she, too, took to the skies. Zana screamed as the air rushed past her, stealing her breath, her dark hair whipping around.

Yet after the initial fear left her, she breathed deeply, a tingle running through her body. It felt...*natural* to be flying. Zana smiled as the gentle light of sundown kissed her cheeks, warming her skin. She leaned into Tanwyn's claws, casting her gaze over rolling hills overgrown in ancient evergreens and flat fields covered in waving stalks of corn. She knew that if the Titans had not attacked, little specks—farmers—would be toiling in the fields, and horse-driven carriages would be bustling in and out of the castle. The Myrtel river twisted through the lands, swelling in the generous rains of spring, its rapids stealing life from the unwary. *My beautiful Arinta.*

The Wyrms roared as they neared the grassy plains of the battlefield, where the giant Titans and Rocs overwhelmed the Arintan forces. Tanwyn dropped Zana near the heart of the battle, and she stumbled to her feet. Gasping, she looked up, the hair on her skin raising. A frozen Titan stood slack-jawed as he stared at the Wyrms circling above.

The Titans began to shout and grovel as the Wyrms descended onto the battlefield, the earth shuddering as they landed. The Rocs screamed, their razor-sharp talons reaching for the Wyrms, but the Wyrms batted them away like flies, rending their flesh. From Gurgaran's snarling maw flashed bolts of white lightning, from Tanwyn's crystal ice, and from Naryth's jaws seethed sanguine fire of scorching intensity. The enemies attempted to flee, but Gurgaran pounced on them, her teeth tearing through flesh like a knife through butter as Tanwyn crushed them beneath her paws.

When all Titans were dead and the Rocs had fled, the battlefield grew silent. Not a single soul made noise until King Tarin dropped his weapon. He threw his arms into the air and the soldiers of Arinta cheered, banging their weapons on their shields in triumph.

The Wyrms bounded back to Zana, looming over her petite form, baring their teeth. "Release us now, as you promised!"

"You promised what?" roared King Tarin, stomping over to Zana. His soldiers arranged themselves in formation behind him with furrowed brows.

Zana licked her lips, her mouth suddenly dry with fear. "They spoke of treachery, Father. They said…that you killed Mother."

Tarin shook his head. "Are you really going to believe the lies from such creatures? Order the Wyrms back to their prison!"

Why had her father simply brushed her away? His behavior was strange, sending prickles of doubt up the back of her neck.

"Tell me, why did Mother want to free the drakes?" Zana demanded, challenging her father with a glare.

"She—this is madness, Zana! Do as you're told! I will not tell you again!"

"Wyrmsblood," whispered Tanwyn, "follow your heart."

My heart.... My heart beats too haphazardly, too loud with fear to follow. Yet I know what song it sings.

"I will free the Wyrms," she declared.

Tarin's grizzled face, frozen with shock, contorted into an ugly sneer. "I should have killed you when I killed your pathetic mother," he spat. "If you will not control them, then I have no use for you anymore, baseborn wretch!"

Zana's breath caught in her throat. Impossible! She wasn't the king's daughter? Memories of happiness with the man she had called 'Father' turned dark, wretched, corrupt, oozing within her mind. She watched the soldiers look to one another, murmuring, whispering. "You lied to me for all these years?"

"You think I would lie with a wretched dragon woman? I only needed you for the dragon blood that flows in your veins. When your mother dared disobey me, at least I still had you to control. But now I will slaughter you as I did your mother and father, and the Wyrms of Avasal will never be free!"

Tarin brandished his axe and leapt forth. Zana stepped back, her blood rushing to her head, her body frozen with fear, yet a sliver of anger started to build. Gurgaran bellowed, slamming her tail in between a charging Tarin and Zana, who gritted her teeth.

"I already bested you once, you snakes! You think I cannot defeat you twice?" boomed Tarin, brandishing his axe.

The Wyrms hissed, muscles tense. "Through trickery! You had no honour, no true triumph in your victory over us!"

"Ha! You speak of honour, you vile creatures, when you have none! Brainless, baseless, bloodthirsty—"

Zana stepped forward and raised an arm, interrupting the king. She held her head high, clenching her hands into fists. She would never forgive the man who stood in front of her. Never. "Naryth, Tanwyn, Gurgaran. I command you to do me one last task."

The Wyrms were silent as their tongues flickered out, awaiting Zana's command. Fire burned through her body, so fierce it threatened to erupt, but she hesitated as her eyes met Tarin's. No longer were they warm toward her.

"Soldiers! Attack!" shouted the king.

The soldiers looked to the Wyrms, then to the shredded Titans and bloodied feathers that lay on the ground. They dropped their weapons, backing away.

"Treachery!" bellowed Tarin. "I will deal with this myself!"

"Butcher this wretch, this false king, this murderer!" Zana screamed.

Tarin roared and threw his axe at her, but Naryth deflected the weapon with his claws. Together, the drakes unleashed their fury on the King, their Wyrmsbreath combining into a silver stream. Zana screamed with them, the Wyrm's roars carrying years of pain and betrayal. Her heart ached, the taste on her tongue bitter, yet sweet.

Once the blaze died away, she gasped. The only remnant of Tarin's existence was a pile of ashes. The wind took pity on Zana, chilling the hot tears that cascaded down her cheeks, whisking the ashes away until nothing of the king was left. She fell to her knees, sobbing, as the soldiers crowded around her. Some wept with her, or perhaps for her.

"My Lady!" said one. "Who will lead us now?"

Zana shook, looking down. "Though he was terrible, and lied, and killed my mother, he was still my father," she whispered. "He was still…"

"Littler One," whispered Tanwyn.

Zana hesitated, then looked up. The Wyrms were trembling.

"Free us," they whispered as ghostly chains materialized. The chains traveled from the Wyrm's necks and over the blood-stained, scorched grass to the castle. Zana knew that they were anchored in the Dragonspool.

She wiped at her tears, gritting her teeth as she trudged to the king's axe, gripping the smooth wooden handle. Arms quivering, she slashed at the ethereal chains. Scathed, the chains turned to glowing dust, twinkling up into the sky as if to join the stars.

Naryth and Gurgaran shrieked their ecstasy, surging into the sky. Tanwyn hesitated, nudging Zana with her nose.

"Dearest child of Wyrmsblood. Find the vessel that contains your powers, your dragonsoul, and you shall be free of this earthly form."

"I must rule this kingless kingdom; bring light to the darkness, happiness to the sorrowful, and heal the wounds that my fa—that the king has created. But when the time comes, I shall fly with you," declared Zana.

Tanwyn bowed, then leapt into the air. Zana watched them fly away until they were but specks in the distance.

Then she cried.

∼

ZANA TAPPED her chin with her fingers, looking down at her court. How many years had it been since she had taken the throne of Arinta, since she had freed the Wyrms of Avasal, since she had slain the king? She had given her life to her country and had grown wise and learned over the years.

She nodded to the weathered man who stood before her, and he cleared his throat.

"And so, we ask for aid," he concluded.

Zana nodded, raising a quivering, wrinkled hand. "And aid you shall have, Sir Daran of Aiswel. Chancellor Rosal, please provide this man with the necessities," she croaked.

"As you will, my Queen," murmured Rosal with a low bow. Zana clapped her hand on the armrest of her throne, ending the hearing, and the next began.

When court finished, Zana shuffled to her chambers. She looked into the polished surface of a crystalline looking-glass and smiled. Her once-thick, dark curls were now wispy white threads, her skin mottled and lined with multitudinous wrinkles, but her earthy eyes were still bright and vivacious.

Zana played with the necklace she wore: a stone of deep, dark garnet tied to a string of gold. She recalled sifting through the king's bedchambers all those years ago, finding the soulstone carrying her dragonsoul within a pile of other jewelry. Once she had seen it, she had known it was hers.

The air was heavy with the scent of spring, but it carried with it a hint of sorrow. It was a strange sort of sorrow, resting on her shoulders—not heavily, but giving her a sense of peace and finality, with an undertone of excitement.

Avasal called to her.

"Perhaps it is time..." she whispered.

With a trembling hand, she wrote a note of farewell and a declaration of her heir to her chancellor before she crept her way to the Wyrms Gate. Each step took its toll, her limbs growing heavy and her heart heavier. She loved Arinta and its people, but she knew she belonged elsewhere. She hauled herself up the stone steps, clawing at stone and reaching for the intricately embossed iron doors.

The raven waters of the Dragonspool, silent and still, called to Zana. With shaky fingers, she tore the stone from the gold, clutching it close to her chest, rising to her feet. Then she let herself fall into the ink.

The viscous liquid assaulted her nose and mouth, slick and slimy against her skin, tasting of brimstone and charred wood. Choking on the water, she breathed in, struggling for air, feeling the waters flooding her lungs. Through the darkness, she saw a crimson light. The light grew until it enveloped her, driving the thick water away and out of her body.

The light grew stronger yet, blinding Zana. She screamed as her bones cracked and snapped, growing, multiplying, reshaping, strengthening. Her skin crawled, smooth scales forcing their way through to the surface. Her cries turned to guttural roars, her nails to claws, her teeth to spikes. From her back burgeoned wings of satin and bone, and a sleek tail lined with deadly spikes.

When the transformation was complete, Zana burst out of the pool in obsidian glory. She climbed higher, panting as she made her way into the open skies, the light of dawn washing over her, inviting her to reach out for new life. As she flew, she remembered the wind in her hair, the kiss of sunset on her cheeks, the smooth touch of ivory on her skin.

Farewell, beloved Arinta. I have served you with loyalty and compassion. I have wished only for your prosperity, and have dedicated my lifeblood to your safety. Now, I must find my path—my peace.

To the Land of Wyrms.
To Avasal.

ABOUT THE AUTHORS

The authors of this book descended into the realm of darkness in order to write these stories.

Some never came back.

S. K. SAYARI

Shasyra Kavat Sayari, from B.C., Canada, tends to get lost in the many stories whirling in her head. Though she often daydreams, she never really thought to write them down until she started journaling. The journals turned to larger notebooks, and then to larger documents on the computer. In 2019, she decided to take the leap and write with the intent of publication.

Her inspirations come mainly from the various video games she plays, as well as the books she reads. You can always find her thinking up another story, scribbling madly in a notebook, or trying to beat that final boss without losing any units.

To keep updated, follow Shasyra at:

https://sksayari.com/

facebook.com/sksayari
instagram.com/sksayari

A. M. DILSAVER

A. M. Dilsaver grew up on books and chocolate. As a teenager, she added coffee to the mix and decided to start writing her own stories. Despite majoring in English and teaching for several years, her heart was always drawn back to books and writing. She now works as an editor for a local publishing house in Tennessee, where she lives with her husband and young daughter. "Beauty's Curse" was her first darker fantasy, and she's pretty sure she'll never go back! Follow her on Instagram @amdilsaver for updates on her projects and pictures of funny memes she found when she should have been writing!

instagram.com/amdilsaver

R. L. DAVENNOR

Raelynn Davennor has been creating and discovering fantastical worlds for as long as she can remember—often getting scolded for reading while her teachers were talking. As both an author and composer of music, Raelynn utilizes her creations in her fictional worlds full of darkness, dragons, and sassy heroines. She's made appearances with artists such as The Who, Weird Al, and Hugh Jackman, and performed on many of the largest stages in the United States. Her inspiration takes no mercy on her despite her busy schedule.

Even when completing the most mundane tasks, Raelynn is usually lost in her head, flying across the sea on the back of a dragon or humming a tune she can't wait to scribble down. In her little remaining free time, she enjoys pampering her menagerie of pets and pretending she isn't an adult.

She can be reached @rldavennor on Facebook, Twitter, and Instagram, or her website:

https://www.rldavennor.com/

facebook.com/RLDavennor
twitter.com/RLDavennor
instagram.com/rldavennor

CHRISTIANA MATTHEWS

Christine, who writes under the pen name Christiana to distinguish her from another author, fell in love with words as soon as she learnt to read. Words have power, words are magic. And when they're used to describe realms of magic, their power is increased tenfold.

As a child she was entranced by fairy stories and wonder tales, and after discovering the works of Tolkien as a teenager and realizing that fairy tales for grown ups were a thing, she determined to write her own stories and create her own lore. Thus was born the saga of the Heirs of Aureya, as well as several short stories and a retelling of the Welsh myth of Blodeuedd from the fourth branch of the Mabinogian.

Christiana lives in South-East Queensland, Australia, with three cats and a houseful of books. Visit her Facebook Page for more stories or follow her on Instagram.

facebook.com/ChristianaHMatthews
instagram.com/matthews9913

JAY ROSE

Jay Rose is a fantasy writer residing in the beautiful state of Colorado. When she's not writing or spending time with her family you can find her at her favorite fishing holes or watching her favorite pair of reckless Monster Hunters. Though, don't be surprised if you find her raiding the horde of enemies on whichever game she may be playing. If you enjoy quirky, nerdy gamer, comic loving, camo obsessed weirdos, then she's your girl. Follow her at:

facebook.com/JayRoseAuthor
instagram.com/jayroseauthor

AISLING WILDER

Aisling Wilder writes epic Urban and High Fantasy from her home in the west of Ireland, just on the edge of windswept Connemara. Aisling's favourite stories were always tales of the supernatural. From Fairy Tales of the Brothers Grimm, to the stories of C.S. Lewis to Tolkien to more modern stories of Princes and Princesses, elves and fairies and magic spells, she was transfixed. So much so that she would think about the stories long after they were read, carrying on in her own imagination with things that could have happened after the 'Happily Ever After'. It was a natural progression to becoming a writer from there.

Aisling has always been fond (and a little afraid!) of the dark and the creatures of the night, and is thrilled to include two tales for this anthology. Visit Aisling's website for more information on her books, blog posts and stories.

https://www.aislingwilder.com/

INE GAUSEL

Ine Gausel has always loved writing and making up his own stories. A lot of his childhood was spent writing roleplays with friends, and as he got older his interest progressed into tabletop games. Whether he is out trail riding with his Icelandic pony, cruising down the river in his boat, or listening to his favorite musicals, there is always a story brewing in his mind.

Now, the only thing left to do to complete your reading experience is to introduce the Norwegian way of ending a fairytale – because not all fairytales have happy endings. *Snip, snap, snout, and then the fairytale was out.*

ABOUT THE EDITORS

Emma O'Connell has a First Class Degree in English Literature and has been editing professionally since 2016, launching her own business - Emma's Edit - in 2019. She has worked on a wide variety of media and genres, but she specialises in fiction and particularly fantasy. A writer herself, Emma loves working with authors to help them reach their full potential; her goal is to make the editing process accessible, affordable and most of all enjoyable.

https://emmasedit.com/

Shasyra Kavat Sayari is pursuing a degree in English Literature. Though she coordinated Blood and Betrayal, she didn't exactly compile the stories in Blood and Betrayal—she collected authors, and together they worked on their stories from concept to finish together. Shasyra was involved in every process of creating the anthology, from critiquing to editing to formatting. An aspiring editor, she hopes to work on further anthologies with more incredible authors.

Made in the USA
Monee, IL
22 July 2021